MAN OF WAR
Graham John Parry

For my Wife and Children,

with love.

CONTENTS

Who will stand when danger calls?
Who defends these precious shores?
Who will fight and not ignore
the battle's trial? . . . . a man of war.

Chapter One . . Quarter Moon

Lieutenant-Commander Richard Thorburn braced himself at the swaying bridge-screen and squinted at the windswept darkness. Salt laden spray swept the platform and he grimaced, well aware of what confronted him. For this was the infamous North Sea, deceptively tranquil on a fine mid-summer day, but as now, not to be relied on. One moment a benign expanse of quiet water lapping gently against Britain's eastern foreshore, the next a wild, inhospitable wind-lashed body of angry waves. And on this night in the July of 1942, the sea had become a restless, foam tossed wilderness, driven on by a northerly gale.

He bent to the wheelhouse pipe. 'Port ten.'

Acknowledgement of the order echoed up the tube. 'Port ten, aye aye, sir.'

Thorburn waited for the bows to come left and meet the waves, and as he felt the ship rise to the next roller he called for the wheel to be centred.

'Midships . . . , steady.'

'Wheel's amidships, sir. Steering oh-one-oh degrees.'

'Very well,' Thorburn said, and straightened from the pipe. He frowned at the waves, the horizon lost in a swirl of mist, and wondered if those in charge truly understood what they asked of men under their command. Not that Thorburn questioned the validity of sending a single lone warship on a search of the North Sea. For this was a mission of mercy. Somewhere out there was the crew of a Lancaster bomber that had bailed out after a raid on Bremerhaven, and he'd been despatched to attempt a rescue. If they had a dinghy there might be a chance of finding some alive, but in this weather? It didn't look very promising. After all, the last known coordinates were probably wrong by God knows how many miles, and even if they'd been accurate, these winds would make fools of anyone trying to predict their current position. And now, in the blackness of a stormy night, he worried they might never be found. But it wouldn't be for a lack of trying, and he determined to stick it out on their behalf.

H.M.S. *Brackendale* shuddered to the next onslaught, and then corkscrewed wildly before thumping into the following trough. Thorburn's grimace tightened as she rolled heavily to starboard, an urgent reminder of nature's unpredictable power, demanding his attention, testing his seamanship. He flexed his knees as the steel bows heaved through a wall of wave tossed spume, steadied on the crest, and dropped headlong into the flank of an oncoming roller.

And so Thorburn waited, the subconscious instinct of a sailor coming to the fore, and then, judging the moment, he lunged swiftly across to the raised compass binnacle. Feet apart, left thigh pressed against the housing, he balanced against the ship's motion and raised his binoculars.

For the second time in as many minutes he sensed danger, not from the ever present rigours of the sea, but more an indefinable sensation that all was not well, that an enemy might lurk unseen in the swirling night. Try as he might, his sharp eyes failed to locate anything other than the breaking crests.

'Time?' he asked, the words snatched away on the wind.

'Two thirty-two, sir,' came a raised voice.

Thorburn nodded and glanced over at the dimmed chart table.

'Thank you, Pilot,' he said, 'well past my bed time.'

Lieutenant Martin half smiled. 'Yes, sir, mine too,' he said, and swivelled the dividers across the chart.

Thorburn let the moment pass, instinctively traversing the binoculars, scouring the blackness ahead. Heavy spray hit the screen and he blinked under the peak of his cap. At this latitude, where summer nights were short, the first hint of dawn wouldn't be long coming, and it would bring with it a welcome relief from strained eyes as night gave way to semi-daylight. And in addition to the nervous tension permeating through the minds of the watchkeepers, the haunting ring of the asdic repeater echoed monotonously in the confined space. Not that he expected a U-boat to be watching in this weather, but nonetheless it served to act as a persistent reminder of their precarious existence.

Brackendale knifed into the next roller, bow-wave shredded and thrown by the wind, driving in over the navigating platform. He lowered the glasses to hang on his chest and wiped moisture from his lips. Beneath his feet the ship settled to an even keel, and he took advantage of the moment to step swiftly down to the forebridge and duck below the dripping glass.

His thoughts lingered on their last boiler-clean, when the ship should have been fitted with the long overdue Radar, which, although by no means perfect, would have been a damn sight better than being without. But at the last minute the dockyard had fobbed him off with some lame excuse over shortages in supply. His vociferous complaints to the senior supervisor fell on deaf ears and he eventually put to sea minus one very important modification. He shook his head at the memory, but fleetingly, it didn't do to dwell on disappointments.

Again that overwhelming sense of hidden danger tugged at his innards and he debated whether it was too soon to alert the crew. This far out in the North Sea he couldn't afford to be caught unawares, but at the same time he didn't want the entire ship's company keyed up for longer than necessary. As was the nature of those at sea, there were already more than the usual compliment of lookouts probing the darkness, none of the crew liked the thought of leaving men to drown.

No, he thought, Defence Stations would have to suffice. Those of the crew who were off watch needed all the rest they could get.

He felt movement at his elbow and turned to find his First Officer standing close.

'Number One?' he said, initiating a response.

Lieutenant Robert Armstrong, tall and rangy, tugged down the peak of his cap and peered at the flying spray. 'Routine signal, sir, a weather report. Force six, increasing force seven.' A note of weary pessimism crept into his voice as he clarified the point. 'Just confirms what we're getting.'

Thorburn smiled, tight lipped. 'Good of them to let us know. Better late than never.' He felt Armstrong turn to look at him, and then heard him chuckle.

'If they'd asked nicely, sir, we might have saved them the bother.'

Despite himself Thorburn grinned. When Armstrong had first joined ship, he'd seemed a touch withdrawn, quiet to the point of being reclusive. But now, almost three years on, he'd proved to be a competent First Lieutenant, someone to rely on. They'd forged a good partnership and his propensity for the occasional cutting remark was all the more welcome.

Lieutenant Martin interrupted. 'Five miles east of their last known position, sir.'

Thorburn wiped water from his cheek and peered ahead. It was time to turn south to complete the square, but he wanted to give this leg a few more minutes.

'Thank you, Pilot. We'll hold this bearing a little longer.'

'Aye aye, sir.'

A gust of wind rattled the halyards and a rain squall swept the open bridge. They ducked from the stinging needles, and when Thorburn straightened he found the bows hidden, visibility down to less than fifty feet. For a long minute the rain lashed in sideways, bouncing off the steel bulkheads, pelting them with a savage malevolence. And then as quickly as it had arrived, it cleared to leave them standing drenched, water streaming down their faces.

'Ship! Bearing Green two-oh!'

Thorburn reacted instantly. 'Action Stations!'

The urgent clamour of the alarm shrilled through the decks, immediately followed by the clatter of boots on ladders, the slamming of water tight doors.

He ignored the commotion and raised his glasses, ahead and fractionally to the right, fine across the starboard bow. Droplets of salt laden moisture refracted on the lens but in the intermittent light of a quarter moon he caught a momentary glimpse of white water, a bow wave head on, and the vague outline of upperworks. Another burst of driving rain and it was gone. He tried to guess the range, two miles? Maybe less, but undoubtedly on a converging bearing. Leaning to a voice-pipe he called up 'Guns' Carling, hopefully already at his station in the Range Finder Tower immediately abaft the bridge.

'Guns?'

The reply was instant. 'Sir?'

'Green two-oh, anything?'

A pause and Thorburn turned to look at the Tower, traversing slowly right. Lieutenant Carling was nothing if not thorough.

'No, sir, wait . . . , yes, I have it; enemy destroyer. Rails on the quarterdeck for laying mines.'

'Well done, Guns. Be ready with starshell.' He retrained his glasses over the bow. No sign of the warship, nor of anything but tossing waves and patchy rain. He cursed silently as seconds ticked by. *Brackendale* plunged on at twelve knots, more than enough in this sort of sea, and the German would probably be doing something similar; it wouldn't be long before they were on top of one another. The ship heeled heavily and he stuck out a leg to compensate, wracking his brain for the best course of action. From the bank of voice-pipes, he could hear reports being called in as men grouped up to their various positions, a tense exchange of acknowledgements. Finally, Armstrong made his own report to the Captain.

'Closed up to Action Stations, sir.'

'Very well, you'd best see to your own.'

'Aye aye, sir,' came the reply, and Thorburn heard him make for the ladder down to the fo'c'sle deck. Armstrong would take charge of Damage Control aft, which served the dual purpose of separating the two senior officers in time of crisis; one available to take over from the other if either were incapacitated.

He rapidly thought through his next move and made a decision, hurriedly considered, but appropriate to the current circumstances. He turned to the compass platform and bent to the wheelhouse pipe.

'Port twenty!'

Chief Petty Officer Barry Falconer had taken over the wheel and gave a firm, unflustered acknowledgement. 'Port twenty, aye aye, sir.'

Thorburn stared at the compass, watching the bearing change as the bows swung to the left away from danger, and as they pushed round to the north-west, forty-five degrees from their original course, he steadied the turn.

'Midships.'

'Midships, sir.'

He let her run on, rolling and twisting away from the enemy, twenty seconds . . . , thirty seconds, and returned to the pipe.

'Starboard twenty.'

'Twenty of the starboard wheel on, sir.'

Thorburn now waited for *Brackendale* to come right, heading north, albeit displaced by a few hundred yards.

'Midships . . . , steady. Steer three-five-eight degrees.'

'Course is three-five-eight degrees, sir,' the Cox'n confirmed, and Thorburn looked up from the dim glow of the compass housing, willing the enemy to appear.

'Guns . . . bridge?' came a call from a voice-pipe.

'Bridge,' Thorburn answered.

'Target bearing Green five-oh, range fourteen-hundred.'

He raised the binoculars, correcting across the beam to the right. And there it was, a ghostly shape in the rain. A thin smile played across his lips, his instinctive reaction had paid dividends, a timely alteration of course.

'Fire starshell!' he snapped.

One of the twin barrels in the forward turret blasted a shot skywards. Moments later, well beyond the target, it burst into a harsh incandescent light, swaying beneath the small parachute. And Thorburn cursed. Silhouetted in the glare, not one German warship but three, the destroyer and two small escorts.

'Open fire!' he called, thanking God he'd made the alteration. That small change had given the main armament the chance of a broadside; and the twin mounted gun turrets hammered out a salvo of four-inch shells. Thorburn felt it through his feet, thumping through the deck plates. Shells hurtled across the intervening space. Three plumes of water, short, and an orange flash as one shell hit the German amidships.

On the quarterdeck above *Brackendale's* galley housing, the four-barrelled Pompom exploded into action, a stream of two pound shells thumping at the destroyer, tracer glistening through the air.

The two German escorts quickly recovered from their initial surprise and peeled out into line abreast, and Thorburn saw their light calibre guns flaming from the bows. And it was then that the enemy destroyer replied, and he heard a shell whip overhead.

Well over, he thought, a hurried salvo or lifted by a wave. In the meantime *Brackendale's* gunnery began to make inroads, scoring hits as the two main warships passed in opposite directions. But the pair of escorts were closing fast. He lifted the binoculars and focussed on the leader. It was an 'R' boat, originally designed as an inshore minesweeper, diesel powered, now a 'jack-of-all-trades'. Light armament and depth charges and he wondered what the hell they were doing out here on a night like this?

Thorburn stepped quickly to the port bridge-wing and called down to the Oerlikon gunner. 'Target dead ahead. Open fire!'

A second starshell flashed brightly, drifting below the scudding cloud, illuminating a wide swathe of ocean.

He glanced at the Range Finder, now pointing across the starboard quarter, following the enemy destroyer as it steamed off beyond *Brackendale's* stern. The forward guns fell silent, fully traversed but unable to sight the target. Then it was the turn of the 'R' boats to find the range, and for all the ferocity of the weather, a hail of bullets swept the bridge. The port wing Lewis gun stammered into action, chasing tracer over the waves.

Thorburn felt the need to make a move, to turn right between the fast approaching 'R' boats and the fleeing destroyer. It would give his main armament more scope.

'Starboard thirty,' he ordered calmly, at pains to keep tension from his voice.

Brackendale responded, her bows clawing round as the ship heeled hard to port. The Oerlikon blasted a fusillade of shells at the nearest boat, scything through men and plating. The boat abruptly turned away, near to capsizing.

Thorburn snatched a glance over the starboard side as the ship continued her turn, still leaning hard over. The quarterdeck guns banged off another salvo, a vivid orange flash lighting the enemy's midships main deck. He nodded at someone's triumphant shout and grinned into the wind.

'Bloody marvellous,' he said, and let the Cox'n hold the turn as the ship drove round after the German. A shell

13

hit the sea close astern, shrapnel rattling the side plates. He leaned closer to the voice-pipe.

'Midships . . . , steady . . . .'

'Wheel's amidships, course one-three-five, sir,' Falconer answered.

Brackendale swung upright, thrusting toward the south-east, cutting across the stern of the German. The Pompom changed target, pumping shells at the one remaining visible 'R' boat. Below the bridge the four-inch guns cracked off another pair of shells, the acrid smell of eye-stinging cordite smothering the bridge.

Thorburn cleared his throat and raised his glasses, catching a glimpse of the destroyer's upperworks. But then in an instant a curtain of rain swept in and obliterated the view. Seconds later the driving rain hit *Brackendale*, lashing the fo'c'sle, and at the same moment the last starshell fizzled out. The forward turret ceased fire and the quarterdeck followed, the entire seascape hidden by rain. A strange silence ensued, only the rain making its presence heard, drumming on exposed steelwork.

'Guns . . . bridge?' It was Carling.

Shoulders hunched against the driving wind, Thorburn ducked below the screen and answered the voice-pipe. 'Bridge.'

'Unsighted, sir.'

'Very well, cease fire. I'll hold this bearing, we might get lucky.'

'Aye aye, sir.'

He forced himself to peer ahead into the swirling darkness, disappointment flooding through him. He'd had the enemy handed to him on a plate and the weather had intervened. But he wouldn't give it up, not yet. With a determined set to his jaw he returned to the voice-pipe.

'Make revolutions for twenty knots.'

Falconer's rasping acknowledgement echoed in reply. 'Speed twenty knots, aye aye, sir.'

Thorburn straightened into the teeth of the gale. Nothing ventured, he thought, nothing gained; he would see if *Brackendale* could cope with these seas. He wondered about the bomber crew, and whether they would see the starshell?

The small destroyer ploughed into a wave, rolled and shipped water, a foaming torrent of sea boiling along her starboard deck. He laughed into the night and grabbed the rail. She thumped again and buried her nose, swaying wildly, and then shook herself free. He wiped his face sensing the rain had eased, hard to tell.

A bulkhead phone sounded and he picked up the handset. 'Captain?'

'Engine room, sir.' It was the warm, Welsh brogue of his Chief Engineer.

'Go ahead, Chief.'

'She'll not take much more of this, sir. The props'll tear themselves apart.'

Thorburn closed his eyes. Bryn Dawkins sounded anxious and he wouldn't make the call without good reason. The propellers were obviously racing in the voids between waves. He cursed silently; the elements were conspiring against him.

'Very well, reduce to twelve knots.'

'Aye aye, sir,' came the relieved reply, and Thorburn clipped the handset to the bracket. He peered sideways into the sheeting spray and sensed the reduction in power, an easing of the ship's behaviour. A wave hit and *Brackendale's* bows lifted, but this time to ride the crest in a more dignified manner. He turned his back on the gusts, still unwilling to break off the chase, but equally aware that it couldn't continue indefinitely. With the enemy making good his escape there was always the chance of running into reinforcements, not an ideal situation given the circumstances. Reluctantly he stepped over to the compass platform and bent to the voice-pipe.

'Starboard ten.'

'Starboard ten, aye, sir.'

The ship leaned a little to port, punching the waves as she turned south-west and away from the immediate danger.

'Midships,' he ordered, 'steer two-two-five degrees.' He vaguely heard the Cox'n's repeat, wondering if he was doing the right thing. Right or wrong, he'd made the decision, his responsibility. His thoughts turned back to their original mission, the downed airmen, and he shook his head. Little or no chance now, and he felt a wave of regret at having to call off the search.

He reached out a hand for the back of the bridge chair and winced as a sharp pain lanced through his shoulder. It eased and he gave a thoughtful smile. The old wound had never healed properly and he was convinced that a piece of shrapnel remained embedded in his shoulder blade. Luckily, the pain when it came didn't have any debilitating effects, and he'd learned to live with it.

Thorburn sat and stared ahead, rubbing his jaw in thought. The squall eased, the rain petering out and the first hint of dawn made itself seen to the east; a miniscule lifting of the cloud darkened night, that infinitesimally small touch of grey that sometimes only a seaman would sense. He straightened in the chair and looked round.

'Damage reports?' he asked of the bridge in general, and heard someone call the quarterdeck.

'Any casualties?'

'None reported, sir, and Lieutenant Hardcastle reports no damage aft.'

'Very well, we'll remain at Action Stations.' He took a final glance over the port side in the direction the German destroyer had taken and accepted the inevitable. 'Pilot, set a course for Rosyth.'

'Aye aye, sir,' Martin said, and bent to the chart table.

Thorburn peered towards the rear of the bridge. 'You lookouts keep a sharp watch astern. The 'R' boats might still be around. The rest of you remember we were searching for that bomber crew.'

Armstrong came onto the bridge and reported.

'We've taken minor damage to the superstructure and there's a few holes in the portside amidships, splinter hits. Nothing serious, sir. The Chief says it's all under control. And one casualty, Able Seaman Denby, flesh wound to his right thigh. Doc's seeing to him now.'

Thorburn nodded, they'd got off lightly. 'Thank you, Number One. I think we'll have hot drinks all round. Give it another ten minutes and then resume Defence Stations.'

'Right, sir, I'll let the galley know.'

And with that, Armstrong departed, and Thorburn relaxed into the bridge-chair. In a few hours they'd be back in harbour.

'Object in the water. Green three-oh. Five hundred yards!'

Thorburn came to his feet and lifted his glasses, that first hint of daylight glinting off the waves.

'Looks like a dinghy, sir.'

And he caught a fleeting glimpse as it bobbed up on a wave, only to be swept from sight in the next trough.

'Slow ahead, starboard ten,' he ordered. Was it wishful thinking or had they really looked like airmen, two of them slumped low, either end of the inflatable. He moved onto the compass platform and steered *Brackendale* to the right of the dinghy. It put the survivors in the lee of the destroyer, protecting them from the worst of the waves. A scrambling net went over the side of the port quarterdeck.

'Stop engines.'

Sailors shouted, and one of the inert figures struggled to sit up, staring at the ship. A line was thrown across the dinghy and the man gathered it in, held on. Willing hands hauled on the rope, rapidly bringing the little boat bouncing into the side. Half a dozen seamen reached to lend a hand while they clung to the scrambling net, half submerged. They pulled the men on deck to where Doc Waverley waited, and Armstrong gave a negative wave to indicate there were no more survivors.

Thorburn bent to the pipe. 'Half ahead, make revolutions for twelve knots.'

Brackendale lifted her bows to pick up speed, and Thorburn waited for Armstrong's report. It was a while before he appeared.

'Navigator and tail gunner, sir. They were the only ones to get out alive. They saw our starshell but had no flares. The navigator's not so good.'

Thorburn nodded at the news, a sadness coursing through him. The bomber crews had a dangerous job. It took brave men to fly into enemy held airspace and their chances of getting home with a damaged aircraft were all but zero. And to make matters worse they had to cross what to many became a watery grave. Knowing the Royal Navy would try to find them must be a powerful incentive to staying alive, a sort of comfort when all else looked so bleak.

'Lucky we came across them, they must have been giving up hope.' He hung his head. 'Two,' he said slowly, 'out of an entire crew.'

Quietly, Armstrong said. 'Yes, sir.'

Thorburn looked up and shook off the mood. No good beating himself up, this was the luck of the draw and a man had to look forward, not dwell in the past.

'Right, carry on, Number One,' he said. 'Defence Stations now if you will.'

'Aye aye, sir,' said the First Lieutenant, and his footsteps faded to the back of the bridge.

Thorburn straightened at the screen, looking down at the fo'c'sle guns. It had been exhilarating while it lasted. He wondered what the new day would bring? Probably back on the East Coast convoys again. He stretched his arms and grabbed the top of the bridge-screen. Could be worse he thought, at least we had some excitement. *Brackendale* slithered across a long roller and settled down to a rhythmic rise and fall, an occasional drift of spray rising over the bridge-screen. The drinks came, Blue watch took over Defence Stations and in the grey light of dawn, with the weather backing off, Thorburn was at last able to order an increase of speed. He decided to remain on the bridge and reached for his cigarettes. He'd write up the report once they were in the Firth of Forth, right now the paperwork could wait. With the coming of daylight the quarter moon faded from view, lost on the far horizon.

He nursed a hot mug of 'kye' and wondered what the new day would bring.

Chapter Two . . . Deception

Far to the east in the German city of Berlin, at Hitler's Reich Chancellery on Wilhelmstrasse, a meeting of the Marine-Oberkommando Nordsee had been convened to implement a strategy of nullifying the Royal Navy's influence in the English Channel. The lights in the Chancellery burned bright through the hours of darkness.

Of those summoned to attend, Admiral Mathias Johann Heinrich Krause, Knights Cross, in company with Großadmiral Erich Raeder, found himself at the forefront of a heated debate on how best to bring the British warships into battle. After all night talks and much considered argument, the eventual decision placed Admiral Krause in overall command of 'Operation Triton', which should be implemented within the next two weeks.

A glimmer of daylight paled the eastern sky as the meeting broke up, and Krause headed for a train to take him back to the North Sea coast.

The interminable journey west via Hanover took a miserable nine hours of frequently disrupted travel, and he arrived at his Headquarters in the German port of Wilhelmshaven in a fowl mood. He ate supper alone in his apartment and sent instructions to his executive officers that a meeting would take place at 11.00hrs the following morning. Krause warned them that the conference was in direct response to a fresh directive from Naval High Command. When all was quiet, he poured himself a Cognac, lit a cigar and pondered his orders. The result of those protracted discussions was that an armed merchantman, the *Holstein,* was to sail from Wilhelmshaven to the French port of Calais. The ship would be used as a decoy to draw in the destroyers of the Royal Navy, to weaken their escort capabilities in the Channel and thus reduce their ability to strengthen the Russian convoys. Before turning in, Krause thought he'd made a constructive start to the Operation.

At 10.55hrs on the morning of Thursday the 23rd of July, 1942, the middle-aged Admiral entered his Naval Administrative block to the east of the dockyard and walked through to the Officer's Lounge. A steward came forward with a tray of coffee, and when Krause nodded, poured a cup and placed it on the bar. A pair of sentries stood guarding the marbled entrance to the conference hall.

Momentarily, a harassed looking flag Lieutnant made an appearance, saw the Admiral standing at the bar, and quickly withdrew.

Krause smirked into his coffee; some of those officers would now be worrying in anticipation. He took a mouthful and savoured the flavour before swallowing, then carefully replaced the cup on the bar. He turned and made for the adjacent room.

The two sentries opened the tall pair of doors, and he marched inside. Four officers snapped to attention and he waved a casual hand.

'Be seated,' Krause said, gesturing to the enormous polished table, and made himself comfortable at the far end. He looked round at the expectant faces.

'I have called you here to pass on an order from Naval High Command. It has been decided to re-instigate surface attacks on the British navy. The Führer has been persuaded that unlike previous attempts to bring the Royal Navy into battle, the armed merchantman *Holstein* can succeed by allowing the enemy spies to report their findings and make certain it is seen in coastal waters.' He paused to gaze at the assembled officers and gave a grim smile. 'I have no doubt the British will rise to the bait, *Holstein's* very presence on the horizon would be too much for them to resist.' His grim smile broadened into a guttural laugh.

'It would give our Kriegsmarine the opportunity to exploit the one weakness to which we know the Royal Navy always succumbs, their willingness to attack, no matter the circumstances. Admiral Raeder is of the opinion that Kapitän-zur-See Baumgartner has the experience to carry out these orders. If there are any of you who have reservations I would value your contribution.'

He leant forward and reached for the large silver cigar box and made his selection. He snipped the end and went through the motions of lighting the finely rolled leaves. The process gave his executive officers time to talk amongst themselves, and as he allowed smoke to trickle from his nostrils he watched them through narrowed eyes. The only dissenting voice came from Hemmelman, a die hard supporter of Hitler's ethos and an outspoken critic of the traditional navy.

'I wonder if Baumgartner is not too soft for such a suicidal mission. It would be easy to find excuses for not attacking. The British are more organised in their patrols, with aggressive use of torpedo boats.' He waved a nonchalant hand in the air. 'The Führer does not have much faith in our Kriegsmarine, only the U-boats are in his favour.'

Krause took another long pull of the cigar and eyed the glowing tip in thought. Hemmelman could be right; he had the same reservations over Baumgartner's willingness to push on with an attack. The man's previous tally spoke volumes for his navigational seamanship and the ability to sink unarmed and defenceless merchantmen. But how would he stand up to warships? No one could deny him the overall command of such a flotilla, but did he really have the capability to stand and fight?

He blew on the tip of the cigar. 'I hear your argument, but I fear we have little choice. In Großadmiral Raeder's eyes he has a proven record, knows the ship and crew. Unless you can give me an overwhelming reason not to have Baumgartner as commander, the order stands.'

Hemmelman glared at him and tightened his lips with annoyance, but also nodded with acceptance. 'No,' he said reluctantly, 'I have only suspicions. His record is unblemished and I can only offer my personal opinion. I do not think he is the man for the job.' And with that he sat back and stared at the opposite wall.

'In that case, gentlemen, I order you to make preparations to sail *Holstein* for Calais at the earliest opportunity. In general terms I expect a full escort for the first leg to Rotterdam. We will have the ships for a reinforcing flotilla before Baumgartner sets out on the second leg. You will keep me informed of your plans and await my agreement before proceeding. The Führer elected to give this expedition his personal seal of approval. In recognition of that he decided on a code name. It is to be called 'Operation Triton'. Clear?'

They were quick to agree, and came to their feet as he stood to go.

He hesitated, resting one fist on the table. 'Don't forget, gentlemen, it is only two weeks since we destroyed the Royal Navy's Arctic convoy. That defeat is still fresh in the minds of the British and the Führer believes that following PQ17 their fear of failure could play into our hands.' He straightened and walked to the door. 'The sooner we are ready, the better.' He left them to it and walked out deep in thought. For Operation Triton to succeed it would be necessary to for him to personally review their plans, and Admiral Mathias Krause had lost none of the cunning for which he'd become famous. Soon, he believed, the Royal Navy would answer the call to battle, a battle in which the Kriegsmarine would have the upper hand.

A hard smile flickered across the solid face and he walked away towards the onshore wind and the distinctive smell of the North Sea.

Chapter Three . . . Firth of Forth

Richard Thorburn had managed three hours of uninterrupted sleep and although not actually feeling refreshed, nonetheless felt a sight better than when he'd turned in. On arrival in the dockyard, the rescued navigator and tail-gunner had been put ashore and whisked away by ambulance. The wounded Denby had been sent to the local hospital as a precaution, Doc Waverley insisting the injury needed proper investigation. A wash and shave had banished the last of the cobwebs, and a thick slice of toast washed down with a hot mug of tea had sufficed for breakfast. Since their inconclusive skirmish with the German destroyer, Thorburn's prediction that they'd be back on the East Coast convoys had proved all too accurate, and within hours of returning to Rosyth, *Brackendale* had once again prepared for escort duty.

A knock on the cabin door made him glance up from the ship's log. 'Yes?'

The Chief Engineer stuck his head in. 'You wanted me, sir?'

Thorburn pushed the log to one side, pleased to see the man from the Welsh valleys.

'Yes Chief. How're the repairs coming along?'

Dawkins rubbed an oily finger down his jaw and left a dark smudge on his chin. 'Well, sir,' he said in that warm baritone, 'all the holes are patched above the waterline.

We were lucky with the underwater hits, a few dents but no leaks.' He hesitated, momentarily at a loss as to how to continue. 'The thing is, sir, a twenty millimetre shell penetrated the starboard fo'c'sle plates and lodged in the line for the steam capstan. The starboard anchor is out of action. We're having to replace that section of pipe.' He spread his hands in a gesture of despair. 'I had to ask the dockyard for a spare part.'

Thorburn grinned behind his hand. If there was one thing Bryn Dawkins hated above all else, it was having to go cap in hand to the shore staff. To him it was an admission of defeat.

'Never mind, Chief, I'm sure we'll survive. Can you blank it off in the interim?'

The Welshman passed a hand over his forehead. 'I can, sir, if you insist.'

'Well, I'm just thinking that if we've got the new bit of pipe we could fit it while we were under way. Can do?'

Dawkins visibly brightened and even managed a tentative smile. 'Oh yes, sir, simple piece of plumbing.'

'And when do we expect to take delivery?'

Dawkins looked at his watch and sniffed. 'Within the hour now, they said before lunch.'

'In that case, I'll proceed on the understanding that the offending article will be installed at the earliest opportunity,' Thorburn said. 'I don't see much use for the anchor in the short term. I take it the Engineering log might well show completion of repair before we sail for duty?' He held up crossed fingers and Bryn Dawkins grinned.

'I can assure the Captain that all necessary paperwork will be completed in accordance with regulations.' He hesitated before posing a question. 'Can I ask where we're off to next?'

Thorburn sighed. 'Yes, Chief, we'll be joining a convoy south for the Thames. Twenty ships, colliers mainly.'

The Welshman rubbed the bridge of his nose, depositing a fresh streak of oil. 'Slow boat to China comes to mind,' he offered with a wry smile. 'Is that all, sir?'

'Yes . . . , thank you Chief. We'll be moving over to Methil docks this afternoon.'

'Right, sir, I'll get on.' He turned to go and paused to glance back over his shoulder. 'And you'd best keep an eye out for wet paint.'

The door closed and Thorburn returned to the ship's log, but stopped with the pen poised. Lieutenant Bryn Dawkins might well display the odd spot of grease, but on the rare occasions Thorburn visited the engine room, there could be no faulting its immaculate presentation. The Stokers took their jobs seriously and he was certain the Chief's habit of leading by example proved well founded.

He put pen to paper and persevered for a while longer before finally succumbing to the need for fresh air. Time to go up top.

On the bridge, the harbour watch had claimed their rightful vantage points with the two lookouts scanning the skies to the east above the Forth estuary. The signalman was keeping a close watch on the dock tower, and Lieutenant Patrick Hardcastle sat in the Captain's chair. He came to his feet as Thorburn's footsteps alerted him.

'Morning, sir.'

'Morning,' Thorburn said. 'All quiet?'

Hardcastle, recently married, and a grandson of Rear Admiral Sir Terrance Hardcastle K.C.B., D.S.O., thought for a moment before replying and Thorburn glanced at him, saw that he was looking at the docks. Faintly, from the innards of a dry docked cruiser, came the sound of rivets being hammered. 'If that's what you mean by quiet, then yes, sir.'

Thorburn hitched himself into the chair and tapped a cigarette from his packet. 'If that's the only thing that interferes with my afternoon, then it truly is my definition of quiet.' He flicked a flame and cupped it to the tip, inhaled and blew smoke. Hardcastle was twenty-five years old and Thorburn had been glad to welcome him aboard, filling a vital role after *Brackendale* had suffered a serious amount of battle casualties. His contribution to the ship as a whole, and his easy going nature coupled with a wicked sense of humour, tended to enliven even the most mundane of escort duties.

Thorburn noticed a bank of cloud building to the west, coming in from beyond Glasgow, building steadily. The met forecast had warned of Force three, visibility good. Rain had not been mentioned and he hoped they were right.

A bright stab of light blinked out from shore.

Brackendale's Aldis lamp clattered in response and the shore light flicked out its message.

'Signal, sir; "Take station on *Warrington* at Methil docks by 15.30hrs." End of message, sir.'

'Very well, acknowledge,' Thorburn said, and looked at Hardcastle. 'Better tell the Chief to hurry up the shore staff or he won't get to see his spare part.' In the starboard wing the signalman shuttered the Aldis to acknowledge the order.

'He's not aboard, sir. Took the motor boat to chivvy them along.'

Thorburn smiled, not in the least surprised, and glanced at his watch. He could afford to wait awhile yet. The continual sound of hammering echoed across from the cruiser and he watched one of the giant dockside cranes lower a bulging cargo net onto the quarterdeck. That ship's company would be scattered to the four winds, taking advantage of an extended shore leave.

He drew smoke and jammed a sea boot against the corner of the fore-bridge. He breathed out, enjoying the relative quiet of harbour activity. Wouldn't be long before the Chief was back and adding his own disturbance to the peace.

Lieutenant Bryn Dawkins cut it fine but duly returned with the 'offending' article. The ship's motor boat was hoisted and secured in the davits and the boilers brought up to pressure. At 14.45 *Brackendale* slipped her mooring, and with the wires coiled and the Special Sea Dutymen clearing away under Armstrong's watchful eye, the ship swung round to the east and headed for the central span of the Forth Bridge.

In Methil Docks they refuelled at the oiler and waited while the next convoy to make the passage south assembled in the anchorage. Not that time passed slowly. Methil had become the busiest port on the north-east coast, with freighters unloading on arrival from far flung countries, or being loaded and refuelled in preparation for sailing to Norway or Russia, or Canada and the American continent. Over and above all that there were the frequent sailings of convoys round Britain's coastal waters. But eventually, from the apparent chaos of disorganised individuals, a convoy began to take shape, a sense of order established.

Thorburn stood leaning against the bridge-screen, binoculars trained over the starboard bow. From his scrutiny of the list of vessels he could see that one of the ships edging out from the quayside was the 2,000 ton S.S. *Lady Maria*, heavily laden with iron ore and making slow progress towards the head of the port column, her single screw working hard to bring her up to speed. Then it was the turn of a collier carrying much needed coal for the London power stations to push across to the starboard column, 3,000 tons of rust streaked hull wending her way cautiously towards a preordained station in line. The ship probably plied the same coastal route as before the war, the difference being she was now under the discipline of convoy procedure.

'Do you think that collier's got enough freeboard, Number One?'

Armstrong shook his head. 'Hand on heart, no, but I guess the skipper knows what she can handle.'

'Mmm,' Thorburn said from behind the glasses, 'let's hope it doesn't get too lumpy.'

And so it went on, ship after ship, until a total of twenty vessels had formed in two long lines ready to depart the Firth of Forth.

Brackendale had been allocated the unenviable task of 'Tail-end-Charlie', the shepherd watching out for the inevitable straggler, and the almost guaranteed mechanical failure, or the ship who simply became unable to sustain their given speed. All too often the owners, intent on the Government's guarantee of a good payment, exaggerated a ship's possible top speed, regardless of the consequences. And those consequences could be lethal, lagging behind and requiring extra effort on behalf of the escort.

At this important time, Thorburn lay broadside on to the two columns, ready to render assistance at short notice, and all the while waiting for the Senior Officer aboard *Warrington* to signal the official moment of departure.

H.M.S. *Warrington* was an old V&W, a veteran of the Great War, and sailed under the command of Captain Hugh Jefferson, R.N., D.S.C., with eighteen months of East Coast convoys under his belt.

A pair of Flower class Corvettes made up the remainder of the escorts; H.M.S. *Cornflower*, a gallant little ship that Thorburn had first encountered in 1940, and the oddly named H.M.S. *Lantana*, such an obscure name for a Flower that he and Armstrong had privately conceded their ignorance of all things botanical.

Then up ahead, the sixth vessel in the right column, an oil tanker, veered off course and *Warrington's* lamp flickered.

'What's she saying, Smith?'

'Instructing *Cornflower* to investigate the *Atlantic Queen*, sir.'

'Very well,' Thorburn said, and watched the Corvette coming back between the two columns. He smiled at the sight of her busy bow wave. She must be making all of her sixteen knots to answer the call. Nonetheless, in a short space of time, *Cornflower* reached the tanker, slowed and turned about to close the ship which had now drifted out to starboard.

Thorburn raised his binoculars. It appeared the two captains were in conversation with hand held megaphones. The discussion went on for some minutes and then *Warrington's* lamp flickered again.

Smith reported. '*Warrington* to *Cornflower*, sir. They're calling up the harbour tug.'

'Very well,' Thorburn said, and wondered if that would be a non-starter or would they wait for a resolution, delay the convoy. The brilliant pinprick of light twinkled again, and this time Smith shuttered a response.

'*Warrington* calling, sir . . . , "*Atlantic Queen* disabled. *Brackendale* to close up starboard column." End of message, sir.'

'Acknowledge!' Thorburn snapped, and leaned to the voice-pipe.

'Port thirty, half ahead both, ten knots.' He heard the wheelhouse repeat, felt the tremor through the deck plates, and the destroyer swept east, swinging round to come inside the right column.

'Midships . . . , steady.' He watched the compass as *Brackendale* bore down on what had been the seventh in line. 'Steer oh-nine-two degrees, slow ahead.'

'Oh-nine-two degrees, slow ahead, aye aye, sir.'

Thorburn gauged his approach, easing up alongside what turned out to be a grain carrier, the M.V. *Elmwood*, running on diesels. The Master came to the bridge-wing, raising his cap in salute, and Thorburn lifted the megaphone. 'Please move up and take the place of *Atlantic Queen*, she won't be with us.'

The florid round face broke into a broad grin and he patted his cap into place. 'Aye, laddie,' he shouted, 'I can see that.' He jabbed a thumb astern. 'They all movin' up too?'

Thorburn gave an exaggerated nod of his head. 'They will be, if I do my job right.'

Laughter greeted his answer and the Master cupped his hands. 'Good luck with that,' he called, and touched the peak of his cap in salute. 'I'll get on with it then,' he finished and turned away to the inner bridge.

Thorburn waited until *Elmwood's* wake began to increase, the extra power easing her ahead of *Brackendale*. He strode to the back of the starboard bridge-wing and eyed up the distance to the next ship in line, probably no more than two cables length astern. She was a collier, heavily laden judging by a familiar lack of freeboard, and already emitting more than her fair share of smoke from the squat funnel, and that before being asked to deliver any more power from the boilers.

'Slow ahead, revolutions for three knots,' he ordered, and *Brackendale* dawdled, idling through the water, waiting for the collier to catch up. He raised his binoculars at the ship's bows, read the name, and smiled. No one who sailed with these convoys could fail to be surprised by some of the names encountered, and this one surely came high on the list. She was the S.S. *Happy Chopper*, and he wondered how many drinks had been consumed before that rather singular name had been nominated and accepted by the alcohol fuelled owner. And in what was a relatively short space of time the collier moved up alongside, and the call went out to her skipper and she pushed forward to fill the space. But as he suspected, the extra input from the boilers sent a concentrated thickening of black smoke spiralling upwards, a clear indication of a ship's passage.

Thorburn frowned, knowing he ought to remind her that it wasn't in the best interests of the convoy for such a signal to be advertising their presence, but he had more pressing matters to attend to, and let it go. All told it took the best part of another forty minutes to reorganise the remainder of the column, but finally he signalled the Leader that order had been established.

'*Warrington* replying, sir. "Resume station as stern-escort." Message ends, sir.'

'Acknowledge,' Thorburn said, and nodded to Armstrong. 'Port thirty, twenty knots. We'll drop back to the left flank.'

'Aye aye, sir,' Armstrong said and passed the order.

Brackendale lifted her bows, sheered away and came round between columns in a satisfying flurry of sparkling foam.

And so, eventually, two hours later then forecast on the evening of Thursday 23rd of July, the convoy pushed out into the waves of the North Sea and the long passage south began. In truth it was just one more convoy out of hundreds, a convoy that in itself held no greater or lesser importance than all the others sailing to and from ports around the British Isles. But Thorburn, after such a lengthy spell on the East Coast convoys, understood the necessity of such routine sailings and was fully aware of the nation's need for these valuable cargoes.

His bigger concern lay with *Brackendale's* crew and the never ending requirement for vigilance. It was all too easy for the Ship's Company to become inured to the dangers, to let slip on the small details that made for a well rehearsed, disciplined response to a dangerous situation. His overriding mantra had to be the maintenance of that willing cooperation to answer the call of battle when it came.

Across the sea in a German held port, the man charged with laying mines in British waters plotted his next course of action. A skirmish in the North Sea had forced the abandonment of the last mission. There would be no repeat of such behaviour.

Chapter Four . . . Enemy Province

Much later that evening, deep in the heart of the French port of Dunkirk, a non-descript man in a flat cap and dungarees shuffled along a bomb damaged alley, and as he paused in front of a door, glanced behind. A soldier of the Wehrmacht crossed from one side to the other and the man waited, watching from the corner of his eye. But the soldier passed out of sight between two tall town houses and the man relaxed his finger from the trigger of the gun in his pocket. A flatbed truck trundled into the road, heavily laden with an assortment of wooden crates, and headed out towards the docks, and again he waited, until it spluttered from sight. Across the way a grubby boy ran out of a house, slammed the door behind him, and ran into another alleyway.

The man was nothing if not patient and checked the street once again, his surprisingly clear eyes alert for the slightest hint of danger. From the harbour a ship's siren gave three short blasts and then, with the exception of the town's familiar background noises, all became still. He pulled a large key from the bib of his dungarees and offered it to the solid wooden door, turned it and entered, stepping hurriedly inside onto the bare boards. A cool silence greeted his presence and he shut the door and locked it behind him. At the end of a small hallway a set of stairs spiralled up to the next floor and the man took them two at a time, his athleticism belying the weary appearance.

He paused at the top and then turned to a door on the landing, and tapped . . . , three times, followed by a pause, then twice more. A metallic scrape and a bolt was withdrawn inside, a key turned in the lock, and the door tugged open. A young woman met his gaze and smiled gently, her dark shoulder length hair framing a beautiful face, dark eyes glinting softly.

She stood aside and let him enter, and he walked over to the large bay window. The alley below remained deserted and he heard her close and bolt the door. He turned to face the room, removed his cap and ran a hand through his hair.

The man's name was Wingham, Captain Paul Wingham, ex infantry officer in the Sherwood Foresters and one time resident of Alderney in the Channel Islands. Now he was a member of the Special Operations Executive and came under the orders of an officer in England that went by the title of General Scott Bainbridge.

'Anything?' asked the woman speaking French, and he shook his head.

'Not specifically, but a couple more destroyers have berthed in one of the basins,' he said in answer, admiring her alluring profile.

Marianne came to stand close, the elegant eyebrows knitted in a frown. 'Must you send a report?'

Wingham smiled to ease her concerns. 'No, not for a while. I need to see more first.'

'And will you go again tonight?' she asked.

The smile vanished from the ex infantryman's lips. To watch the dockyards at night was fraught with danger but he knew the vigil must be maintained.

'Yes,' he said, 'this time the roof.'

Her face crumpled in disappointment, and she moved to the window, folding her arms in disgust. 'It is too dangerous, Paul. You can't get away with this forever.'

'Don't be angry,' he said in an attempt to pacify her irritation. 'This is why I am here, and anyway I said you didn't have to become involved in this one. You could have stayed in Dieppe.'

Marianne shook her head, hair shimmering in the light of the window. 'Dieppe is Dieppe, nothing ever happens in such a place, just too many Bosch.'

Wingham gave a tight smile, softening his tanned features. 'Then I can only ask that you don't argue with me, it won't be for much longer.'

She turned and laid a hand on his arm, looking up into his eyes, and almost whispered her reply. 'Sorry, Paul, I am a woman. I worry for you.'

He swallowed and held her shoulders. 'I know,' he said, brushed her cheek with his lips, and turned away to the kitchenette. 'What will we have for supper?'

'There is some soup, and I managed to get sausage in the market. I am afraid the bread is a little old.'

'More than enough,' he grinned encouragingly, 'I'll check the wireless is in good order.'

She nodded and walked over to select a pot, and Wingham made his way into the bedroom.

Opposite the sash window, in the corner next to the double bed, an ancient wardrobe stood in solitary splendour. Originally stained and polished to a high walnut sheen, the years had added a warm patina round the handles on the doors. He opened the right side and reached down into the third shelf, deliberately selected for being below eye level, and pressed the rear panel. It moved under the weight of his fingers and he carefully prised away the end with his nails. The false panel swung out and he reached with both hands to remove the transmitter receiver.

Carrying it the side dresser, Wingham unravelled the Morse key wires and checked they were securely attached. He then connected two multi spade-end plugs to the power pack, one from the receiver and the other for the transmitter. He flicked the Bakelite switch and watched the needle in the half-moon meter swing round to verify it had powered up, and quickly turned off. Satisfied with his findings, Wingham thought of his boss twiddling his thumbs in London. Bainbridge had recruited Wingham back in 1940 and it wasn't long before enemy occupied France had become the Infantryman's second home. Born and brought up in the Channel Islands, the French language had become a primary part of his upbringing, and following that first foray into the Cherbourg Peninsula, the General had found him three more placements, this one being the longest and thus far, the most dangerous. He returned to the wardrobe and replaced the wireless parts once more behind the false panel and shut the door. He looked at his watch. In a few hours he would be hidden in the darkness overlooking the harbour.

He found a cigarette and wandered back to the living room.

'Smells good,' he said, and sat himself at the small table.

Marianne stood at the coal fired range stirring the contents of the pot, and gave him a sideways glance with a raised eyebrow. 'Don't just sit there, open the wine.'

He rose from the chair and chose a bottle of red from the wine rack, holding it up to the window with a critical eye. It seemed clear enough and he wound in the corkscrew and removed the cork with a satisfying pop. He dashed a small amount into the wine glass and tasted, and for a change found it not too acidic. There'd been a distinct lack of quality of recent times and when challenged the shopkeepers blamed it on the war. These days the war was blamed for anything that wasn't up to scratch; every shopkeeper's excuse for bad quality, but somehow the price still went up.

'Not bad,' he said grudgingly, poured two half glasses and returned to his chair. He drew on the cigarette, blew smoke to the ceiling and made himself comfortable, content to wallow in a warm moment of domesticity.

That night, approximately sixteen nautical miles out into the English Channel, a twenty-one year old Lieutenant by the name of Charles Holloway, skipper of the Motor Torpedo Boat *Forty-Nine*, lowered his binoculars.

Square jawed and athletic, the son of a trawlerman from Hull, he'd grown up with the sound of surf in his ears. Having completed Royal Navy training he'd volunteered for Coastal Forces and shortly thereafter been promoted to captain of M.T.B. 49. It had been an eventful twelve months of night action in the North Sea before he'd been despatched to Ramsgate in preparation for North Foreland convoy defence.

Earlier in the night an urgent call had come into Coastal Forces and he'd been ordered from Ramsgate with two Motor Gunboats in an attempt to intercept an unknown number of E-boats. He glanced at the Cox'n.

'Stop engines.'

In the compartment below, Chief Motor Mechanic Ben Moore heard the ring of the telegraph and threw the levers. The roar of the engines subsided and an unusual quiet descended on the boat.

To port and starboard, the M.G.B.s followed suit and idled to a stop.

Holloway stood still, listening to the darkness. If the E-boats were out there within hearing range then someone aboard *Forty-Nine* might detect the noise of engines. Small waves slapped the wooden hull, the only sound to disturb the night. He looked to port at the nearest boat wallowing uneasily in the gentle swell. The skipper shook his head, as blind to the enemy as Holloway.

But *Forty-Nine's* skipper wasn't about to give in. They'd answered the call following an attack on a north bound convoy off the coast of Clacton-on-Sea. The escort had managed to drive them off with no casualties and Holloway took the calculated gamble the E-boats would head home for Ostend. The report from the convoy also hinted at a possible destroyer accompanying the E-boats, hence the reason *Forty-Nine* was involved.

And then, faintly in the air he heard a low rumble, hard to read a direction, but it sounded as if it came from their left, somewhere to the north. He looked again at his opposite number who nodded, pointing to port.

Holloway turned to the other boat, and the skipper also nodded and pointed north, confirming the bearing.

He glanced at the Cox'n. 'Hear it?'

'Yes, sir, north by west.'

'Right, we're all agreed. Start engines. Half ahead, twenty knots.'

He signalled the other two skippers with a circular motion of his hand, and to the renewed roar from the exhaust, the power came on and the bow lifted in response. Lieutenant Charles Holloway led his little flotilla north by north-east on a course designed to intercept the enemy boats. At 01.35hrs, only sixteen minutes after changing course to the north-east, he made a sighting. His binoculars picked up the faint sheen of disturbed water, and that all important, unmistakable silhouette of an E-boat. Within seconds he counted three more following in line astern, all of them approaching from north-west of his position. He watched a moment longer to be certain of the numbers.

'E-boats,' he warned the crew. 'Red four-five.' He turned to look at the pair of Gunboats, both vessels following close astern to starboard. Alerted by his vigorous wave, they closed rapidly alongside and he called across.

'Four E-boats at Red four-five. Usual drill, line abreast and pick your targets.'

Nods and raised hands acknowledged the order, and Holloway turned back to the needs of his own command.

'Full ahead, Cox'n.'

The boats fanned out, bows lifting to the increase of power, and *Forty-Nine* surged forward. Holloway removed his cap and donned the steel helmet, always the last to do so. Raising his binoculars to the E-boats, he tensed, frowning at their silhouettes. Something had changed and it took a moment for him to realise they'd altered course away, now presenting their starboard quarters to *Forty-Nine's* port bow. He stared hard at their outlines, at the foaming wake. Had the Germans seen them? The distance between flotillas had actually decreased, so it seemed they were still at cruising speed.

Holloway relaxed slightly. On the enemy's present bearing his own boats had the advantage of maximum surprise. *Forty-Nine* bounced and skidded, and Gilman brought her back under control. She was riding high now, skimming the waves, close to thirty knots. The ensign whipped and crackled abaft the bridge, cold night air on the skin. He glanced astern. Jenkins manned the pair of Lewis machine-guns and McCallum stood on the bow gun. Not a lot of fire-power, but the Gunboats made up for it. His torpedoes were the main armament, and in this scenario unwanted, but *Forty-Nine* could still play her part. Initially the E-boats would see three fast attack craft; identifying individual types came later, if at all.

One of the M.G.B.s had eased ahead, closing the enemy from the right flank, gaining ground with every minute.

Then an E-boat opened fire. White and green tracer whipped in towards the leading M.G.B. and she replied with every gun aboard. The second Gunboat joined the fight and the night lit up with a frantic display of glowing tracer.

Holloway saw the last E-boat in line peel away to the left heading north, and gave chase.

'Port ten! Steer three-five-oh!'

The boat swerved under them and steadied, hard on the E-boat's starboard quarter.

'Open fire!' he yelled above the racket, and Jenkins hit the triggers. Both barrels lit up, hammering a stream of shells at the weaving E-boat. Bright flashes showed from the enemy's aft decking, and Holloway hunched as tracer impacted *Forty-Nine's* bow. The bullets swept the bridge, sparking and whining over the noise of the engine.

Gilman gave a yell of pain and sagged at the wheel, then straightened and regained control. Holloway saw a dark patch spread over his left shoulder.

'Alright?'

Gilman nodded, teeth gritted. 'I'll manage.'

An E-boat tore across their bow, flames pouring from the stern, chased by a stream of tracer. A Gunboat came powering in from the starboard side, skipped aft through *Forty-Nine's* turbulent wake, and continued the chase.

The distinctive punch of an Oerlikon joined the mayhem and the returning gunfire from an E-boat stopped abruptly, dense smoke rising from the engine compartment. The other M.G.B. closed in for the coup de grâce, all guns blazing.

Holloway stared over the bows at the E-boat he'd targeted. It poured white smoke, a deliberate screen behind which it twisted and weaved into the night. Only a fool followed into that murk.

He ignored Gilman and bent to the voice-pipe. 'Twenty knots!'

'Twenty knots, aye, sir,' Moore confirmed up the pipe.

He took a quick look round the field of battle. Two E-boats rocked in the waves, one burning brightly, the other smouldering, silent. Of the third boat there'd been no sign and he wondered what had happened. Probably pulled out early he thought, and looked at Gilman. 'Want me to take the wheel, Cox'n?'

There was defiance in the reply. '*No*, sir, I'm fine.'

Holloway grinned. 'Sorry, only asked.' He pointed. 'Make for that nearest E-boat, that's one of ours standing by.'

The boat veered left and *Forty-Nine* closed the E-boat on the opposite side to where the M.G.B. had stopped.

'Slow ahead,' Holloway said, immediately followed by, 'Stop engines.' A scene of utter destruction met their gaze. Amongst the flickering flames bodies lay as death found them, crumpled in the gun tubs or lying broken and burnt. Through the smashed glass of the cockpit lay more distorted figures, darkened patches of glistening blood congealing from their wounds. Other than crackling flames, no sounds came to their ears, no cries from those who may have only been wounded. It didn't take much to understand there were no survivors.

Holloway looked across the flames and shook his head at the other skipper, who nodded his agreement. No need to wait around. They started up and cruised over to the remaining E-boat. The second M.G.B. had stopped alongside and two of her crew were helping a German casualty while another German stood on the bow with his hands in the air, twin Lewis machine-guns aimed at his chest.

Prisoners, thought Holloway, worth their weight in gold. The German showed no signs of aggression and meekly allowed himself to be taken aboard with his shipmate. The E-boat itself, although badly damaged continued to float and Holloway made the decision to sink it, just to be sure. When all was ready, the three power boats pulled back clear of danger and Holloway nodded. The Oerlikon fired, a steady burst spraying the E-boat's waterline, punching holes in the hull. When the firing stopped the boat settled by the stern, the entire length of the vessel sliding slowly into the depths. In the ensuing silence Holloway glanced round at his small flotilla, elated by the victory, but subdued by the carnage they'd witnessed. It wasn't every day that you came face to face with the enemy. He took a lungful of air and straightened up.

'That's it,' he called. 'Time to go home.'

Chapter Five . . . East Coast

Lieutenant-Commander Richard Thorburn, standing tall on *Brackendale's* bridge, trained the binoculars to his right over the starboard wing and found the black outline of England's east coast. It was the second night of the convoy's journey south, and the wind had become an on-shore force three, driving the waves towards the coast. Frowning, he lowered the glasses. With both hands gripping the compass bowl, he glanced again across the starboard bridge-wing. The frown was necessitated by the ship's proximity to that coast, clearly visible through the binoculars but now hidden from the naked eye.

'Aren't we due another marker buoy, Pilot?'

Lieutenant Martin made a quick check of the chart. 'Seven minutes yet, sir.'

Thorburn had no reason to doubt Martin's navigation, and he had to assume that the corvette up ahead, on the convoy's right flank, would be even now congratulating themselves on locating it.

In accordance with his previous orders from Senior Officer of the escorting warships, *Brackendale* maintained her station astern of the convoy, screening the rear echelon. His worries centred around straying beyond the confines of the swept channel; the Germans made a concerted effort to continually sow mines and no ship could afford to gamble. Having seen for himself, and regardless of his navigator's certainty, he decided to err on the side of caution and steer for the middle of the swept channel.

He bent to the bank of voice-pipes, deliberately raising the pitch of his voice for clarity.

'Port ten.'

From the wheelhouse the Cox'n acknowledged the helm order. 'Port ten, aye aye, sir.'

Thorburn peered down at the dimly lit compass, waiting as the bows swung left to towards the south-east.

'Midships,' he said, and hesitated while the ship came upright, giving her time to stabilise. 'Steady . . . , steer one-five-five degrees.'

'Steer one-five-five degrees, aye aye, sir.'

Straightening up from the bell-mouthed pipe, Thorburn stepped down from the raised platform and moved forward to the bridge-screen. Balanced against the ship's pitching roll, he peered ahead beyond the pair of four-inch guns and into the darkness, his sharp eyes probing the murk. Beneath his feet, a wave slapped heavily against *Brackendale*'s steel forefoot, and the small warship veered off course.

Down in the wheelhouse the Cox'n felt the hit and saw the bearing fall off to starboard. He cursed, and corrected with a half turn to port. He fought to hold it, hung on, and as the ship lifted to the following sea, his experienced hands eased the wheel back to steady the bearing. The compass returned to one-five-five and he relaxed the tension from his shoulders. Glancing round at the leading hand, he gave a wry grin and accepted a sympathetic nod in return. They understood the complexities of small ship handling, the lively, agile behaviour, and the ability needed to predict her often unruly behaviour. With both hands on the wheel and his eyes glued to the compass, the barrel chested veteran returned to the task of holding *Brackendale* on a heading of south, south-east.

On the bridge, Thorburn, attuned to the ship's performance, grinned at the thought of the Cox'n's undoubted struggles, then lost the smile.

To his left in the port bridge-wing, he found the shadowy outline of Robert Armstrong, binoculars up and exploring the seas off the bow.

'Number One,' he called quietly, and saw him look round.

'Yes, sir?'

'A moment, if you will.'

Armstrong swayed across to join him at the forebridge. Thorburn glanced at his ill-defined presence and smiled to himself. Armstrong was ever the professional; and at this moment displayed a serious frown.

'I'm minded to take station on the left flank, we're not much use inshore.'

Armstrong hesitated before answering. 'I think *Southern Spirit's* last in line in the port column, sir.'

Thorburn stared into the night and pictured the five-thousand ton freighter, an old red painted collier, thumping along at seven knots. He'd seen her Master in daylight, a large man with a cheery grin and a ready wave. And Armstrong was right to bring it to his attention; there were a total of nineteen ships left in this convoy, steaming ahead in two columns, and collisions were a common occurrence in the narrowness of the swept channel.

Brackendale held her position as tail-end-charlie, while H.M.S. *Warrington* remained on the port flank. The pair of Flower class corvettes, *Lantana* and *Cornflower* held station ahead and to starboard.

He nodded. 'Let's hope no-one else has dropped astern.' Mind made up he looked round in the darkness and found Lieutenant Martin. 'Port ten, Pilot. Make revolutions for six knots.'

'Aye aye, sir,' Martin said, and Thorburn heard the order passed to the wheelhouse.

Beneath their feet the 'Hunt' class destroyer seemed to sag as the speed came off and she wallowed round towards the left flank. The wind drove in on her starboard side, caught her beam-on and the bridge tilted before she swung upright and steadied.

'Midships,' Thorburn said.

The small warship settled, cutting across the tail of the convoy's passage at forty-five degrees.

A lookout gave a quiet warning from the starboard bridge-wing. 'Ship, bearing Green two-oh, six-hundred yards, sir.'

Thorburn raised his glasses and found the stern of *Southern Spirit* fine on the starboard bow. 'Very well,' he acknowledged and watched the distance close. *Brackendale* would pass clear of her stern, after which he could alter course and steam parallel with the freighter's port quarter.

They pushed through the vessel's foaming wake and Thorburn chose his moment.

'Starboard twenty, steer one-six-oh. Make your speed seven knots.'

A faint shaft of moonlight appeared from behind the scudding clouds and Thorburn watched the bows come round, her sharp stem throwing up drifts of spray. With the course finally re-established, *Brackendale* settled at her new station, a cable's length clear of *Southern Spirit*'s port side.

A strident shout called in alarm. 'Ship! Bearing, Red one-seven-oh! Range six-thousand yards.'

Thorburn leapt to the port bridge-wing and raised his glasses to the stern quarter. The call from the lookout had been specific. Red for port, and one-hundred and seventy degrees from the bows, coming round from the ship's centreline, tracing aft . . . , should be fine over the stern rail. For an instant he searched and then caught a white glimmer, the faint sheen of a bow wave.

'Action stations!' he called, and heard the alarm bell shrill through the decks. He kept focus on the unidentified stranger and picked up the trail of disturbed water, the phosphorescent wake of propeller turbulence. This side of the convoy, approaching from the enemy shore, it must certainly be German, crossing *Brackendale's* stern from east to west. How it had penetrated the British laid minefield, God only knew. He turned to a voice-pipe.

'Guns?'

In the tower, Carling answered the call. 'I heard, sir, we're tracking.'

'Range?' Thorburn asked.

'Five thousand yards . . . , increasing.'

Thorburn hesitated; a lone target, or were there more?

Carling added to his initial sighting. 'Looks to be a 'T' class destroyer. Speed eighteen knots, course two-seven-oh.'

Thorburn narrowed his eyes, and made the decision. If the target had company they'd soon find out.

'Hold fire, Guns, I'm turning to go after him.' He stepped up to the compass platform, figuring the angles. If he brought *Brackendale* round to port he could attack the German's left flank as he emerged from crossing the convoy's stern.

'Hard-a-port! Make revolutions for twenty-five knots.'

The Cox'n's acknowledged, echoing up the pipe. 'Port three-five. Speed twenty-five knots, aye aye, sir.'

Brackendale answered the helm and heeled hard over to starboard, vibrating to the increase in power, punching through the breaking seas.

Throughout the ship men already prepared for action came alert at their stations; the gun crews closing up in readiness, and below the waterline men in the ammunition magazines prepared to feed the hoists. In the engine room, the veteran Bryn Dawkins, watched his dials and gauges, and kept one eye open for the telegraph. His Stokers checked and double-checked the revolutions of the spinning shafts, alert to the slightest change in the hundred and one components turning steam to power. The heat inside their steel-walled compartment began to rise.

Amidships, positioned high on the galley deck-house, the four-barrelled Pompom trained round in its mounting. Leading Seaman Gunner 'Taff' Williams settled to the back sight and glanced at the ammunition feedrails ensuring there was a ready supply. His primary role was 'layer', the oft abused 'up and downer', and along with his eight man gun crew they'd notched up a total of six confirmed 'kills'. It was a remarkable tally; 'eyeshooting' through a ringsight required an extraordinary amount of skill, and Williams had a natural flair for dispatching enemy aircraft.

Thorburn stood tall on the compass platform and bared his teeth to the wind. The chase was on, any minute now they would engage the enemy. *Brackendale* gathered speed, powering through the water, a welter of flying foam. He brought the glasses up and found the target, growing in size as the ship came round. A drift of salt spray soaked his face.

'Midships,' he ordered, careful to control his voice. Beneath his feet she swept upright, the mast swaying beyond the perpendicular before settling with her bows to the north.

'Steady.' He waited for the compass to react. 'Steer three-five-oh.'

Falconer replied; calm, measured. 'Steer three-five-oh degrees, aye aye, sir.' *Brackendale* thumped a wave, and another. A fine mist engulfed the open bridge and Thorburn turned away to query the Control Tower. 'Range?'

Carling answered. 'Four thousand two-hundred and closing. Definitely a 'T' class, sir.'

That was the confirmation Thorburn needed. 'Yeoman!' he called.

The man appeared from the back of the bridge. 'Get a signal off to *Warrington* copied to Admiralty. "Enemy in sight. Engaging," and send in clear. Got that?'

'Aye aye, sir,' said the Yeoman, and confirmed the instruction, then headed for the wireless room.

Thorburn squinted in thought. No point in sending a signal in code with the enemy in sight, their proximity to one another just helped the Germans with their code breaking. Vital seconds ticked by as Thorburn refreshed his memory. The German was similar in size to *Brackendale* but almost ten knots faster; a single four-inch gun on the fo'c'sle supported by a lot of 20 millimetre anti-aircraft stuff, and a main armament of six torpedo tubes. Not to be taken lightly. And any moment now they must catch sight of *Brackendale*. Only luck had brought the enemy in behind the convoy and not in amongst the freighters. Time to engage and he gave the order to Carling.

'Open fire!'

Thorburn heard the faint call. 'Shoot!'

From the forward turret he heard the fire-gong, immediately followed by the blast of both barrels. A pair of four-inch shells hurtled towards the target, the bridge engulfed in smoke. He coughed.

Another blast from the guns, and more shells whipped away over the dark sea. He glimpsed two plumes of water rising short of the target, and pursed his lips. It was imperative he get the quarterdeck guns in action, turn *Brackendale* to port between the German and the rear of the convoy. That would give Carling the ship's starboard beam facing the enemy, and give all the guns a line of sight. He bent to the wheelhouse pipe. 'Port five!'

He vaguely heard the Cox'n's reply, and the ship commenced a turn to the left. From the corner of his eye he caught a dull flash from the German destroyer, immediately followed by a column of water lifting off *Brackendale's* bow.

'Midships . . . , steady . . . , steer two-one-oh,' Thorburn called, and raised his binoculars. As the ship centred, 'Guns' took full advantage. All four barrels of the main armament crashed out a broadside, a full salvo whistling towards the target. Water spouts straddled the enemy, but with no obvious result. Thorburn spotted the German turning away to starboard, circling back for German waters. He *must* intercept, cut off their means of escape.

'Port thirty, full ahead both!' he called to the pipe.

The Cox'n' reply was lost to the noise of the guns, a sustained barrage hammering from the muzzles.

Brackendale heeled heavily to starboard, foaming sea cascading down her quarterdeck.

Thorburn raised his glasses. With the change of positions the range had closed and he smiled grimly. A ripple of tracer rose from the enemy destroyer, lazy lines of brightly coloured beads arcing through the night. Then they flattened, hissing close overhead. Bullets hammered into the upperworks, ricocheted around the bridge, and he ducked.

On the raised platform above the galley housing, the four-barrelled Pompom traversed right and rejoined the fray. The distinctive thumping punch of synchronised gunfire accompanying the burst of tracer, the 2lb shells whipping out at the target. Below the starboard bridge-wing the Oerlikon hammered into life, spewing tracer at the enemy.

A voice-pipe shrilled. 'Guns . . , bridge?'

Thorburn acknowledged. 'Captain.'

'Range increasing. Enemy speed thirty-two knots, heading east on oh-eight-five degrees.'

Thorburn frowned.

'Very well,' he said, and forced himself to concentrate through the noise of gunfire. The speed differential had been at the back of his mind and he was now confronted with his original dilemma; that of straying beyond the swept channel and into a minefield.

A starshell burst into dazzling brilliance, lighting up the fast moving German, H.M.S. *Warrington* had entered the fray. She opened fire with her 'A' and 'B' guns, shooting on the rise, bow-wave flying.

But Thorburn was quick to notice she came in tight to the channel buoys. Fast she might be, maybe thirty-four knots all up, but *Warrington* wasn't straying outside into the risk of those mines.

'Signal from *Warrington*, sir.'

He turned to the Yeoman. 'Read it.'

'Discontinue pursuit and take my station.'

Thorburn swallowed as the forward guns cracked out another salvo. *Warrington* had asserted her authority, ordering *Brackendale* to fill the gap in the screen. A tower of water shot up close to the starboard bow, a faint noise of shrapnel against the steel hull.

A lookout shouted excitedly. 'A hit! We've hit 'em, sir!'

Thorburn glanced up and caught the end result, the remnants of the explosion glowing red beneath the mast. Flames flickered briefly, quickly brought under control, and his momentary hope of serious damage faded. He raised the binoculars for one last look, the range increasing rapidly. The hit might well have belonged to *Warrington*. He cursed under his breath and lowered the glasses, it was galling but he had to call it off. Reluctantly he gave the orders.

'Cease fire.' And then to the Cox'n. 'Starboard thirty. Half ahead, make revolutions for twenty knots.' *Brackendale* eased down from her headlong rush, the bow wave less prominent, heeling hard over as she turned south again.

'Midships!' he called to the wheelhouse. He heard Falconer's reply, and changed voice-pipes. 'Guns?'

'Sir?'

'We'll hold fire. Leave it to *Warrington*.'

'Aye aye, sir.'

'Cox'n . . . , revolutions for eighteen knots.'

Falconer's metallic reply echoed up the pipe. 'Half ahead, speed eighteen knots, aye aye, sir.'

Thorburn waited while the ship settled, squinted at the compass and nodded, satisfied they were on a course.

Feeling somewhat dejected he looked round at the crowded bridge.

'Number One, any casualties?' he asked.

'None reported, sir,' Armstrong said.

Thorburn nodded and stepped down to the screen. Beneath his feet, *Brackendale* settled into a rhythmic rise and fall, that old familiar feeling of a small destroyer cruising on through a rolling sea. He sighed and moved to the bridge-chair. Easing himself into the high-backed wooden seat, he rubbed his eyes with thumb and forefinger. Another few hours and he might get a chance to snatch some precious sleep.

A lurid flash lit the night ahead and Thorburn whipped up his binoculars. He found it to be a vessel in the starboard column, down by the head, a fire raging abaft the funnel, and slewing out of line.

'E-boats! Red four-five, two-thousand yards, sir.' The call came from Leading Seaman Allun Jones.

Thorburn swept his glasses seaward and immediately picked out the deadly shape of a German torpedo boat powering in towards the convoy. Beyond it another boat turned away from an attack, torpedoes gone.

'Starshell!' he demanded of the voice-pipe. A muzzle lifted in the forward mounting, traversed left and blasted a shot at the sky. Seconds later the flare burst white, drifting on the small parachute, and revealed three E-boats, two of them still on their attack runs.

'Open fire!'

At a range of eighteen-hundred yards *Brackendale*'s guns roared into action.

Thorburn moved to the compass housing, bending to the voice-pipes.

'Full ahead both!'

The Cox'n repeated. 'Full ahead together, aye aye, sir.' And Thorburn heard the faint ring of the telegraph.

He felt a vibration through his boots, the power of the turbines transmitting through the ship, the bows lifting as the propellers found purchase.

Far ahead, peeling out from the left column, the Flower corvette *Lantana* joined the fray. Her single four-inch gun belched flame, the Pompom letting go a stream of tracer at the fast moving boats.

A freighter in the right column exploded, a great plume of water rising from her fo'c'sle.

Brackendale's bow-chaser hammered into life, tracer arcing across the waves. A second starshell burst, floating in the air, and the nearest E-boat made a violent turn towards *Brackendale*. Twin lines of German tracer hissed over the fo'c'sle, found the forward gun shield and smothered it in flashing sparks. The bow-chaser latched on to the E-boat, a fusillade of shells striking home, the boat's guns falling silent. It turned away sharply, bouncing in the waves, and a four-inch shell from the quarterdeck mushroomed off the boat's port side.

Thorburn heard the sound of *Warrington's* guns and glanced quickly astern. The destroyer had left the swept channel, curving out beyond the marker buoys.

A bright orange flash lit *Brackendale's* bridge and he looked to port. The E-boat had taken a direct hit, blasted into fragments, a machine gun spinning end over end, splashing beneath the waves. Bits of hull rained down on the sea.

The third E-boat launched torpedoes and skidded away in a tight turn, directly into the path of *Lantana*, and the corvette let loose with everything she had. Oerlikons, machine-guns, the Pompom; a mass of bright coloured tracer chasing the target.

Somehow it survived unscathed, racing into the darkness.

Thorburn turned to watch the convoy, waiting for the inevitable explosion, but keeping one eye on his own situation.

'Half ahead, make revolutions for twelve knots.' No more explosions followed and as the last of the starshell sputtered out they were left with the pale light of the moon.

On the far side of the convoy, the last ship to be hit glowed red, flames flickering about the waist, low in the water, and Thorburn raised his glasses for a closer look. The stark outline of H.M.S. *Cornflower* closed to give assistance and Thorburn turned his attention to the first casualty. His binoculars showed her after section riding high in the water, ships of the column astern taking urgent avoiding action.

'*Warrington* signalling, sir.'

He turned and spotted a small, shaded Aldis lamp flashing a message, and waited.

'Message reads, "Enemy withdrawn, resume station". End of message, sir.'

'Very well, acknowledge.' Thorburn said. With *Warrington* approaching at speed he took the least complicated option to return *Brackendale* to her station.

'Slow ahead,' he ordered, and as the ship reduced speed the convoy plodded past, each vessel stubbornly pushing on with a precious cargo.

Warrington rushed by, all bow wave and flying ensign, her Aldis lamp flickering with more instructions. When his Yeoman of signals remained silent he prompted a response.

'What's she saying?'

'It's for *Cornflower*, sir. "Stand by and recover survivors." End of message.'

Thorburn looked across at *Cornflower*, dwarfed by the freighter's upperworks even though she lay low in the water. The pair of ships had already lost touch with the convoy, drifting astern of the last in line. And then *Brackendale* herself dropped astern of *Southern Spirit* and Thorburn matched his speed to that of the convoy.

Armstrong came up to the bridge with his report.

'Two walking wounded, sir. Gunners Foster and Grant from the forward mount. Doc Waverley has them in the sick berth, nothing serious he said. We have superficial damage that Mr Dawkins says we can repair ourselves.'

'Very well, Number One,' Thorburn said, peering round the dark bridge.

From overhead he heard the throbbing pulse of aero-engines, bombers judging by the noise, a dull rumble, flying southwest towards London.

'Number One,' he called softly. 'Allow the crew to relax but hold them at Action Stations. No one to leave their posts,'

'Aye aye, sir,' Armstrong said, and Thorburn heard him descend the ladder to the flag deck. They pushed on through the night, alert to the danger of the darkness, knowing many more hours of vigilance would yet be required.

On the departing enemy destroyer, Korvettenkapitän Wolfgang Schulze nodded with satisfaction, his job done. As advised from aerial reconnaissance, and with carefully plotted charts, he had managed to penetrate the East coast minefield barrage. And the British had taken the bait, drawn into a meaningless fight. The damage to his own ship, unfortunate, a very minor hit amidships.

One crewman killed, two injured; a small price to pay for such a successful night's work. The ruse to draw the Royal Navy away from the Schnellboats had worked far better than he had dared hope.

From what he'd seen, at least two freighters had been hit. No reports from the Schnellboats as yet and a garbled signal indicated one might have been destroyed. He nodded and allowed himself a cynical smile; the Kriegsmarine had outwitted their British counterparts. Raising his binoculars he searched for the distant outline of Bolougne harbour. Not yet in sight but they would soon be within the safety of the shore guns.

'Signal the defences we are coming in,' he ordered. Tomorrow he would be entertained by the base Kommandant. It would be a good day.

On the southern edge of the British laid mine barrage, close to where Schulze's destroyer had slipped away from the engagement, a single Royal Navy deployed contact mine, disturbed by the warship's passage, broke free from its mooring and wobbled to the surface. The lethal trigger horns rolled with the waves, and driven by the prevailing westerly winds, began to drift north.

Chapter Six . . Thames Estuary

On the coast of Kent, nine hundred yards southeast of Jos Bay, a battery of eight 3.7inch anti-aircraft guns sat pointing at the night sky. The gun emplacements had been dug in and protected by walls of sandbags. From the unit's Command Centre the alarm went out to man the guns, dozens of soldiers pouring out from the sleeping quarters, shouted orders bringing sense to the apparent chaos. Within minutes fused shells waited to be set and a bank of searchlights prepared to pinpoint a fleet of German bombers. The gun captains were well aware that when the Heinkels crossed the coast they would be flying at nigh on sixteen-thousand feet, descending to ten-thousand before releasing their bomb loads. High over the Channel the sound of their engines filtered down to the waiting gunners. They held their breath, concentrating on the dark skies.

Two kilometres out to sea, a German warship throttled back and turned towards the north. Oberleutnant Heinrich Vogel ordered 'slow ahead' and the vessel almost lost steerage, nosing erratically ahead in the wind driven waves. He looked to the heavens and waited. The planned diversionary air raid should arrive any time now. Binoculars searched the immediate vicinity, on the lookout for roving British patrols. And then the commander heard the distant rumble of engines in the sky and glanced at the time. He smiled coldly, his operation could begin.

'Half ahead,' he ordered, and with the noise of the aircraft engines growing louder, the ship's propellers gained purchase, and in the comforting cloak of darkness the vessel steamed north past Margate's headland towards the Thames Estuary.

The anti-aircraft battery opened fire on the bombers and the night sky burst into splashes of fiery colour. The powerful beam of searchlights criss-crossed the blackness, latching on to a Heinkel, target found, concentrating the flak and chasing the aircraft inland towards Canterbury.

And hidden in the Channel waters, the minelayer steamed out into the approaches to the Thames Estuary and began to lay its 'eggs'.

On a recent stormy night Vogel had escaped the attentions of a Royal Navy destroyer, and on reporting the skirmish to his superiors, had been summoned home for repairs before attempting further forays into British waters. It had taken a lot of planning and a fair share of luck, but when he finally turned his ship away from the English coast, he left an additional twenty-four underwater contact mines moored across the mouth of London's principal maritime artery. It had been a good mission.

It was Sunday the 26th and in the early morning, fog-shrouded waters of England's eastern coastline, eighteen nautical miles north-east of Sheerness, H.M.S. *Warrington*'s small convoy of seventeen remaining deep-laden freighters, steamed slowly south towards the outer reaches of the Thames estuary. By the grey light of dawn they comprised a motley collection of rust streaked hulls and smoke blackened funnels, all the tell tale signs of long usage, the accumulated dents and scrapes of years spent navigating the worlds seaways. Eleven of those ships carried coal, a vital replenishment to the dwindling stocks of London's power stations, and preceded a small five-thousand ton oil tanker. The remainder hauled general cargo, a combination of grain and raw materials.

Approaching Foulness Island the convoy changed course to the west and followed *Warrington* in towards the mouth of the city's great River Thames. As they slowed to negotiate the static barges that tethered the floating armada of barrage balloons, an Admiralty 'Pilot' tugboat and a small Sloop appeared from the skeins of patchy fog, and signal lamps began to flicker. As leading escort destroyer, *Warrington*, released her charges into the tug's capable hands, and then made a signal thanking *Brackendale* and the two Flower class corvettes for their co-operation and gave them permission to disperse. The 'Hunt' blinked in response and surged away to the west, bow up, white wake foaming astern, fading into the haze.

H.M.S. *Cornflower*, overcrowded with survivors, acknowledged with her Aldis lamp and peeled away to port, heading for her home station of Sheerness.

It was 04.43hrs when the captain of *Warrington* pushed his cap to the back of his head and breathed a gentle sigh of relief. One more convoy delivered, three less than expected and sadly two short by way of enemy action, but the remainder of the vessels with their valuable cargoes were on their way up river. He raised his glasses for a last look round the stragglers, pleased to find they were well closed up, probably glad to be so near home. *Southern Spirit* trailed in last. He watched as the new escort took station, busying themselves with guiding their charges through the moored barges. A final glance in the direction of the departing destroyer, already swallowed up by the mist, and he turned to the bridge chair.

He fished out his pipe, found a morsel of tobacco, and turned to his First Lieutenant. 'Hot drinks all round I think, Number One.' He tamped down an errant strand of leaf into the bowl, struck a match and managed to secure a glowing ember. To add to his sense of well being the morning sun broke through the haze and he watched the ships as might a shepherd counting the flock onto fresh pasture.

An explosion shattered the quiet dawn, rolling across the sea, a heavy, rumbling roar.

Warrington's captain froze, staring in disbelief at an enormous column of seawater, fragments of a ship's carcass hurtling through the air. As the deluge subsided, where once there'd been a small corvette turning for home, the sea had already risen to her gunwales, and only the splintered remnants of her bow plates could be clearly seen above the waves.

The captain jumped for the compass platform.

'Port thirty! Half ahead both!' He looked over at the sinking ship. There would be survivors, only a few, and he wasn't about to leave men in the water. But unlike so many they'd rescued before, there was a difference with these men. A lot of those on board had only just survived one sinking, and now they'd suffered another. And then there were those who wore the same uniform, performed the same vital task and suffered the same hardships in protecting the merchantmen from a similar fate. They were comrades, unknown by name, and yet familiar from an occasional wave of the hand. *Warrington's* captain was no fool. He was risking his ship and her crew by going to the aid of another. What had happened to

Cornflower? A torpedo? If so, where was the U-boat? If not, it could only be an underwater mine, and where there was one . . . ?

And then with a gurgling upsurge of rushing water, the remains of the corvette succumbed to the sea and she sank from sight. The turbulence at the surface spread slowly, smoothed, and the ripples died away.

Warrington ran on, closing the distance. A scrambling net appeared over the starboard quarterdeck and the whaler swung out from its davits on the port side. The remaining corvette circled wide, hunting for signs of a U-boat.

'Slow ahead,' the captain said, and the destroyer eased to nose slowly in amongst the first signs of wreckage. His crew were quick to spot some of those in the water, the few who still had strength to swim. The whaler splashed into the waves and rowed out from the side. Faint calls for help guided their efforts and an oil sodden sailor was dragged over the gunwales. While the boat searched for more, two survivors reached the scrambling net and found enough energy to haul themselves up the side, gentle hands helping oil blackened, retching men over the side.

But as the captain had suspected, there weren't many who made it. Sixteen altogether, and five of those were merchantmen from the freighter. Of *Cornflower's* crew, only eleven out of an entire ship's company, and one of those might not live to see the end of the day. When he was certain there were no more to be found, the captain sadly turned his back on the sunken warship, and *Warrington* set course for home. With *Brackendale* long gone, *Cornflower's* sister corvette searched the surrounding area for over an hour; in the end the assumption was it had been a mine. If you were in a ship on the east coast convoys, the most unnerving thing for a sailor was the terror of striking an unseen enemy, the stealthily laid underwater killer; and it was all down to the luck of the draw.

Before the old V&W destroyer tied up to her berth, the ship's doctor reported one more death amongst H.M.S. *Cornflower's* survivors. Just ten of the original eighty-five man crew, finally made it ashore.

On the far side of the Channel, the commander of a German minelayer slept soundly, unaware of the carnage he'd inflicted on a small warship.

Daylight found *Brackendale* tied up to the quayside in the shelter of Sheerness harbour. Action reports signed off, the ship's log brought up to date, stores replenished, re-ammunitioned, and harbour watch established; the officers and crew snatched what sleep was offered before duty called again.

Richard Thorburn lay with his eyes closed, unable to sleep. The ship sat quietly enough and the only sound that might have disturbed him were the muted footsteps of a watch keeper on the bridge above the wheelhouse overhead. But that was the background noise of harbour routine, an all too familiar normality for him to be disturbed. No, he thought, his mind racing over a dozen different problems, even though the last few months had been a frantic merry-go-round of alarms and patrols, another anxiety kept him awake. It was a woman by the name of Jennifer Farbrace and it had been a long time since they'd last met. She had become more than just a pleasant distraction. He found her attractively beguiling, impulsive, more than enough reason to keep a man awake. He smiled ruefully in the grey light from the scuttle.

From his earliest memories he'd always wanted his own command. He was a sailor, the sea was where he belonged, and time spent anywhere on water was never wasted. He relished every opportunity to take *Brackendale* out of harbour. Seamanship, and all that it entailed, had become Thorburn's natural environment, second nature. He sighed, if he couldn't sleep he may as well be up. The clock showed 06.45hrs and he swung from the bunk and padded across to his desk. Impatiently he lit a cigarette and opened his file of requisitions, the mundane non-urgent inventory that arose through the normal course of repair and maintenance.

The engineering department required a signature to their list of spares and he reached for the fountain pen. As he signed with a flourish the watchkeeper walked from port to starboard across the bridge. He frowned at the tip of his pen, and wondered if Jennifer had slept soundly, and then rebuked himself for the thought. Of course she'd slept, no woman in her right mind would be losing sleep over a sailor. He pulled over the next request and studied the 'Gunner's' carefully itemised request form, any vague possibility of feeling tired banished to the back of his mind.

At 07.00hrs a priority signal arrived ordering *Brackendale* to proceed Dover where Thorburn would await instructions from Captain (D). He put out a call for Armstrong to warn the ship's company, and an hour later, with breakfast cleared away, the crew set about preparing to put to sea.

In the captain's cabin, Thorburn looked up as a pipe echoed through the decks.

'Hands to station for leaving harbour! Special sea duty men close up!' A glance at his watch told him it was 08.15. He tapped the paperwork into a neat pile, placed them to one side and came to his feet. The sounds of boots on ladders accompanied his movements, a flurry of activity around the ship. Lifting his seagoing jacket from the back of the chair, he shrugged into its faded comfort and ran a finger round the inside of his roll-neck jumper.

He turned to a knock on the door.

'Come.'

The lean face of First Lieutenant Robert Armstrong peered inside.

'Ready to proceed, sir.'

'Thank you, Number One. I'll come up.'

Armstrong nodded. 'Very good, sir,' he said, and hesitated.

Thorburn saw it. 'What?'

'The lads are very tired, sir. Action stations held for some hours.'

Thorburn looked at him in sympathy, and with good reason. They were all tired. This sector of the English Channel was overworked and undermanned. If it wasn't East Coast convoys it was defensive patrols, or like the other day, a rescue sweep into the North Sea. The constant demands on too few ships and the never ending alarms wore a man down, frayed the nerves. And Armstrong broached the subject because someone had got to him, maybe the Cox'n, warning him of the ship's morale. Sleep had become a luxury that seemed confined to those with proper beds.

'I know and I'm sorry, Bob, but not much I can do other than cruise down on defence stations and hope there's no alarm. We might get a break at Dover.'

'Yes, sir,' Armstrong said and Thorburn waited for him to leave. He picked up his cap, settled it on his forehead, took a quick look in the mirror to check, and straightened his jacket. For a split second he took note of

67

the tanned, lined face staring back, grinned at the reflection, and reached for his pair of Barr and Stroud binoculars. He slipped the leather strap over his head and let the familiar weight hang on his chest. Feeling for his cigarettes, he patted a pocket for the matches and headed for the bridge.

In bright sunlight he clambered lightly up the ladder and as he emerged onto the back of the navigating platform, a quietness descended over the gathering of officers and watchkeepers. He pushed through the crowded space to the glass screen at the fore-bridge and looked down on the fo'c'sle party, already busy coiling a greasy wire. Armstrong stood in close attendance, hands behind his back, alert to the possible need of a swift correction in case of mishaps.

Thorburn moved to the port wing and looked down at the quayside, and then astern to where Sub-Lieutenant George Labatt stood waiting with the quarterdeck party.

'Let go aft!' he ordered, and a moment later men down on the hard released the wires attached to the bollards and dropped them to the water. The Special Sea Dutymen hauled them aboard and once clear of the ship's side and the propellers, the call came to the bridge. 'All clear aft.'

Thorburn took a breath and began the business of extricating *Brackendale* from the harbour wall.

'Slow ahead.'

The ship eased forward and he watched the bow-spring tighten, pulling the ship's stem in towards the dock, the stern swinging unrestrained out into the harbour. He waited until she reached a forty degree angle.

'Stop engines.' He ordered the spring wire to be released and waited while it was hauled aboard.

'Slow astern.'

Cautiously, *Brackendale* eased sternfirst out from the quayside and into the flotsam covered oily water of the harbour. Thorburn made a cursory check for clear water and leaned to the voice-pipe.

'Stop engines.' He allowed thirty seconds grace. 'Slow ahead both. Starboard fifteen.'

'Slow ahead, fifteen of the starboard wheel on, sir,' the Cox'n answered, and the ship veered gently away into open water.

'Midships . . . , steady. Steer two-seven-five degrees.'

'Two-seven-five degrees, aye aye, sir.'

Brackendale turned west toward the Isle of Grain, cleared the sheltered waters of the Medway's outer reaches and met the open sea. 'Half ahead together. Make revolutions for twelve knots.'

Falconer acknowledged and the ship lifted to the first of the long rollers, winding her way through the waves.

Thorburn glanced astern, gauged they were far enough out to make the next turn and passed the order. 'Starboard fifteen, steer three-five-five degrees.'

He heard the repeat and moved to the bridge chair. The sparkling waters of the English Channel glinted under the warmth of the sun and he reached for his pack of cigarettes. He extracted one and glanced over his shoulder.

'You have the ship, Pilot.'

'Aye aye, sir,' Lieutenant Martin said, and the warship steamed north to clear the Isle of Sheppey, then east, before turning south for Margate and the North Foreland.

Thorburn smiled into the breeze and wondered, not for the first time, why the Admiralty had ordered a small 'Hunt' class destroyer to report to the Captain of Destroyers in Dover. The only tangible outcome to the detachment was that *Brackendale* would, in all probability, not now be called upon for escort duty tonight. He breathed smoke and closed his eyes, lulled by the hot sun and the ship's swaying motion. It was good to be out on the open sea.

Korvettenkapitän Wolfgang Schulze climbed the steps of Bolougne's Kriegsmarine Headquarters, passed through the ornately carved doors of the old municipal building, and then descended the stairs to the cellar. In the cold, dimly lit corridor he found the door marked, 'Port-Kommandanten', and knocked.

'Ja?' came a bark from inside, and Schulze strode into a sumptuously furnished office. He came to attention and saluted, not with Hitler's high thrown hand, but with the Navy's traditional touch of fingers to the peak of his cap.

Kapitän-zur-See, Erich Deitricht Richter, looked up from behind his desk and allowed the faintest of smiles to brighten his otherwise leathery face.

'Relax, Schulze, we will not stand on ceremony. I hear all was well?'

'It was, Herr Kapitän. Your reading of the Royal Navy's tactics left them totally at the mercy of the Schnellboats. I am understanding two ships were sunk, a third maybe damaged.'

'And your ship?'

'One hit on the afterdeck, slight damage, repairs are almost completed, sir.'

Richter nodded and Schulze felt the full force of his probing stare. When the Kapitän spoke again, he did so in measured tones.

'Good,' he said slowly, 'that is very good. And now I have news. You and your ship are wanted.' He glanced away for a moment. 'If I remember correctly, you formed part of the defensive flotilla for the breakout in February. Your experience will be valuable. We have been given the honour of forming an attack force to stand by while the *Holstein* sails from Rotterdam to Calais. When the ship leaves Wilhelmshaven you will prepare for sea.'

Schulze felt a surge of anticipation. It would be the second time he'd been involved in an escort flotilla, the first had been the triumphant dash up the Channel with the *Scharnhorst*, *Gneisenau* and *Prinz Eugen*. The British had thrown everything available at the Kriegsmarine's capital ships and failed. And he'd heard of this armed merchantman, the *Holstein* had proved itself more than capable with 45,000 tons of shipping already credited to its tally.

But this time Schulze would be steaming in the opposite direction, east to west. He grinned, unable to contain his excitement.

'And who commands the *Holstein*, Herr Kapitän?'

'Gerhard Baumgartner,' Richter replied, 'Kapitän-zur-See Gerhard Erich Baumgartner.' He sounded envious. 'Oberleutnant Vogel will also be with you, plus two of our minesweepers and all the available Schnellboats.'

Schulze thought about the validity of using the inexperienced Vogel but guessed it was all to do with the number of guns. 'When will the *Holstein* come?' he asked.

Richter narrowed his eyes, the wrinkled face furrowed in thought. 'Soon, I believe . . . , within the week.'

Chapter Seven . . . Hellfire Corner

In the rubble strewn streets of Dover, less than a hundred yards from the sea, a heavily bearded Royal Navy officer stepped down from his staff car and cast a critical gaze over the sandbagged entrance to his new headquarters. Captain James Pendleton had not set eyes on Dover since the Royal Navy had made the strategic decision to withdraw from the vulnerability of Admiralty Harbour. But with the Royal Air Force now in control of the skies, Admiral Ramsey had taken the decision to reinforce the remaining Motor Torpedo Boats with a significant force of destroyers. Normally on a Sunday he would have attended the church service in Chatham's dockyard. Today was different. He'd deliberately chosen the weekend to make the move, allowing him therefore to be back in harness for the week ahead.

He turned and looked along the street running parallel with the waterfront, where Dover's proximity to the German guns at Pas-de-Calais became all too evident. The red brick masonry of a once fashionable hotel lay scattered across the far end of the road. A bath tub hung precariously from of the remains of an upper floor, the plumbing swaying vertically in space. Tattered curtains fluttered behind the broken glass of a once ornate window, polished wooden furniture discarded in the debris flung across Liverpool Street. Members of the local fire brigade, assisted by passing volunteers, were bent to the task of clearing up.

Pendleton glanced out across the harbour and tried to envisage the German heavy artillery sitting on the cliffs twenty-two miles away. With little or no warning a shell would arrive and obliterate everything in its path. The innocent men and women of Dover had much to fear.

The sound of an engine made him turn, and a Bedford lorry trundled out from a side street and pulled up behind the staff car. Three seamen jumped down from the cab, dropped the tailboard and disappeared under the tarpaulin. Within moments they began transferring a varied assortment of paraphernalia into Pendleton's new quarters.

He turned to the car. 'Miss Farbrace . . . , perhaps you would be so good as to oversee the correct placement of our files.'

The young woman, Second Officer Jennifer Farbrace, W.R.N.S., stepped away from the back door of the car and smoothed her uniform skirt into position. She smiled, her usual cheery self. 'Of course, sir. The basement you said?'

Pendleton nodded, admiring her graceful poise, the natural elegance that even a plain uniform couldn't hide. 'I'm afraid so, and I doubt we'll have much in the way of daylight.'

She laughed in response, a sparkling show of white teeth. 'I'm sure we'll be fine, sir. At least you're back where you should be.' She walked lightly up the steps into the dark interior of the building, and Pendleton rubbed his beard in thought. She was right, of course. Ramsey, probably acting under Churchill's direct orders, had finally decided to reinstate Captain of Destroyers 'Captain (D)' to Dover's defences; albeit underground, hidden from view and protected from the worst of any German activity. He hoped it wouldn't be a short lived exercise. With a resigned shrug of his shoulders he stuck out his bearded chin and strode off towards the inner harbour of Wellington Dock. It was time to see for himself.

He walked on, weaved between a row of light ant-aircraft gun emplacements, reached Granville Dock and made for the Prince of Wales Pier. The outer waters of Admiralty Harbour beckoned.

Pendleton rounded the western end of the inner basin and stepped across the steel tracks beyond the railway station. A short distance to his left the Prince of Wales Pier jutted out into the inner harbour. Beneath his shoes the concrete of Admiralty Pier stretched out to meet the distant southern breakwater, which in turn met the Eastern Arm that enclosed the bay of mooring buoys.

A half-smile lit up his bearded cheeks. It was good to be back, he thought, even though his new position was a bit of a double edged sword. Way beyond the far breakwater, below the dominant presence of Dover Castle, the tall, chalk white cliffs shone in the sunlight. But Pendleton wasn't here to admire the scenery. A variety of ships swung to their moorings, mostly merchantmen waiting for onward passage with a passing convoy.

And there in the distance, dwarfed by an old tramp steamer, he found the small outline of a 'Hunt' class destroyer. *Brackendale* had entered harbour.

Approaching footsteps made him turn and Jennifer Farbrace arrived beside him. She saluted and he touched the peak of his cap. Formal customs satisfied, particularly in full view of the public, he pointed across the water.

'She's here,' he said. 'Other side of that old rust bucket.' He glanced down and watched her face brighten with pleasure. It had been a few months since Richard Thorburn had made an appearance, and Pendleton was well aware of her attachment to the maverick young commander. A thought struck him and he grinned, a mischievous twinkle in his eye.

'Fancy a boat trip?'

Jennifer looked up, pensive.

He saw the hesitation. 'No? . . . , I thought we'd pay them a visit.'

She glanced down at her skirt and he guessed what was going through her mind. Small destroyers were not equipped with companionways, only a Jacob's ladder slung over the ship's side.

He gave a short chuckle. 'You've climbed those ladders before.'

She glanced at him quickly, and he could see the annoyance. 'In dungarees, yes sir, but not in a skirt like this.'

Pendleton stood back and pretended to give her a thorough appraisal. The pleated skirt came down well below her knees so if she was worried about decorum only a shapely calf would be visible. As for her Navy issue shoes, they were as stout and sensible as his. He turned away, looked out over the harbour and rubbed his beard.

'Well, if you'd rather be in the cellar checking filing cabinets, don't let me stand in your way.'

There was silence, but when he looked round she giggled, her face lit up. 'That, sir, is blatant blackmail. But you win, I'll come on your ruddy boat trip.'

Pendleton clapped his hands. 'Good girl, let's see if we can find a vacant jolly boat.' And with that he strode off ready to apply the full authority of a Captain's rank.

He found the harbour motor launch berthed at her old station in Granville Dock. Pendleton's narrowed eyes swept critically over the boat's presentation and he nodded with approval. She was primarily used to deliver mail, but her duties included ferrying officers and crewmen from ship to shore, and vice versa, and they were amongst the busiest craft in a harbour. Sometimes they let standards slip. But in this case the lines were neatly coiled, fenders well placed, boat hooks secured; all in all a good turnout.

A rating on the quayside smartened to attention, surprise on his face at the appearance of a Captain.

'Who's in charge?' Pendleton asked.

'Cox'n, sir. Petty Officer Roper.'

A head appeared from the cockpit and a veteran seaman snapped up a salute. 'Roper, sir. Boat's at your disposal.'

Pendleton beamed. 'In that case, Cox'n, perhaps you'd be so good as to take us out to *Brackendale*. She's the 'Hunt' moored off the southern breakwater.'

'Aye aye, sir,' the man said, and stepped over to offer a helping hand.

Pendleton stood back for Jennifer to board, then dropped easily into the waist.

'Cast off!' the Cox'n ordered, and with the lines coiled, a sailor standing fore and aft with a boathook apiece, he throttled up the engine and peeled out from the quayside.

Pendleton stood tall in the waist of the boat, eyeing each vessel in turn, sizing up their lines with all his experience of years at sea. Big or small, new or old, there weren't many he couldn't find a classification for. Tramp steamers, rust buckets, ocean going grain ships, and coastal steamers with freshly painted company liveries. They all had their role to play, but for now they swung to their moorings awaiting transition to an east or west bound escort to continue their journeys.

He noticed Jennifer watching from the cockpit, craning her neck to look out beyond the bows.

In minutes, Pendleton realised they were approaching the 'rust bucket', the old steamer which was obviously empty of cargo and in ballast, the tips of her single propeller showing above the water. From her bridge, a merchant seaman in a soiled white vest waved a hand, and Pendleton nodded respectfully in return. The men who manned these ships were worth their weight in gold and they lived a precarious existence. Without them, as Churchill well knew, Britain would be starving.

The motor-boat cleared the rust streaked bows and turned gently to port under the huge overhanging forepeak. And Pendleton straightened his shoulders with a sense of pride.

H.M.S. *Brackendale* sat quietly at her mooring buoy, the calm waters of the harbour lapping gently round her sleek hull. The twin four-inch gun barrels pointed forward in neat alignment, and her two-pounder 'Bow-chaser' in the eyes of the ship pointed threateningly at the sky. Twenty millimetre Oerlikons offered close range anti-aircraft support beneath the bridge-wings, and amidships on the galley housing, Pendleton could see the multi-barrelled Pompom undergoing routine maintenance.

His sharp eyes picked out movement on the bridge and he watched with anticipation as the ship began to show signs of life.

In the port wing of *Brackendale's* bridge, Sub-Lieutenant George Labatt stood and stared out at a small convoy plodding up the Channel. The merchant ships slowly clawed their way towards the North Foreland, a sight which until recently, had become altogether unfamiliar during daylight hours. Only since the Royal Air Force had established air supremacy over Britain's coastal waters, had the Admiralty hesitantly given the go-ahead for a smattering of daylight convoys.

'Motor-boat approaching, sir.' The warning came from the bridge watchkeeper.

Labatt turned and spotted the harbour launch nosing out from the far side of a freighter and raised his binoculars. From *Brackendale's* time at Chatham dockyard, he instantly recognised the stocky figure of Captain James Pendleton, and unclipped a handset from below the screen.

'Captain, sir?'

He heard Thorburn answer. 'Yes, Sub, what is it?'

'Captain Pendleton approaching, sir.'

Thorburn hesitated for a few seconds. So Captain (D) must be Pendleton, at long last returned from Chatham to his rightful command of Dover's forces. 'Very well,' he said. 'Man the side.'

'Aye aye, sir,' Labatt said, and returned the handset onto its bracket. He passed the word for the Cox'n and tugged his jacket into some sense of uniformity. It wasn't everyday that a Captain R.N., took time out to visit one of His Majesty's small destroyers.

Richard Thorburn hastily shuffled some papers into the desk drawer. He'd only just dismissed the crew from Sunday Divisions and the prayer service, and changed back into his older uniform. He checked his appearance in the mirror. What he saw made him lift a critical eyebrow, a wry grin spreading over his tanned features. This uniform he wore, his sea-going outfit, wasn't exactly what the Royal Navy had in mind for their design of a captain's wardrobe. It had long since succumbed to the daily wear and tear of life on the open bridge, and now hung somewhat misshapen and threadbare from his shoulders. His battered cap sat squarely, the peak shading his lined forehead, and the prominent wrinkles at the corner of his eyes betraying constant hours spent scanning the seas.

He tucked his unruly hair under the peak of his cap and chuckled. There'd been no warning from the dockside so Pendleton could either like it or lump it. A final glance round the cabin and he stepped out into the linoleum laid corridor, and out to the starboard side. He slid down the ladder from fo'c'sle to main deck and caught sight of the harbour motor-boat heading bow on for *Brackendale*.

A side party had mustered amidships between the galley housing and the guardrail and the Cox'n chivvied them into line. He was pleased to see Sub-Lieutenant Labatt, his Officer-of-the-Day, already in attendance. A movement at his shoulder made him glance sideways, and he hid a smile as Armstrong arrived in a hurry, brushing off the front of his tunic.

Out on the water, the motor-boat swung wide and then turned to make her approach from the stern, throttling down at exactly the right moment to drift her gunwales alongside the Jacob's ladder. A boathook latched on and Thorburn watched the Captain hesitate and peer into the cockpit. A shapely ankle stepped into view and Thorburn straightened in surprise.

Second Officer Jennifer Farbrace ducked out from the canopy and lifted her face to the ship. Before Thorburn had time to react, Pendleton reached for the ladder and the Bosun's pipe shrilled as he came up over the side. He stepped aboard as the wavering call died away and Thorburn snapped up a smart salute. Pendleton touched the peak of his cap, then reached out a hand.

'Morning, Commander,' he said, his gruff, bass voice resounding along the deck.

Thorburn shook the extended hand, held the strong grip.

'Good morning, sir. An unexpected pleasure.'

Pendleton peered at him with a jaundiced eye. 'More for me than you I suspect,' he said with a wicked grin, and he then recognised Armstrong standing in line. He shook hands.

'Number One,' he said by way of acknowledgement. 'Still keeping your captain in order?'

'Trying to, sir,' Armstrong said, and Pendleton turned as the Cox'n bent forward to lend Jennifer his support. Thorburn caught the crew of the motor-boat looking up grinning, nudging each other at the sight of her shapely legs.

She managed the final step up the swaying ladder, pushed the Cox'n's hand away, and then with a touch of colour flushing her cheeks, smoothed her skirt into place.

Pendleton turned to face Thorburn, a wicked twinkle in his eye.

'Your cabin if you please, Richard.'

'Of course, sir. This way.'

Leaving Armstrong to dismiss the side party, and with the motor-boat curving out across the harbour for its berth in Granville Dock, Thorburn walked forward beneath the davits holding the ship's boat and climbed the ladder to the fo'c'sle deck. He led them down the corridor, opened his cabin and stood aside for Pendleton to enter. As the Captain stepped in, Jennifer hesitated and gave Thorburn a secretive smile.

He smiled in return, placed a protective hand in the small of her back and ushered her into the cabin.

Pendleton stood surveying the cabin and removed his cap.

Thorburn gestured at the table and chairs. 'Can I have the steward bring you anything, sir?'

The Captain glanced at Jennifer and nodded. 'We're parched. A nice cup of tea would be excellent.'

Thorburn passed word to the steward and wondered why *Brackendale* had been singled out for an unannounced visit.

Pendleton squeezed himself into a chair and propped his elbows on the table. 'Busy times, Richard,' he said, stroking the heavy beard.

Thorburn waited, knowing there was more, and not just idle chatter.

The Captain peered up from beneath the bushy eyebrows, a veil of sadness in his eyes. 'You know we lost *Cornflower*?'

Thorburn nodded. And that corvette would not soon be forgotten. She'd sunk a U-boat while on escort duty with an Atlantic convoy, a convoy which had lost five merchantmen in as many days. But that little ship had doggedly pursued a contact for almost twelve hours before finally depth-charging the submarine to the surface. It had eventually slipped back under with no survivors.

Then more recently she'd been transferred to East Coast duties, and finally, in the early hours of this morning, H.M.S. *Cornflower* and the survivors she'd rescued, had paid the ultimate price.

'Yes, sir,' Thorburn said, feeling some of Pendleton's pain. 'She ran out of luck.'

'Indeed,' Pendleton said slowly, 'but part of her misfortune is the Kriegsmarine's continued success in sowing those bloody minefields!' He shook his head a little, obviously frustrated, and glanced guiltily at Jennifer. 'Sorry, let my tongue get the better of me.'

A knock on the door and Thorburn's steward entered balancing a pot of tea on a tray of cups and saucers.

'Thank you, Sinclair, we can manage.'

Jennifer took charge and began to pour, and Pendleton sat back and clasped his hands over the thickening paunch.

'The thing is, Richard, something's brewing.' He paused as Jennifer passed him the tea, took a sip, and very deliberately replaced the cup in its saucer.

'I've been warned of an impending mission which might entail the use of a small flotilla. It would need an experienced commander as Leader.'

Thorburn narrowed his eyes, the first inklings of something out of the ordinary grabbing his interest.

'They've suggested a destroyer for starters combined with M.T.B.s and Gunboats.'

Thorburn nodded, attentive to his every word.

Pendleton produced a pack of cigarettes, offered one to Thorburn and lit for both of them. 'This all comes from a Commodore Lawrence Collingwood. Never met the chap but he arranged a meeting for tomorrow. We'll go by train.'

Thorburn nodded politely. Typical Pendleton, an order casually dropped into the conversation.

'I assumed I'd be on escort duty tonight, sir.'

'No, *Brackendale's* detached until further notice. Give the ship's company a run ashore. They probably need it, and then you'll be fresh for London.'

'Yes, sir,' Thorburn said, 'the crew might take the opportunity to catch up on some sleep,' and he grinned, 'well, the older ones anyway.' Personally he wasn't overly excited by the prospect of going to the city. Too many people, too many buildings, and too much traffic.

Pendleton scraped back his chair and stood, cup in one hand, cigarette in the other, and walked over to the scuttle. 'Are you going to show me round your ship, Richard?'

'As you wish, sir.'

The Captain swung round from the scuttle with a grin. 'Good, the bridge I think.'

Jennifer came to her feet. 'Are you sure, sir?'

Thorburn saw her hesitation, guessed at her reluctance to be climbing ladders. 'My cabin is at your disposal if you wish,' he volunteered, and she nodded.

'Thank you, yes, I'd prefer to wait.'

Pendleton laughed gently. 'Alright, young lady. We won't be long,' and he walked out.

Thorburn caught Jennifer's eyes. 'How about a drink tonight? Must be somewhere we could go.'

She nodded. 'I'll be in the Wren's quarters up at the castle. Ask for me there.' She blew him a kiss and Thorburn hurried to catch Pendleton with a grin on his face. There were definitely benefits to not being at sea.

Chapter Eight . . Hostile Intent

On the Nazi occupied northern coast of France, just south of Boulogne, a temporary airstrip for the Luftwaffe had recently been constructed from a swathe of gently rising farmland. Situated seven kilometres inland, the runway ran from a low point in the east to the highest ground due west nearest the sea. A large ancient woodland served to camouflage a squadron of Messerschmitt 109's.

Hauptman Karl Jäeger, credited with a personal tally of nine kills, resulting in the award of an Iron Cross, now found himself in command of sixteen fighter aircraft. The blonde haired Jäeger counted himself blessed to be among the few to have escaped the mayhem of 1940's desperate summer. Many of his comrades had perished. And worst of all, only seven months ago, Friedrich, his younger brother had lost his life during an attack on an enemy cruiser off the Isle of Wight. Anti-aircraft guns had destroyed his Stuka and he'd been seen to explode into the sea.

But since Reichsmarschall Hermann Göring's botched attempt to wipe out the R.A.F., the Fuhrer had stripped most of the Luftwaffe away from the British theatre in support of Operation Barbarossa. These days the news from Russia seemed to indicate many losses.

In theory, Jäeger's Staffel acted as an independent squadron, but in reality formed a loose alliance with the fighter wing based at Calais, and he operated under the immediate guidance of a local radar, known simply as the 'Freya' command. The radar section, in conjunction with an as yet still incomplete network to be rolled out all the way south along the French coast, monitored all shipping sailing between British ports. When given a worthwhile target to attack, Jäger was at liberty to use his initiative, often co-ordinating with a nearby Stuka dive bomber squadron. His biggest worry centred on the R.A.F. Their reaction time had always proved to be unbelievably short, so some cloud cover had become imperative.

'Morning, Herr Major,' came a voice from the trees, and Jäeger turned to greet his Flight Controller, the man with a patch over one eye, the end result of aerial combat over England's Kent coast.

'Morning, Hans. Do you have good news for me?'

'A weather report. Intermittent cloud at 10,000 metres over the sea and light fog over Kent.'

Jäeger nodded thoughtfully. 'So good weather for hunting, no?'

Oberleutnant Hans Wiemar hesitated. 'The British have become cautious, less and less ships in daylight. But there are reports of a destroyer in Dover harbour.'

'And . . . ?'

'A minesweeper clears the channel to the east.'

Jäeger grinned. 'Then there is a chance. On Sunday the British will have their guard down for prayers. See that the ground crews are ready and the pilots warned.'

'Jawohl, Herr Major,' Wiemar said, and turned for the trees where his office lay hidden.

Hauptman Karl Jäeger very much wanted the chance to avenge his brother, and the destruction of an enemy ship would go a long way towards fulfilling his mission.

On *Brackendale's* bridge, Captain James Pendleton stood with his hands braced on the screen and looked down on the fo'c'sle, the twin barrels of the forward gun mount meeting his gaze. Beyond that, the anchor chains and the capstans, and the 'Bow-chaser' pointing skywards, a proven addition to a ship's defences. It had the advantage of being able to point down over the bows and engage targets the main armament couldn't depress low enough to sight. Somewhat incongruous on a modern warship but worth its weight in gold.

A breeze ruffled the surface of the Channel and he breathed deeply, luxuriating in the salty tang. From somewhere in the bowels of the ship the noise of hammering reached him and he raised an eyebrow in query.

'Nothing major, I hope?' he asked.

Thorburn shook his head. 'No, sir. The Chief's on a bit of maintenance, while we've a moment to ourselves.'

The Captain nodded and rubbed his hands together. 'And how's the wardroom? Will your cook have enough for two more?'

Thorburn glanced at his wristwatch. 'I'm sure it can be arranged, sir. If you'll excuse me, I'll see to it now.'

'Don't worry about me, my boy, I'll just have a wander round deck.'

Reluctant to leave him unsupervised, Thorburn slid down the bridge ladder and found the Cox'n on the boat deck.

'Get a message to the galley, Captain (D) and Miss Farbrace are staying for lunch. Warn him to make the effort. Same goes for the stewards.'

The Cox'n grinned at his Captain's obvious irritation and saluted. 'Aye aye, sir,' he said and hurried away.

Thorburn heard a commotion behind him and turned to see Pendleton descending the ladder. The Captain stepped down on deck and smiled. 'Not as nimble as I was, eh? How about the quarterdeck, the after guns I think.'

'Of course, sir. This way,' and Thorburn led him aft beneath the ship's motor boat. He hoped the Cox'n had got to the cooks; for that matter, he hoped the cooks had something decent to offer his guests.

Hauptman Karl Jäeger tickled the throttle of his Messerschmitt and kicked the rudder to taxi down the far end of the runway. He had decided on a flight of eight Messerschmitts combined with nine Stukas and the attack would be a simple low level hit and run. They would discard the safety of the clouds in preference of wave-hopping for the entire distance to Dover.

The Stukas, primarily known for their devastating dive bombing capability, had also proven themselves in ground attack and on this occasion, Jäeger had designated the nine aircraft into that role. They would rendezvous over Boulogne-sur-mer before dropping to sea level and flying directly for Dover.

He glanced in his mirror, swivelled his head either side of the cockpit and waited for control to signal take off. With his Messerschmitts paired up for takeoff he sat ticking over and finally received clearance. Applying a steady increase of power his fighter accelerated up the grass runway, hopped once, found the air, and climbed over the trees for the coast. A quick check showed him all the pilots airborne and he banked north along the shoreline.

Three minutes later, a little north of Boulogne, Jäeger made rendezvous with the flight of Stukas. He banked his fighters northwest, stationed himself ahead and below the dive-bombers, and then led them all down to within a few metres of the sparkling wave crests. He narrowed his eyes through the goggles; at this height concentration became critical. Cruising at 280 kilometres an hour, weaving gently above the sea, the phalanx of warplanes skimmed the Channel toward their target.

Leading Seaman Allun Jones had taken over as watchkeeper, and on *Brackendale's* bridge all was quiet. The two senior officers had gone on an inspection of the ship, now somewhere astern on the quarterdeck. Once again he began a systematic sweep of the hazy blue skies to the south, his binoculars ranged at the middle horizon of the Channel waters. Dover harbour, with the castle standing sentinel on the hills above, was nonetheless not a place to relax. Even with a battery of ant-aircraft guns arrayed on the heights and the radar station above the white cliffs, the speed of low flying aircraft could take the best prepared by surprise.

The sound of steps on the ladder made him stiffen, and Sub-Lieutenant Labatt stepped onto the bridge.

'All quiet, Jones?'

It was a routine question and Jones kept the glasses to his eyes. 'Yes, sir. Nothing to report.'

'You taking shore leave later?' Labatt asked from the other side of the bridge.

Jones nodded behind the binoculars. He liked Labatt, respected the man even when he'd first joined ship as a young Midshipman learning the ropes. And his early promotion to Sub-Lieutenant after the battle with *Stefan Saltsburg* had been well deserved.

'Hope to, sir,' he said. 'Me and the lads from the depth-charge crew, we're wanting to try the Crown Inn.

New barmaid, sir.' He grinned under the binoculars and swung them back to the east.

'Thought you were due to be married, Jones?'

'Not for a while yet, sir. Ain't no harm in looking.' He heard Labatt chuckle and they fell silent, basking in the warmth of the sun.

The binoculars slowly panned across the narrow sea, up and down, from sky to waves, focussing and refocusing as Jones thought fit. He wondered how long Captain (D) would stay aboard.

Jäeger's Messerschmitt powered in towards the Kent coast, his eyes glued to the high ground over the white cliffs, surmounted by the dark shape of Dover Castle. He eased the stick back, fractionally, to give more height above the waves, and swivelled his head to snatch a glimpse of the dive-bombers. They weaved in formation, rising and falling above the water.

He looked through the spinning propeller at the fast approaching harbour and gauged the distance, near to three kilometres, and made the call.

'Staffel Nine, this is Red leader. Make altitude.'

A crackle in his headphones. 'Red leader, Staffel Nine, climbing now.' The dive-bombers clawed their way skywards.

Jäeger flicked the switch on his mouthpiece. 'Red Eagles, this is Red leader. Follow me in.' He waggled his wings, adjusted the throttle for more power and pulled on the stick. The 109 soared up from the wave tops. He levelled off at three-hundred metres. Range to harbour, twelve-hundred. A check of the sky, left and right, above, mirror behind. He spotted the JU87s soaring into the air, their inverted gulls wings menacingly black against the bright sky.

Oberleutnant Karl Jäeger picked out the shape of a destroyer, dropped his nose into a shallow dive and began his attack run. The memory of his brother returned; this might be his best opportunity for revenge.

Allun Jones jerked with surprise as he saw the fast flying shapes climbing and diving. 'Enemy aircraft! Red nine-oh, attacking!' he shouted. He'd seen the Stukas first, climbing rapidly from the sea.

Behind him, Labatt lunged for the button to sound Action Stations, and the alarm shrilled though the decks. Those of the crew not ashore, Blue Watch, answered the call. They scrambled to their posts, boots pounding along corridors and up ladders. Hatches banged shut, watertight doors slammed and secured. Ready reports began pouring into the bridge. From the dockside, late off the mark, came the haunting wail of an air raid warning.

Sub-Lieutenant George Labatt, with no other officer immediately to hand, made his own decision. 'Open fire!' he yelled, needlessly pointing at the enemy aircraft.

Thorburn, on the quarterdeck abaft the four-inch gun mount, took one glance at Pendleton and turned for the bridge.

'We're no use here, sir,' he called, and ran forward along the starboard side, Pendleton's footsteps close behind. One of the Pompom crew appeared on deck, fumbling his helmet onto his head, and Thorburn squeezed over to the guardrail as the man dashed past. From all around came the sound of aircraft engines, louder and louder. Thorburn made it to the foot of the ladder, and then flinched.

Cannon shells ripped into the steel upperworks, tracer fizzing, lethal shards ricocheting in all directions. A

Messerschmitt roared in low overhead, banked sharply to the right, and accelerated towards the sea.

He hauled himself up the ladder and sprang onto the bridge. He found Armstrong answering the telephones. Leading Seaman Jones had the port Lewis machine-gun at his shoulder.

The high pitched scream of a Stuka caught the attention, plummeting in a vertical dive. A pair of bombs dropped from the wings, wobbling their way through the air. Then the thumping bark of the multi-barrelled Pompom joined the noise, hurling shells at the enemy aircraft.

Thorburn grimaced at the fighters, too many to count, wheeling and diving through the tracer. The nose of a 109 sparkled with canon fire, lancing in towards the ship.

Brackendale's Oerlikons added their staccato rattle to the fight, pumping rounds at fleeting targets. At the fore-bridge, Thorburn saw a figure running towards the bow. It was Labatt, bent double and sprinting for the Bow-chaser. He made it unharmed and settled at the rear sight, traversed left out to sea and hit the trigger mechanism. A stream of two pound shells banged out at an inbound Stuka, accurate, forcing the pilot to pull out of his dive.

From round the breakwater, light anti-aircraft guns stammered into action, and a curtain of shells reached out to the enemy.

A dull red flash blossomed into an orange ball of fire and a dive bomber disintegrated in mid-air. Smoking wreckage fell harmlessly into the harbour. A bomb near missed *Brackendale* and hit the water a few yards from the starboard side. It exploded and showered the plates with shrapnel.

Thorburn turned as he heard a cursed exclamation; Pendleton lay crumpled in the starboard bridge-wing. He hurried across and knelt at the Captain's side. The eyes were open, cap askew, and he gave a bashful grin. 'I'm alright, just lost my footing. Give me your hand.'

Thorburn reached out and hauled him to his feet, and Pendleton sheepishly centred the cap on his forehead.

In that moment the noise of battle receded, the enemy fighters chasing out across the Channel, the dive bombers gone. Thorburn looked after them, two trails of thick smoke lingering in the air, the tell-tale signs of damage. A final burst of gunfire from a shore based muzzle and silence descended on the harbour.

'Number One, check for casualties, and get someone to look at the starboard side.'

Armstrong nodded. 'Aye aye, sir,' he said, and made for the bridge-ladder.

Thorburn looked at Pendleton. 'My cabin if you don't mind, sir. I think that's more than enough excitement for one day.'

Pendleton pushed out his bottom lip and tugged the end of his beard. 'Indeed, Richard. Haven't seen that sort of action in a long time.' He walked to the rear of the bridge and before Thorburn could follow, raised a hand to wave him away. 'I can manage, you have your ship to see to.' And with that, he disappeared down the ladder.

At R.A.F. Hawkinge the shout went out for a 'scramble' and within minutes, six Spitfires roared along the grass strip and took to the air. But even under maximum acceleration, by the time they swept across Dover's harbour, the German aircraft had fled the scene, fast disappearing dots above the sea.

The Spitfires powered on in pursuit and midway across the Channel caught and attacked five Stukas. In the ensuing dogfight four of the dive-bombers were despatched into the sea, with only two of their pilots managing to deploy parachutes.

Pilot Officer Teddy Whitlock, Section Leader, checked his pilots were all accounted for, and having expended all his ammunition, called the flight together and headed for home. Not altogether satisfactory but at least they'd doled out a bit of punishment on the enemy formation. As he flew in over the harbour, he waggled his wings in reply to a waved arm. Seconds later the six fighters soared over the Western Heights and turned for the airstrip. The ground crews would be waiting, counting them back in.

Somewhere in the town the 'all clear' sounded and Thorburn stepped over to the bridge-screen. On the Bow-chaser, Labatt stood waiting, eyeing the skies to the south.

Thorburn called. 'Well done, Sub. Leave it and come up.'

A hand saluted in acknowledgement and Thorburn turned to look round the harbour. Over by the Prince of Wales pier a tug lay heeled over at an odd angle, a wisp of smoke rising from her bow. Nearer too, the old 'rust bucket' had suffered obvious shrapnel damage and now displayed a large hole in her funnel. Elsewhere a Lighter that had been ferrying stores to a merchantman had turned turtle, no sign of her crew. On the southern breakwater, a sandbagged machine-gun emplacement had been savaged and two soldiers lay dead, crumpled amongst the ruins.

A voice-pipe squealed. 'Bridge?'

Thorburn frowned and leaned to the pipe, unsure of who was calling.

'Bridge,' he answered.

'This is Captain Pendleton. Tell the Commander to come to his cabin. It's urgent.'

'This is Thorburn, sir,' he said for clarification.

'It's Jennifer, Richard. She's wounded.'

He straightened from the voice-pipe and interrupted Armstrong speaking into a telephone.

'Number One,' he snapped. 'You have the bridge.' And leaving his First Lieutenant open mouthed he ran for the ladder. Dropping quickly to the fo'c'sle he tore through the corridor and flung himself into his cabin.

Jennifer lay on the bunk, her face pale, eyes wide staring at the deckhead. Pendleton pressed a bloodied towel to the side of her neck.

'Shrapnel,' he explained with a shake of his head. 'She needs a doctor. I sent your steward to find him.'

Thorburn took a pace closer and her eyes flickered with recognition. She tried a smile, wincing instead.

The door to the cabin banged inwards and the portly figure of Surgeon-Lieutenant 'Doc' Waverley entered with his bag. He showed no signs of surprise at the sight of a woman patient, dropped his bag on the table, and immediately bent to hold the towel.

'Alright,' he said to Pendleton,' let me see.'

Pendleton tentatively let go and Thorburn peered over Waverley's shoulder to see the extent of the wound. Her jacket and the collar of her blouse were a mess of blood and 'Doc' found a clean portion of towel and dabbed it on her neck below the ear. 'Just a scratch, young lady,' he said, smiling gently at her shocked eyes. He looked round with a Doctor's authority.

'My bag, please.'

Thorburn reached to the table and placed the case on the bunk. He frowned at the amount of blood; didn't look much like a scratch.

Waverley removed her tie, loosened the jacket and undid the first few buttons of her blouse. He delved inside his bag, came up with a roll of bandage and a large gauze pad. Intermingled with a strong smell of antiseptic, he wiped the laceration clear of blood and applied the gauze wadding. He looked at Thorburn.

'Lift her head for me,' he said, and Thorburn came round and carefully raised her from the pillow.

With accomplished ease, 'Doc' unrolled and wrapped the bandage round her neck to hold the pad in compression over the wound and straightened up.

'There,' he said, beaming at his handiwork, 'that'll suffice till we get you ashore. They'll make a proper job at the hospital, needs sutures.'

Thorburn reached for the bulkhead phone and heard Labatt's voice answering from the bridge.

'Is Number One with you, Sub?'

'Yes, sir, I'll hand you over.'

'Armstrong, sir,'

Thorburn cleared his throat. 'Have the ship's boat swung out level with the deck. Second Officer Farbrace is wounded and she's going to hospital. Captain (D) will be accompanying her to the shore.'

He heard Armstrong's acknowledgement of, 'Aye aye, sir,' and turned his attention back to Jennifer. She gave him a wan smile, a little colour returning to her cheeks.

Pendleton coughed loudly making Waverley look round. 'Well done, Doc. I think we deserve a pick-me-up.' He slanted his head at the door with a frown, and Waverley took the hint. He closed his bag, grinned, and the two officers scurried from the cabin.

Thorburn looked at Jennifer and gave her an encouraging smile. He sat and touched her arm. 'Looks like we'll have to leave that drink for another time,' he said gently, and received a warm smile in response.

'There'll be other days,' she said, and the smile disappeared. 'Does the wound look very bad, Richard? I mean, will it be a big scar?'

He shook his head and met her eyes. 'Not from what I saw. Below your ear, beneath your hair and probably under the collar.'

There was a knock on the door.

'Come,' he said, and Waverley re-entered leading two of the crew.

'Right, young lady, we need you to sit up, and then we'll get you to the boat. Think you can manage? You might feel a bit light headed.'

Between them all, they sat her up, got her to her feet, and Waverley instructed the two seamen to support her either side.

Thorburn, feeling utterly useless, followed in their wake, hoping Armstrong had the motor-boat ready. When they got to the boat-deck, Pendleton had already climbed aboard, and with Jennifer now more able, began to assist her over the side.

Thorburn could see her pain and pushed aside the two seamen. He swept up her legs, cradled her weight in his arms and carried her into the waist of the boat. He lowered her to her feet and Pendleton sat her down.

When all was ready, Thorburn turned to Armstrong and the waiting line of crewmen. 'Lower away Number One.'

Steadily the boat swung down to meet the rippling water, touched, and the engine purred into life. Jennifer managed to look up and give a little wave, and Thorburn nodded with what he hoped was a reassuring smile. He saw Pendleton reach out and offer his support, and with that, the boat turned out from the side and pushed off towards the inner harbour.

Thorburn watched for another few seconds and turned away. It was the first time the war had personally impinged upon someone for whom he had a close relationship and he shook his head in frustration.

'Number One,' he said brusquely, instantly regretting his severity, and changed his tone. 'Be so kind as to ask Mr Dawkins to come to the bridge. We need to asses the damage.'

Chapter Nine . . . Commodore's Orders

Late that afternoon a Bangor class minesweeper, H.M.S. *Faversham,* steamed out from Southend and into the broad expanse of the open estuary. She began to sweep ahead of what would be the evening convoy heading north. At a point four miles south-east of Shoeburyness, having completed the second leg, she made a turn north to commence the third sweep.

A violent explosion caught her amidships and broke her back. The fore and aft sections drifted apart, the stern sinking rapidly, the upturned bows floating in the waves.

An anti-aircraft observer on the coast of Foulness witnessed the explosion and reported the incident. An Admiralty tug departed Sheerness and arrived on the scene thirty-five minutes after the detonation. She picked up eight survivors from a crew of sixty-two. An hour after the initial explosion the bow section eventually slid beneath the waves. It was assumed she'd been hit by a mine.

A second minesweeper, despatched from Harwich, took over the clearance, and the delayed convoy of twenty-four ships sailed three hours later.

Well after sunset, in the streets behind Dover's waterfront, Thorburn walked to the junction of Union Road. With the blackout strictly enforced he was grateful for the moon's grey light. He found the entrance to the

Infirmary, an old brick building which had become a sort of cottage hospital.

'Can we help you, sir?' asked a middle aged woman wearing a white starched cotton cap and what Thorburn took to be a Sister's uniform. He removed his cap, uncomfortable under her stern gaze.

'Second Officer Jennifer Farbrace?' he began, 'she came in with a neck wound.'

'Are you sure? She might have been taken to the Military hospital under the castle.'

'I was told she came here.'

The Sister crossed to a reception desk and consulted a file before turning back to him with a suspicious glance. 'And you wish to see her?' she said brusquely. 'You realise visiting hours are over?'

'Sorry,' he said lamely, 'I've been dealing with damage to my ship. Can you at least tell me if she's alright?'

The woman looked at him for a long moment and then her hard expression softened into a compassionate smile. 'I think we can do better than that, follow me.'

Sister led him through a door and along an empty corridor. At a junction they turned right past a male ward and stopped in front of a pair of doors with round windows. She paused and turned to face him.

'This is a ward for ladies. Wait here while I check they're presentable.' And with that she swept through to leave him feeling like a naughty schoolboy. But he couldn't resist a quick glimpse. Through the glass he saw a long room, down either side of which lay a row of metal framed beds. The ward appeared to be half empty. The Sister, all hustle and bustle, beckoned a nurse and pointed to a patient. Thorburn looked away and stepped back to wait.

She returned more officious than ever. 'Right, young man. Nurse will show you to Miss Farbrace's bedside. You have five minutes and no longer. Are we clear?'

The Lieutenant-Commander, captain of His Majesty's ship-of-war, and a man who exercised full authority over a ship's company of a hundred and forty men, nodded meekly. 'We are,' he said.

With a final frosty look she pushed open a door. The nurse was waiting and turned on her heel.

'Five minutes,' came a harsh reminder from behind, and Thorburn followed the nurse to a bed against the right hand wall, overlooked by a blacked out window.

Jennifer lay propped up against the crisp white pillows, a fresh bandage round her neck, and managed a warm smile.

'Hello, Richard. I'm surprised Sister let you in.'

Thorburn grinned, perched on the side of her bed and reached for a hand.

'She couldn't resist my charm,' he said with a slow wink. He dropped the grin and frowned. 'But how are you?'

He felt her fingers squeeze his and returned the pressure.

'A bit sore, it's difficult to turn my head, but they're letting me out in the morning. The surgeon said I'm to stay overnight as a precaution.'

'Good,' he said, and added, 'Pendleton's taking me up to London in the morning so you won't have him to worry you.'

'I thought so,' Jennifer said slowly. 'He hinted at a meeting before we came to see you.' Her eyes searched his face with concern. 'Not to worry,' he smiled. 'Pendleton likes to impress me with all the trappings of the Admiralty. He's trying to get me to show a bit more diplomacy.'

She pressed his fingers again, her eyes smiling. 'And we both know that wouldn't do any harm.' She let her head sink back in the pillow and for a while they stared at one another in comfortable silence.

The nurse broke the stillness, came over and made a point of looking at the watch on her pinafore.

Thorburn raised a hand to acknowledge the hint and stood. 'I'd better go. Sister didn't give me much leeway.'

She reluctantly released his fingers, her eyes fixed on his own. Very gently, he leaned forward and kissed her lips, a brief moment of intimate closeness in the austere surroundings. He straightened up and she giggled shyly.

'They're all watching,' she said, embarrassed.

Thorburn glanced round at the nearest smiling faces, the nurse grinning broadly. He gave them all a nod and looked back at Jennifer's liquid eyes.

'At least I know you're alright,' he said. 'Don't over do it when they let you out.'

'I won't,' she said, her elegant eyebrows knitting together in a worried frown. 'And you be careful around Pendleton, he's a sly old fox.'

He laughed. 'True, but the trouble is he outranks me. Not much I can do about that.' He backed away to the end of the bed and turned to go. As the nurse walked ahead he took a last glance over his shoulder.

'Take care, Richard,' she said, and pursed her lips in a tiny kiss.

He gave her a confident smile and the nurse pushed open the door.

Alone in the corridor his smile vanished and he strode off for the exit. In hindsight, Pendleton had probably made a bad decision to bring her on board, particularly bearing in mind Dover's vulnerability to air attack. Done with the best of intentions, no doubt, but not very responsible.

Outside he lit a cigarette. Standing in the dark, Richard Thorburn felt a surge of anger towards the enemy. It wasn't as if he hadn't seen colleagues killed and maimed, even carried his own painful reminder of being wounded, but to have Jennifer injured in such a way, a relatively innocent bystander, and to cap it all, on his own ship; well God help the next bloody German to come in range.

Stamping out the last of his cigarette he set out for the harbour, forcing the pace, using the strenuous exercise to work off the anger.

It took ten minutes of hard walking before he began to calm down, the physical exertion finally having an effect. By the time he reached Granville Dock his thoughts had returned to *Brackendale* and Pendleton's impending trip to London. Reluctantly he wondered if the break wouldn't do him some good, but London wasn't the place he'd have volunteered to visit.

He found *Brackendale's* motor boat sitting quietly at the quayside, and Leading Seaman Rafferty saw him coming. The engine rumbled into life, and as Thorburn dropped into the waist, the bows swung out from the side and Rafferty steered for the outer harbour and towards the familiar shadowy outline of a 'Hunt' class destroyer.

The following morning, on Monday the 27th of July, Captain James Pendleton sat by the window of a First Class carriage and looked up as the train squealed to a shuddering halt at London Victoria station. A hiss of steam escaped the coal fired boiler, the pungent smell of oil and smoke permeating the atmosphere. Two grey haired men in pin stripe suits and bowler hats folded their newspapers and reached for leather briefcases. They slid back the door and stepped out into the corridor, and Pendleton sighed, rising to his feet. He looked down at Thorburn and nodded. 'All change.'

He smoothed his full, grey-flecked beard between thumb and forefinger and frowned, his bushy eyebrows closing over the bridge of his nose. On the platform, barrow boys walked busily to and fro, touting for customers, and porters pulled hand-towed trucks, or pushed sack-barrows bulging with suitcases.

Pendleton allowed the worst of the congestion to thin before venturing into the corridor and letting himself out onto the platform. Thorburn stepped down behind him.

Carrying only his small briefcase Pendleton strode out of the gloomy station and into the brightness of a blue sky day. On the pavement he paused to stare at the vast array of barrage balloons floating above the city, then stepped back quickly as a lorry crawled past belching exhaust smoke. To his right a parked staff car sat waiting at the kerbside, and as he made a move towards it the driver stepped out and saluted.

'Captain Pendleton, sir?'

'Yes.'

'I've been detailed to pick you up, sir,' he said, and opened the nearside rear door.

'Good,' Pendleton said, 'but I prefer the front,' and lowered himself into the passenger seat, grinning at Thorburn as he climbed in the back.

The driver closed the doors and pulled out between a bus and taxi, and Pendleton settled back for the ride.

London's war torn streets reflected the suffering her people had endured over the past year. The majority of buildings and warehouses in the immediate area bore witness to the devastating attacks unleashed by the bombers of the Luftwaffe. But the nightly attacks had eventually petered out and the city began to recover.

Vast swathes of ruins remained to be cleared and James Pendleton looked out from his staff car and marvelled at peoples' resilience. The car jolted over a badly repaired section of tarmac and his driver came off the throttle, choosing a less damaged tract of roadway.

Pendleton glanced at his watch; they'd made good time. He turned to check on Thorburn and received a grim smile. It was much as they'd expected, a stark reminder, if needed, as to why the Navy put to sea.

After what seemed an age negotiating the bombed out streets, the car finally drew up outside the sandbagged entrance to the Admiralty buildings. Pendleton let himself out and they walked up the steps. Two guards snapped to attention, bayonets glistening, and Thorburn touched the peak of his cap.

Inside the spacious office, Commodore Lawrence T. Collingwood, R.N., D.S.C., D.S.O., sat with his back to the room, a spiral of blue smoke rising above his head.

Thorburn stood inside the door, cap under his arm, and marvelled at how quickly Pendleton's suggestion had been progressed into this meeting. The ornately carved oak panels gave a dignified solidity to the history of the room, impressively solemn.

The Commodore slowly turned to face them and puffed again on the burr walnut pipe. His face projected power and authority, lean and angular with a prominently hooked nose. He stood from the chair, carefully placed his pipe in a large ashtray, and then stepped forward.

'James, isn't it?' he said, shaking Pendleton's hand. 'Good to meet you.'

Thorburn steeled himself as the glare of piercing blue eyes turned on him. 'And this must be Richard Thorburn.' The broad smile revealed a set discoloured and badly misshapen teeth, but it had warmth and the handshake a firm strength. 'Heard a lot about you.' He released the grip and turned to his desk, waving a hand at the chairs. 'Have a seat.'

Thorburn sat and settled, and watched Pendleton do the same, the briefcase placed across his knees.

The Commodore took his time, flicking open a buff coloured file and glancing at the foolscap sheets within. He retrieved the pipe and struck a match, drawing on the flame until the tobacco glowed red. He blew smoke, leaned back and crossed his knees. He stared hard at Thorburn, the shocking blue eyes narrowed in thought. Smoke trickled from his large nostrils and he jabbed the stem of the pipe at Thorburn.

'My sources tell me you're a bit of a firebrand, Commander.' It was more a statement than a question, and Thorburn swallowed, not quite knowing how to respond.

Pendleton saved him from answering. 'Independently minded,' he said, and the Commodore nodded, a brief smile lighting the sallow cheeks.

'One way of putting it.' He tapped the folder and turned his gaze to Pendleton. 'Sorry to be underhand, James, but these are copies of your reports on *Brackendale* and her captain. From when you first recommended the Commander for Special Operations.'

Thorburn cringed at the thought of what they might contain. He'd not exactly endeared himself to the Royal Navy's hierarchy.

If Pendleton was surprised by Collingwood's bland appraisal, he didn't show it.

'Yes, sir,' was all he said.

'And . . . ,' Collingwood continued, 'there's also a personal assessment by a certain General Bainbridge, with reference to a mission off the Cotentin Peninsula.'

Thorburn looked down at the floor. Collingwood obviously wasn't too impressed, and Thorburn privately conceded he had never really seen eye to eye with the General.

'But then of course,' Collingwood said, studying the papers, 'this young man gets himself a D.S.O. for sinking an enemy warship.' He glanced again at Pendleton. 'Seems your judgement proved correct.'

He leaned back from the papers and pulled on his pipe. He gave a short chuckle. 'I might argue these opinions till the cows come home, but I can't quarrel with the King.'

Thorburn squirmed in his seat, unaccustomed to being the subject of discussion, embarrassed by the Commodore's discourse.

'That being said . . . , to business.' He looked at Pendleton.

'The Admiralty have got wind of a possible forthcoming Kriegsmarine deployment. Our intelligence sources are convinced this is a real threat and I've been authorised to take steps to intervene. My problem has been convincing them to release enough of our limited resources to have a flotilla with which to combat the threat.'

He scratched an eyebrow.

'It's been decided to procure four Torpedo boats and four Gunboats, giving us three of each type on patrol, and one as back up. I've already spoken to Coastal Forces Command and they're detaching individual boats from established flotillas. They'll report to Dover and come under the office of Captain (D) until further notice.' He paused to take breath. 'In addition, I've persuaded the C/O of Harwich submarines to divert H.M.S. *Trophy* from her previous North Sea patrol to stand off the Dutch coast. They agreed she might be better employed in that area. And after due consideration, I have accepted Captain Pendleton's recommendation that *Brackendale* will assume command of these ad hoc forces.'

Thorburn straightened in his seat and glanced sideways at Pendleton. The Captain stuck out his beard and nodded, smoothing his moustache. 'A wise choice, sir, ideal man for the job.'

Richard Thorburn nibbled at his bottom lip. If only he felt so certain, after all, what did he know about fast patrol boats? Once, in Weymouth, he'd had the privilege of a short trip round the Isle of Portland followed by a quick dash to Lyme Regis and back. He'd never forgotten the thrill of the ride, but handling a destroyer didn't exactly compare to the agility and speed associated with power boats. And what about tactical deployment?

He raised a hand. 'If I may, sir?'

Collingwood tilted his head to one side. 'What is it?'

Thorburn winced; he had to be diplomatic. 'I'm just wondering if I'm best suited for this?' He splayed his hands in a gesture of supplication. 'It's not as if I've ever worked with them before, and I understand they have a rather unorthodox method of operation.'

Silence greeted his statement, and then Collingwood looked at Pendleton, smiled, and burst out laughing. Pendleton also obviously saw the funny side and joined in, leaving Thorburn to sit in bewildered ignorance.

Eventually, Collingwood caught his breath and pointed a finger at Thorburn, grinning broadly. 'Did I hear correctly? The rebel in our midst complaining about someone else's unorthodox methods? Good God above.' He dissolved into more laughter.

Pendleton took over. 'Don't worry, Richard, there'll be plenty of time to work out the whys and wherefores.'

Collingwood nodded, losing the smile. 'Simply put, Commander, your job will be to give fire support to our little brethren when they come up against heavy firepower. Covering fire if you will, while they take up positions to make their attacks. No different really from battleships and destroyers; the big boys rely on the little boys to dash about, and then take on the other big boys when needed. Self explanatory.' He dismissed the objections with a wave of his hand, then sat back and folded his arms, the beak like nose twitching in satisfaction.

Pendleton sat forward. 'Where is *Brackendale* likely to be used, sir?'

Collingwood grimaced and rubbed the bridge of his nose. 'Ah . . . ,' he interjected, 'that is the crux of the matter.' The Commodore stood and walked to the window, then wandered back and perched on the end of his desk. He brought his gaze up to rest on Thorburn. 'Our sources tell us a new German flotilla appears to be gathering in Wilhelmshaven.' He touched the side of his face and Thorburn watched his gnarled profile. 'We have agents on the German and French coast, in Belgium too.' He lifted his head. 'That General we spoke of, Scott Bainbridge. Those agents come under his unit of Special Operations. They're tasked with reporting all ship movements . . . , if they can,' he finished ominously.

'By the make up of warships this is not a threat to the Russian convoys. In fact the biggest ship involved appears to be a merchantman, somewhere in the order of five-thousand tons. Whether it's armed is another matter.' He stood and moved to a hanging chart of the North Sea. 'The remainder of the flotilla is made up of a couple of minesweepers, two Elbing destroyers, two 'T' class, and an armed trawler.' He turned and thrust his hands in his jacket pockets. 'I make that eight vessels, not to be sneezed at.' He ambled back to his desk and eased himself into the chair.

Thorburn watched him rub his jaw.

'We have good reason to believe that the flotilla is destined for the Brittany coast, and probably Brest. As for the merchantman, we've yet to establish exactly what's going on. Either way the Admiralty have decided to take the bull by the horns. They came to the conclusion that nightly sweeps off the Dutch coast might prove very worthwhile.'

Thorburn blinked but kept quiet.

Collingwood pursed his lips, looking from one to the other. 'My argument is that one destroyer and a few boats isn't enough. I think we could do with at least two more destroyers.' He let his gaze land on Pendleton.

The Captain smoothed his beard, obviously thinking through the possibilities. 'I believe there's a 'Hunt' in Chatham dockyard finishing a boiler clean. We might be able to reallocate her before she returns to duty.'

'Anybody we know?'

'Not specifically, but I hear she had a hand in sinking a U-boat.'

'What ship?'

Pendleton frowned and looked down. 'H.M.S. *Cranbrook* I think, R.N.V.R. captain.'

Collingwood smiled thinly. 'Good enough, I'll make the arrangements. Any more?'

'Sheerness has a 'Hunt', sir. The *Darrow*, east coast convoy escort.'

'Mmm . . , not sure I could get her released. We've already pinched *Brackendale*,' he said pointedly. 'Took all my diplomatic skills to convince them you'd be more useful elsewhere.'

Thorburn leaned forward. 'I know *Darrow* is reporting to Chatham for a modification tomorrow, sir. Sheerness are getting a V&W as temporary replacement.'

'And *Darrow's* commander?'

'Lieutenant-Commander Hudson, an Australian reservist, sir.'

Collingwood smiled his approval. 'We might make that work, and it should ensure you maintain seniority without any awkward standoffs.' He pushed himself up from the chair and paced across the room, hesitated and came to stand by the desk.

'Now I don't wish to labour the point, but this is top priority. Churchill is adamant that the Germans will not have free reign of the Channel. Personally I have my doubts as to our capacity to stop them entirely, but the Admiralty have been toying with the idea of something called 'Operation Tunnel'. Broadly speaking, to mount offensive sweeps in the region of Brest and up round the coast to Le Havre with the intention of severely disrupting their convoys.' He paused and Thorburn felt the full force of the man's eyes. A curl of smoke rose from the pipe and Collingwood stared at the floor.

'Our operation might well be viewed as a test run for how 'Tunnel' is utilised, if it ever gets off the drawing board, so a lot hangs on the outcome and,' he gave Thorburn an enigmatic smile, 'not just your immediate future.'

Thorburn nodded slowly and fixed Pendleton with an amused stare. 'As you said, sir, busy times.'

Pendleton stroked his beard and grinned. 'Didn't want you getting bored, Richard. Need to keep nice and sharp, eh?'

'Yes, sir,' he said, and sat back.

Lawrence T. Collingwood grunted his approval and bent to retrieve his pipe, pausing before grabbing his cap. 'Right, that's sorted, time for a bite.' He strode to the door and waited for Thorburn. 'Now, Richard, this D.S.O. of yours. Tell me all about it.'

And with that, the Commodore led them out into the echoing corridor and along to a well attended canteen.

Chapter Ten . . . A Foreign Shore

At 7pm on that Monday evening, far out in the dangerous waters of the North Sea, the diverted Royal Navy submarine, H.M.S. *Trophy,* arrived at her new patrol area. Approximately twenty-five miles from shore, she lay north-west of a chain of islands known as the Dutch Frisians.

Lieutenant-Commander Craig Mitchell, R.N., captain of the boat and now on his fourth war patrol, stood on the bridge of his conning-tower and gauged the moment to submerge. Fair haired, medium height, and with a disarming smile that belied a steely resolve, he nonetheless skippered *Trophy* with a relaxed formality that had long since brought a devoted loyalty from the boat's crew. Together they'd survived three war patrols and the men under his command had come to trust his judgement.

With no land in sight they took a fix, initially by his Navigator, then repeated by the First Officer, and finally by his own rudimentary endeavours. Having pooled the information and established their position, he now prepared to dive before the final approach. The prevailing weather conditions were in his favour, a force three south-westerly imparting just enough wind to create a short choppy sea, ideal for taking regular periscope observations of the surrounding area. Too calm and there was always a risk during daylight hours of being seen by aerial reconnaissance, the dark shape of the boat visible thirty-two feet below the surface.

Mitchell raised his binoculars in search of the island of Terschelling, a low lying, sixteen mile long strip of land running approximately north-east to south-west. In the back of his mind he was remembering the order to take station off the islands and report all German seagoing activity. More specifically he would be looking for an armed convoy, eight or twelve ships strong and with a large merchantman in their midst. Should the opportunity present itself he was directed to attack that ship. Whatever the outcome he must signal the convoy's whereabouts, speed and course. More pertinently for a Royal Navy submariner, he was at liberty to attack any U-boats on sight.

As always when approaching a fresh patrol area, he'd adjusted *Trophy's* speed to coincide with the need to dive at a safe distance from shore, and now prepared to take her under.

Unable to find any sign of land which would have added one more parameter to their navigational calculus he lowered the binoculars. In other circumstances he would have used *Trophy's* radar but it was common practice for the German coastal stations to monitor for just such an event, and all skippers on surveillance had been warned of the implications. It was time to submerge.

'Lookouts below, clear the bridge.' He waited as they scrambled through the hatch and disappeared into the conning tower. A final glance round the visible horizon and he gave the order.

'Dive.'

He secured the voice-pipe and dropped through the hatch, clipped it tight and slithered down the ladder. The

Control Room held an air of expectancy and he nodded to Crawford.

'Eighty feet, Number One. Slow ahead'

'Eighty feet, slow ahead, aye, sir.'

The submarine took on a down angle by the bows and *Trophy* slid quietly beneath the waves. With the batteries grouped down and the electric motors giving them an economical three knots, the boat slowly closed in toward the island in preparation for night time operations.

On the Kent coast, the lengthening shadows of a setting sun spread long fingers across Dover's waterfront, and when Thorburn arrived back from London and returned to *Brackendale*, his first thoughts were for her state of repairs. He requested both Armstrong and Dawkins report to his cabin.

'Where are we, Chief?'

'Just the one job outstanding, sir. The searchlight requires a replacement lens. I've placed the order and Chatham are sending one over. Should be here shortly.'

Thorburn nodded and turned to Armstrong.

'Number One?'

'Re-ammunitioned and 'Guns' reported all main armament in good order, sir.'

Thorburn breathed a sigh of relief, the comfort of knowing that as forthcoming Leader to a new flotilla, at least his own command was up to scratch. He returned his gaze to the Welshman, the ship's engineering wizard.

'You'll let me know as soon as the replacement's fitted, Chief?'

Dawkins wrinkled his eyebrows in mock shame at the captain's insinuation that the Chief Engineer would not inform him of when the work completed.

'You'll be the first to know, sir.'

Thorburn allowed them a smile. 'In that case, I can tell you we've been singled out for a new operation. Bit hush-hush at the moment, but I'll fill you in as soon as I know more.'

Dawkins face beamed. 'Then I'd better tend to my duties, sir. I expect you'll not be sparing the horses.'

Thorburn grinned in return; there was something infinitely reassuring about the Welshman's enthusiasm. 'Thank you, Chief. Please carry on.'

'Aye aye, sir,' he said, and stepped outside.

To Armstrong, Thorburn said, 'I'd appreciate it if you'd have the Officer-of-the-Day log everything flying a White Ensign that enters harbour.'

Armstrong raised an inquisitive eyebrow in response, but Thorburn didn't offer any clarification, and so he acknowledged the order. 'Aye aye, sir. Is that all?'

'Yes, thank you Number One, we'll talk later.'

The First Lieutenant slipped out, closing the door with a soft click, and Thorburn turned to his desk. There was much to think about, not least the complication of leading an unrehearsed flotilla into action at a moment's notice. He settled down to fathom out a few possible scenarios. The sun sinking below the horizon barely penetrated his consciousness as he bent to the task of finding solutions.

It was ten o'clock that night in No2 repair basin of Chatham's Royal Navy Dockyard, when the destroyer, H.M.S. *Cranbrook* began clearing away in readiness for a return to duty.

Her captain, Lieutenant-Commander Roger Sullivan, R.N.V.R., a squat, chunky Yorkshireman, answered the knock on his cabin door.

'Enter.'

Leading Signalman Evans looked in. 'Confidential message, sir.'

Sullivan wrinkled his brows in suspicion and held out a stubby fingered hand. 'Alright, let's have it.'

Evans stepped forward with the brown envelope.

Sullivan took it and tore open the flap. The words stood out in stark contrast.

"On completion of boiler clean *Cranbrook* will proceed Dover at earliest opportunity. On arrival ship's Commander to report Senior Officer, Captain (D). Notify Dover of ETA."

He read it again and then glanced at his watch. The last of the ship's company would not return aboard until 23.00hrs.

'Where's Number One?'

Evans raised an eyebrow and tilted his head, thinking. 'Last I seen he was on the quarterdeck, sir.'

'Right . . . . Well, you'd better acknowledge this, and get someone to find the First Lieutenant. Ask him to come to my cabin.'

'Aye aye, sir,' Evans said, took the pink slip and disappeared.

Sullivan walked over to the scuttle and peered into the darkness of the repair basin. The boiler clean had been carried out much as the dockyard had promised and *Cranbrook's* Chief Engineer reported initial firing had proved satisfactory. He frowned, reflecting on the signal. His assumption prior to berthing in the repair basin was that *Cranbrook* would rejoin her two 'Hunt' class sisters of the Harwich Flotilla and resume duties as escort for the East Coast convoys.

He looked round to a tap on the door and the florid face of Lieutenant David Randall stuck his head in. 'You wanted me, sir?'

'Yes, Dave, sailing orders. We're to report to Captain (D) at Dover. I've not heard of him, you any the wiser?'

Sullivan's First Lieutenant pursed his lips and then grinned. 'I think it's a chap called Pendleton. He was here until recently, supposed to be a stickler for the rules.'

Sullivan sighed. 'That's all we need.' He shook his head. 'Be prepared for an early start in the morning, and let's hope there aren't too many sore heads amongst the crew.'

Randall nodded. 'Yes, sir, I'll have a word with the Cox'n.'

'And we'll take a walk round the ship, for our own peace of mind. Take the chance to see for ourselves, have a quiet word with heads of departments.'

Randall bobbed his head. 'Aye aye, sir. Time?'

'Oh . . . , straight after breakfast I should think, the dockyard people ought to have shoved off by then.'

Randall closed the door and Sullivan seated himself at his desk and pondered the signal. He must warn his navigating officer, the ship had never entered Dover harbour.

In northern occupied Europe, the Kriegsmarine began sending operational signals.

Chapter Eleven . . . A Gathering

The following morning on Tuesday the 28th of July, as daylight came to the top floor of a run down, ivy-clad hotel in Ramsgate, Lieutenant Charles Holloway awoke to a bang on his door.

'Lieutenant, sir?'

Holloway half sat up propped on one elbow. 'Come in, what is it?'

A Telegraphist from Operations poked his head in. 'Message, sir. M.T.B. *49* is to make ready for detachment and proceed Dover at 10.30hrs. Report to Captain Pendleton, Officer Commanding. It's from Senior Officer, Coastal Forces Operations, sir.'

Holloway rubbed his face and sighed, half awake. 'Very well, acknowledge and wake the others.'

'Aye aye, sir,' the man said, and withdrew, leaving him to ponder on his new orders.

Twenty minutes later he stepped out onto the landing and called for his crew. Doors creaked open and the eight men of Motor Torpedo Boat *49* made their appearance.

'You all right, Cox'n?' he asked, looking at the bandaged arm.

'I'm right as rain, sir. Just a scratch.'

Holloway nodded, not really convinced but accepting the statement at face value. 'We all here?'

Gillman counted heads and nodded. 'All present, sir.'

Holloway turned for the stairs. 'Right, time to go.' He led them down the worn steps, out through the overgrown porch and down to the ancient quayside. A well used fishermen's jetty stretched out from the inner dock. Berthed half way out along the wooden decking, M.T.B. *49* rocked gently to the ripples of Ramsgate's crowded basin. Two other Navy craft sat alongside. They were the Motor Gun Boats that had accompanied the urgent foray into the Channel last Thursday night. As his crew scrambled aboard, Holloway stood for a moment admiring *Forty-Nine's* sleek lines. A seventy foot, wooden hulled Vosper, mounted with three powerful Packard Marine petrol engines, she could achieve thirty-seven knots all up. Fitted with a pair of 21inch torpedo tubes, two half-inch machine guns and a 20mm Oerlikon, the boat made for a formidable weapon.

The Cox'n made a final adjustment to the compass housing and straightened at the controls. 'Ready, sir.'

Holloway stepped on deck. 'Start her up.'

With a grumbling cough the engines kicked into life, blue smoke swirling astern.

'Let go for'ard.'

Seaman Gunner Sam Jenkins unhitched the line and jumped onto the bows.

'Let go aft.'

A rope snaked inboard over the stern rail, and Ordinary Seaman Jock McCallum followed. 'All clear, sir.'

Holloway settled his cap squarely over his eyes and gave the order.

'Slow ahead, take us out, Cox'n.'

The boat burbled to the muted snarl of engines, and then gracefully peeled out from the jetty. Gillman put the helm over and with practised ease steered her away for the harbour entrance.

Pushing out between the towering breakwaters, *Forty-Nine* lifted to the incoming waves, and Holloway glanced astern. Once clear of the harbour he turned to face the waves. The wind blew in from the southwest, driving the sea into a rolling chop, and he set the boat's speed accordingly.

'Half ahead, eighteen knots.'

'Eighteen knots, aye aye, sir,' the Cox'n said, and rang up the telegraph.

In the engine compartment, Chief Motor Mechanic Ben Moore, heard the ring and pushed on the throttles. As the motors picked up he grinned at Leading Stoker Albright and nodded. Now they were under way.

Holloway felt the bows lift and bounce into the open waters. *Forty-Nine* was back in her natural element. 'Steer south, Cox'n.'

'One-eight-oh degrees, sir.'

The skipper reached out for a hand hold, knees bent to the lively hull. He squinted into the spray. Dover here we come.

A short distance up the Channel, amongst the warships at Sheerness on the Isle of Sheppey, a Motor Gun Boat slipped her moorings and swung north in the lee of the land. Sub-Lieutenant 'Ginger' Lambert bellied up to the bridge, checked his bearings and brought the boat round due east to clear Margate's headland. His orders were to report to the Captain of Destroyers at Dover, no later than 17.00hrs. Plenty of time.

In Portsmouth, two more M.G.B.s pushed out through the opening in the anti-submarine boom, turned for the

Eastern arm of the Solent and throttled up to power out beyond Hayling Island. On the bridge of the lead boat, Sub-Lieutenant David T. Richmond, 'Richie' to his close associates, set a course for Dover. He glanced over the starboard quarter where Sub-Lieutenant Kenneth Stokesley had taken station and waved a hand.

He received a theatrical salute in reply, and then grinned as Stokesley's M.G.B. squirmed in the wake from his own boat and screwed awkwardly to port before the Cox'n regained control.

Clearing the southern shore of Hayling Island the boats came up against a choppy sea, to such a degree that they began thumping and flying between crests. Richmond checked on the other boat, could see the punishment it was taking and ordered a reduction in power. They'd be no use to the new flotilla if they damaged themselves before arriving. He found twenty knots a lot more manageable and settled down for the journey. A few hours and they should catch sight of Dover Castle.

From Harwich, a pair of M.T.B.s lifted their bows to the sea and turned southeast for Margate, The young skippers had received orders to proceed Dover as part of a newly forming flotilla. Their 'Leader' would be a certain Lieutenant-Commander Richard Thorburn in the 'Hunt' class destroyer *Brackendale*. The younger of the two captains had heard gossip that Thorburn had sunk a two-thousand ton German destroyer. No mean feat for a small 'Hunt'.

On board *Brackendale*, Richard Thorburn sat in his cabin and poured himself three fingers of gin. In front of him on the desk lay a file containing the list of boats joining his new flotilla, and the rank, name and a brief summary of each skipper's experience. A knock on the door interrupted his reading.

'Come,' he said.

Armstrong looked in. 'You wanted me, sir?'

Thorburn nodded, gestured towards a chair, and opened a drawer to produce a fresh tumbler. 'Help yourself,' he offered, pointing to the gin, and he waited while Armstrong got comfortable.

'We'll not be on patrol for a few nights,' Thorburn began. 'Pendleton has been given the go-ahead to tackle German convoys over the other side.' He fished out his pack of cigarettes and extended them to Armstrong. They lit up and Thorburn grinned through the smoke.

'*Brackendale* will be Senior Officer of a newly formed flotilla.' He paused for a reaction.

Armstrong waved away the smoke and sat forward with renewed enthusiasm.

'To do what, sir? Who are we getting?'

Thorburn took a swallow of gin and studiously returned the glass to the desk. 'That, Robert, is the crux of the matter. Their Lordships have reacted to a report of probable enemy activity in the shape of an armed convoy assembling in Wilhelmshaven. Commodore Collingwood, that's who we went to see in London, wants us to carry out offensive patrols. And as for who we're getting . . . , hopefully two more 'Hunts', M.T.B.s and gunboats, three of each type, plus two spares, one of each. The spares are what remains of Dover's boats. And us, of course.'

Armstrong rubbed his hands together, obviously pleased. 'Three 'Hunts' and six boats, that's serious.'

Thorburn agreed. 'It is . . . , provided the weather's on our side. The boats can't operate in anything too severe. In that case we end up with just three 'Hunts'.

Armstrong tossed down the last of his gin and studied the coil of blue smoke rising from his cigarette. 'Well let's pray for good weather,' he said. 'Those M.T.B.s can inflict some serious damage.

Thorburn sighed and nodded. 'My thoughts exactly, although that's really what we'll be there for. Anyway, they should arrive here during the day, then it'll be a case of all captains meeting with Pendleton.'

Armstrong rubbed his forehead and stubbed out the cigarette. 'Do we have a time limit on these operations?'

'Not specifically,' Thorburn said. 'I think it'll be more a case of until we frighten them off . . . , or we beat them in battle.'

Armstrong grinned in turn. 'Isn't that always the way?'

Thorburn chuckled his agreement, and for a short while they sat in companionable silence. Then he pushed back from the desk and came to his feet.

'Right, Number One. Let me know when they've all arrived and we'll have a meeting in the wardroom, break the ice and get to know them. Then I'll see how Captain (D) wants to proceed.'

Armstrong stood and nodded. 'Aye aye, sir. Will there be a run ashore for the port watch later?'

'I should think so, yes, but no later than seven this evening. In case Pendleton wants anything.'

Armstrong stiffened in acknowledgement. 'Sir,' he said, and walked out.

Chief Petty Officer Barry Falconer climbed down the ladder from the fo'c'sle and ambled aft along the main deck. Subconsciously, his critical eye passed over the numerous small details of ship board fittings. Were the Carley floats properly secured? Was the motor-boat's canvas tarpaulin stretched as taut as it should be? A coiled rope looked neat enough, but he noticed the whipping on the end had frayed. All these things he took note of automatically, logged as satisfactory, or as in the case of the rope's end, requiring further attention, a word in someone's ear.

Between the funnel and the searchlight housing, he crossed from starboard to port and paused to lean on the guardrail, gazing down at the oily water of the harbour. The iridescent, multi-coloured sheen sparkled in the sunlight, lapping against the ship's side and leaving a line of dark scum with the gentle movement of water. He smiled gently. As a young lad he'd first noticed the same effect on the River Tyne near his home in Newcastle where he played with his school mates outside the perimeter fencing of the docks. And it was there, in the waste ground on the banks of the river, that his lifelong fascination with ships had come to the fore, nurtured amidst the north-east heartland of shipbuilding. Having joined the Navy at the earliest opportunity, he'd eventually found his way from the big battleships and cruisers to the Fleet destroyers and then to the smallest destroyer in the Royal Navy, *Brackendale*, one of the first 'Hunts' off the slipway.

He remembered his mother standing on the steps of their terraced house, scalding him for being late home from school, and then spoiling him with a treat from the sweet cupboard. She worked in the dockyard canteen now, as well as being a member of the Women's Institute. And his old man was a foreman in the same dockyard, having originally apprenticed as a ship's carpenter. They were hard working people, typical of their northern generation, and although they'd been reluctant to wave him off to the Royal Navy, he'd seen pride in their faces when each of his promotions had been awarded.

Footsteps approached from the stern and he straightened from the guardrail. It was Bryn Dawkins, the garrulous Welshman, overalls covered in dark patches and rubbing his hands clean on a piece of waste rag. He slung the dirty cloth over a shoulder and delved into a pocket for his pipe. An officer now, but he'd come through the ranks from stoker to Petty Officer, and then been rewarded with the rank of Lieutenant (E), the most senior Engineer aboard ship. Informally, he and Dawkins were on first name terms, got on well with one another.

Dawkins lit the pipe and blew smoke, turned and leaned on the guardrail. 'Any news?' he asked.

'Nothing to write home about,' Falconer said, staring at the shore. 'Number One says we'll get a run ashore, but no later than seven.'

Dawkins took another pull of smoke and jabbed the stem of his pipe at the dockside. 'Something's afoot, mark my words. Captain (D) coming aboard, the skipper swanning off up to London,' and he nodded, worldly wise. 'Don't take a genius to work that out.'

Falconer grinned. 'No argument from me. You coming ashore for a quick one?'

The Welshman looked at his watch and pulled a face. 'Might manage to finish up by five. Where'd you have in mind?'

The Cox'n thought for a moment and pursed his lips. 'First port of call with beer on the pump and a welcoming landlady. Agreed?'

Dawkins knocked out the embers from the bowl of his pipe and glanced up at the town. 'Beggars can't be choosers. I seem to remember a pub called The Rose and Crown, and the landlady pulls a fine pint.' He tested the pipe for any remaining warmth and dropped it into his pocket, then retrieved the cloth from his shoulder. 'Six o'clock,' he said, and wandered off.

Falconer watched him go with a warm smile, just one more good reason for being in small ships.

An M.G.B. puttered into the protected waters of the harbour and made her way over to the Admiralty Pier. Falconer watched her tie up, and then walked aft to his small office in the afterdeck housing. His paperwork awaited.

On the far side of the Channel isolated warships of the Kriegsmarine's north coast flotillas began preparing for action. Wolfgang Shultz kept a watchful eye on the loading of extra provisions. Ammunition was of paramount importance.

Chapter Twelve . . . North Sea Passage

At five in the afternoon in the industrial German port of Wilhelmshaven, an armed merchantman awaited the moment to put to sea.

Kapitän Gerhard Baumgartner, a man steeped in all the old traditions of the pre war Navy, had just celebrated his thirty-seventh birthday. His craggy, lined face bore witness to his years spent at sea and the hair at his temples showed a hint of premature grey. Unfortunately, his lack of zeal in all matters Nazi had been noticed by the hierarchy and his prospects of promotion severely restricted. But although he detested the arrogant swagger of Hitler's modern Kriegsmarine, he nonetheless strived to maintain the standards to which he'd sworn allegiance. If nothing else, Gerhard Baumgartner knew full well where his underlying loyalties lay and, given the opportunity, he would more than prove his worth.

'Herr Kapitän?' The query sounded anxious.

Baumgartner turned from the screen and nodded warmly to his First Officer. 'Ja, what is it, my young friend?'

'Admiral Krause has arrived on the quayside, getting out of his staff car.'

Baumgartner frowned; it was an unusual departure from protocol. 'Not to worry, Konrad, it's too late for a formal welcome. I'll go down and meet him myself. Wait here.' He strode across the bridge and stepped outside onto the port wing. Below him on the dock he could see Krause emerging from the car, a small escort of senior officers accompanying him towards the ship's gangway, not yet hauled in and stowed.

Baumgartner shook his head in disbelief at the late interruption to his schedule. After all, it was the Admiral's own timetable to which he adhered. He hurried inside for the stairs at the back of the bridge and made his way down to the main deck just in time to meet the uninvited guests as they stepped aboard.

He saluted and made his excuses. 'An honour, sir, but you gave me no time for the usual formalities. I am about to take passage.'

Krause scowled and nodded. 'I am well aware, Baumgartner, but there will be a delay,' he said abruptly. 'Your cabin . . . , lead on.'

'Of course, this way,' Baumgartner said, the first flicker of concern coursing through his veins. What had happened to cause the delay?'

At the door to the Grand Cabin, he stood aside to allow them in, called his servant and turned to Krause. 'Can I bring you anything?' he asked. 'Coffee perhaps?'

'No, we are not here for pleasantries,' he snapped, and stared pointedly at the servant. 'Leave us,' he demanded, and waited for the door to close.

Baumgartner stood uncomfortably, holding his silence, careful to wait for whatever came.

The Admiral stared at him for a long moment, frowning. 'There has been a change in the plans, necessary to the overall strategy. You will time your arrival at Rotterdam for dawn tomorrow . . . , daylight, you understand?' Baumgartner made no pretence of appearing to comprehend the dangerous instruction, it flew in the face of all standing orders for navigating that stretch of coast.

'No, sir, I do not understand. We will be open to air attack.'

'A small possibility, I grant you, but we must be certain the British know *Holstein* is on the move, that you are a threat to their shipping. Be in no doubt Kapitän, your ship is being monitored, there are many spies working for our enemies.' He paused to glance at his officers and smiled thinly. 'This time we can make it work in our favour. You will be like the wounded bear, the bait to draw in the hunter while a separate flotilla springs the trap.'

Baumgartner clenched and unclenched his hands behind his back, twisted his fingers. He would be like a lamb to the slaughter. He doubted his ship would be much use up against warships, that was never the intention in the design. And if his escorts or the supporting flotilla failed to engage quickly enough, then his chances were slim. But he was determined not to show Krause any sign of weakness, and smiled.

'I see,' he said slowly, 'and if I may ask the reason for all this?'

The Admiral gave a short explosive laugh.

'Annihilation, Kapitän, annihilation. The Führer wishes to remind Churchill that we are the rulers here, not the Royal Navy. Just because we fight the Russians in the east does not mean the Führer has forgotten to defend the west.'

Baumgartner wondered if Krause really believed the propaganda and he felt astonished by the revelation; outwardly he managed a nod of agreement. 'Of course, sir,' he managed lamely, after all, the man was speaking for Hitler, how could he argue?

The Admiral drew in a deep breath and rubbed his hands with satisfaction.

'So . . . , Kapitän, for a little delay now, we reap rich rewards later, no?'

Baumgartner struggled to find something positive to say. 'I'm sure it will be a great success,' he lied, desperate for the meeting to end, to be left alone.

His wish was granted. Krause grinned triumphantly and walked to the door.

'Good,' he said, 'very good. The British will come looking for trouble, they will find it, no?' he laughed at his own humour. 'The Führer will be pleased.'

Baumgartner escorted them to the ship's side and saluted as they made their way down to the dock, and as the big black Horst drove away, he dejectedly went back to his cabin. *Holstein's* chances of success were no better than fifty-fifty, probably worse. The British would never risk attacking in daylight and a night engagement usually proved to work in their favour. He found the decanter of brandy and poured himself a generous measure, carefully replaced the glass stopper and raised the glass in a solitary toast. Gulping a mouthful of the fiery liquid he grimaced and straightened his shoulders. It would not do for the men to see him worried, after all, he was their Kapitän and there must be no doubts as to his certainty. He contacted the bridge to inform them departure would be delayed for two hours, drained the last of the brandy and relaxed onto his bunk. He closed his eyes and began thinking of what he might do to outwit the Royal Navy.

Fifteen minutes before their new time of sailing, Baumgartner breezed into the bridge and called for his First Officer.

'What news, Konrad?'

'We are cleared to get under way, sir.'

'Wunderbar,' he said, giving the impression he was in high spirits. 'Make ready.'

'Jawohl, Herr Kapitän,' and he turned to execute the order.

'And, Konrad,' Baumgartner called with a thin smile on his lined face, 'when we are clear of the harbour we will exercise the men on the guns.'

Oberleutnant Konrad Neuman looked over his shoulder, touched the peak of his cap and grinned. 'Of course, sir,' he said, and dropped down the ladder.

Baumgartner crossed the bridge to stare down at the port mooring lines and watched as the crew let go the cables and freed all but two from the quayside bollards. He checked the time,

Neuman reappeared. 'Ready to proceed, Herr Kapitän.'

'You may take us out, Oberleutnant.'

Neuman crossed to the screen and called out the first order.

'Release cables.' The shore men let go the last of the lines.

'Wheel to starboard. Slow astern.' With no other ships at the quayside they reversed slowly away from the side, gave the ship enough room to manoeuvre and idled to a stop.

'Slow ahead both,' Neuman ordered, and with the helm hard to starboard *Holstein* found the safe channel and made for the open sea. Next stop Rotterdam, to coincide with dawn the next day. His anti-aircraft gunners would have to be on their toes.

Kapitän Baumgartner received a routine weather report from his messenger and noted the next twenty-four hours would bring strengthening winds from the west. He signed the pad, returned it, and then wandered over to the bridge-wing. Out there in the darkness an old 'between the wars' destroyer-escort pushed ahead, eight-hundred metres off the starboard bow. An intermittent flash of bow wave told him the warship held station and for a moment he watched the trailing wake.

'Konrad,' he said, turning to confront his First Officer. 'I will go to my cabin. Call me before we alter course for Rotterdam.'

'Yes, sir,' Neuman said, and straightened his shoulders. He glanced at the ship's compass and checked the time. 'We make the turn shortly before midnight, Herr Kapitän.'

Baumgartner nodded his approval. 'Good,' he smiled, 'I leave the ship in your hands. You will keep us safe, Konrad, and make certain the lookouts remember the British torpedo boats. On a night like this they will be active, you can be sure of that.'

'Jawohl, Herr Kapitän,' Neuman said and saluted.

Baumgartner touched his cap and turned away, the bunk in his Grand Cabin awaited.

He awoke to the call from Neuman and swung his feet to the deck. He rubbed his eyes and reached for his jacket. The row of medal ribbons made him pause, reflecting on life as it used to be. He sighed and shrugged into the familiar comfort, collected his cap and headed for the bridge.

On his arrival, Neuman stiffened to attention. 'We must alter course in four minutes, Herr Kapitän.'

Baumgartner nodded. The fitful sleep had left him feeling lethargic and he crossed to the bridge-chair.

'Anything more to report?'

There was the faintest of hesitations and Baumgartner jerked his head round. 'Tell me,' he demanded.

'It is nothing, Kapitän, a possible target reported from the underwater sound office. The idiot thought he must be mistaken, very short and not repeated. I could not wake you for such a reason, sir.'

'When was this?'

'Twenty minutes ago.'

Baumgartner thought for a moment. The *Holstein* was not equipped with the most advanced set of transponders; the latest equipment awaited their arrival in Brest, along with a fresh crew of operators. His existing crewmen were not the Kriegsmarine's best. 'Has our escort signalled? Their equipment is much more modern.'

Neuman now looked thoroughly crestfallen. 'I'm sorry, Herr Kapitän, I did not think to ask.'

Baumgartner rubbed his forehead in exasperation. 'Alright, Konrad. Let us make the change of course. I will assume that no contact from the escort indicates all is well.'

'Jawohl, Herr Kapitän,' Neuman said, and gave the order.

'Come left to one-ninety degrees.'

The helmsman swung the wheel. 'Left to one-ninety degrees, sir,' he repeated, and *Holstein* swung ponderously towards the south. The helmsman held the wheel over watching the compass, and then slowly allowed it to return to the midships position. 'One-ninety degrees, sir.'

Baumgartner stood and walked to the starboard wing, lifting his binoculars to where his escorting destroyer should be. He found the ship broadside on to *Holstein's* beam and nodded his approval. The young commander kept good station. He lowered the glasses on the leather strap and turned his head. From past reports, Baumgartner knew that these waters off the Dutch coast were prone to attacks by the Royal Navy. Of recent times their success rate had become progressively more intrusive, to such an extent the Kriegsmarine had reduced the number of convoys, and he felt extra precautions would be wise.

'Konrad,' he said slowly, following through with his thoughts. 'Get me the wireless operator.'

The man arrived with his notepad and clicked his heels.

Baumgartner paced the bridge. 'Send this to our escort. "Take station six kilometres to the west. Be prepared for attack by British torpedo boats", and tell him to report when in position.'

The man finished writing, saluted and turned away.

'Coffee!' Baumgartner barked. 'Let us have some strong coffee, Konrad.'

Neuman called for the liquid refreshment and slunk to the back of the bridge. It would be better to keep away from the Kapitän until his humour was restored.

The ship lifted to a long roller and slid majestically into the following trough, and Baumgartner glanced at his watch. On course and on time, and he smiled in the darkness.

Chapter Thirteen . . . Contact

Eight miles out from Terschelling and hovering sixty-feet below the surface of the North Sea, *Trophy* began preparing to commence operations. Lieutenant-Commander Craig Mitchell eased his way into the Control Room and stopped to look at the chart.

Crawford pointed to show their latest position. 'Sea state's the same, sir, moon's up.'

Mitchell nodded his approval and glanced inquiringly at his Hydrophone Operator who squinted and slowly shook his head. 'No sound, sir.'

For Mitchell, the time had come to surface the boat and proceed with diesels. It would be better to use the cloak of darkness to gain distance and charge the batteries; never assume *Trophy* wouldn't run into trouble and be forced under. He stepped across to stand by the vertical tube and reminded himself of the boat's current position and bearing. North-west of the island steering east by south. He gave the men around him a meaningful glance and gave the order.

'Periscope depth.'

Once again, as on so many previous occasions, the submarine rose through the waters and levelled off beneath the waves. He tensed at the eyepiece, well aware how danger might be lurking, the ever present threat of an enemy warship stopped on the waves. The lens broke the surface and Mitchell made the obligatory fast sweep of the horizon. What little cloud cover obscured the stars left him with a surprisingly good field of vision and he continued with a second search, slower this time, to all points of the compass. He finally returned the lens to dead ahead and stood back.

'Down periscope. Surface.'

Trophy broke through the waves in a swirl of foaming water and Mitchell took command from the navigating bridge. His lookouts swarmed up to their respective posts and commenced searching the port and starboard quarters. Having established they had the ocean to themselves, he activated the voice-pipe.

'Start the diesels.'

With a subdued roar the main engines kicked into life, sucking fresh night air into the bowels of the submarine. 'Obey telegraphs,' he said, and ordered a speed of ten knots. The galley began to prepare hot drinks, and those who smoked took advantage of the open boat.

'Ship, sir! Dead astern.'

Mitchell whipped round and rammed his eyes into his binoculars. He found it immediately, bow on and the sharp stem throwing up a clearly visible wave, so pronounced it had to be making at least thirty knots. He lowered the glasses, screwing his eyes at the darkness, and just managed to pinpoint the distant target. He judged the range as something over three miles, an Elbing class destroyer bearing down on them at speed. But why hadn't it opened fire? Had it really spotted *Trophy* or was it making best speed for another reason?

He wasn't about to take a chance. 'Prepare to dive,' he called. His natural instinct told him to go deep and make a ninety-degree turn to the south-west.

'Clear the bridge,' he ordered to those around him.

The lookouts dropped through the hatch, instantly followed by the Cox'n, and Mitchell raised his glasses for a final look. The enemy held his course, visibly closer.

A gun spat flame from the German's fo'c'sle and a plume of water shot up off the starboard quarter. Any lingering doubts as to a course of action were immediately dispelled.

'Dive . . dive . . dive!' he called, and threw himself into the conning tower. Hatch cover closed, clips secured, and Mitchell landed in the Control Room.

'Starboard thirty, one-hundred feet. Group up, full ahead.' He would risk the noise for two minutes.

In just under sixty seconds *Trophy* had left the surface.

'Fifty feet, sir.'

'Midships . . . , steer two-two-five degrees,' he ordered.

'Eighty feet, sir.'

He checked the time.

'Group down. Slow ahead, three knots.' As the acknowledgement was repeated he closed his eyes, conjuring up the relative positions between vessels. *Trophy* now moved silently south-west and he'd last seen the German moving south-east; that meant a ninety-degree difference in direction.

'Quiet in the boat,' he said, and heard it whispered through the compartments. He looked at the Hydrophone Operator.

'Twin screws, high speed at oh-five-five degrees, sir.'

Mitchell nodded at the confirmation and looked down at the deck plates. The German held his course. . , for now. Every second counted.

'One-hundred, sir.'

Trophy slid silently south-west, levelling off at one-hundred feet below the surface, and Mitchell looked inquiringly at the man with the earphones.

'Moving to port, sir.'

The Captain nodded, his brain computing the next move. The ideal scenario would be to keep the enemy astern, reducing *Trophy's* profile, end on to the enemy destroyer. Right now it had crossed their stern and he reacted accordingly.

'Starboard twenty.'

'Starboard twenty, aye, sir.'

The bearing swung through west towards the north. 'Midships . . . , steady. Steer three-five-oh degrees.'

'Three-five-oh degrees, aye aye, sir.'

Silence followed.

Cole spoke softly. 'Going away, sir.'

Mitchell inclined his head, watching, yards gained. A muffled rumble resonated along the pressure hull and Cole eased the earphones from his head. 'Depth charges,' he said, matter of fact.

Mitchell looked round the Control Room, expressionless faces concentrating on their stations. That destroyer had lost *Trophy's* signature, but lobbed a pattern of charges just in case, more to frighten than with any chance of hitting. More rumbles traversed the hull, and he guessed that the enemy destroyer would be deafened by the explosions. Time for a calculated gamble.

'Group up, full ahead both!'

He peered at his watch, at the sweep of the second hand, and gave it fifty seconds before ordering a reduction in speed.

'Slow ahead, three knots.' He vaguely heard the repeat while he tried to envisage the German hydrophone operator waiting for the water to settle. In the meantime *Trophy* had gained valuable distance.

'Propellers fading, sir,' Cole said.

'Very well.' He waited in the tense silence remembering they were moving a few points west of north.

'Eighty feet,' he ordered.

'Eighty feet, aye, sir.'

Mitchell rubbed his mouth with the back of his hand. He would prefer to be surfaced with the boat running on diesels. It was a risky proposition but he felt confident night would cloak their escape. He felt the boat level off.

'Eighty feet, sir.'

He looked inquiringly at Cole.

'Going away south-east. Very faint, sir.'

Mitchell grimaced. 'Sixty feet,' he ordered and *Trophy* answered the angle of the hydroplanes. She reached the required depth and cruised on at three knots. He caught Crawford's eye and nodded.

'Periscope depth.'

They rose and levelled, the depth gauge indicating thirty-two feet.

'Periscope depth, sir. Trim is good.'

'Thank you, Number One. Up scope.'

The tube came up and he gripped the handles and made the obligatory sweep. There was little to see, only enough to be certain no ship lay waiting in the immediate vicinity. He closed the handles and stepped back. 'Prepare to surface.'

The warning travelled through the compartments and the Control Room tensed.

'Ready, sir.' He moved to the base of the tower. 'Surface.'

The lower hatch opened and he climbed to wait beneath the upper hatch.

Crawford called out the depth and finally gave the important one.

'Ten feet, sir!'

Mitchell unclipped, relieved the internal pressure, and the hatch swung open. He moved swiftly onto the bridge, a hurried visual all round and then binoculars over the stern towards the enemy's last bearing. The lookouts squeezed up, checking their sectors and Mitchell moved forward focusing ahead, allowing time for night vision to fully function. This was the moment of greatest danger and he repeated the visual . . . , they'd almost been caught napping once, and that was once too many. Satisfied all was clear he turned to the voice-pipe.

'Start main engines.' And in moments the exhaust coughed and roared, and settled into a rhythmic pulse. 'Twelve knots, Number One.'

He chose to remain for a while longer, enjoying the occasional splash of spray, riding with the swaying tower. After five minutes he was about to leave the bridge for the Control Room, when he froze to a lookout's alarm.

'Ship! Bearing, Red one-hundred!'

Mitchell straightened, lifting his binoculars in disbelief. He refused to accept that the German destroyer had somehow reached that bearing, it had been going away on the starboard quarter. Try as he might, he found only darkness, a few breaking wave crests.

'Did you say Red one-hundred?'

'Yes, sir.'

'Can you still see it?'

'Yes, sir. Just.'

Mitchell gathered himself and concentrated through the glasses. He rolled the knurled wheel to focus at maximum range . . . , and found it. Exactly on the lookout's bearing. He studied what little he could detect but from the size of the vessel quickly concluded the target must be a merchantman. It most certainly was not a warship, wrong shape, too bulky, not sleek enough. A convoy then, and the destroyer had been part of an escort screen. And by sheer luck they were inside the screen. And that ship would cross *Trophy's* stern. He swivelled to the voice-pipe.

'Number One?'

'Sir?'

'There's a German freighter coming across our stern. Have the stern tubes readied.'

'Aye aye, sir.'

Mitchell mulled it over. He was caught by the mission brief. Was that ship greater than five-thousand tons? And what of the convoy, if that's what he'd located? He rubbed his forehead in frustration. A stern shot would be a gamble and in any other circumstances well worth the risk, but right now his orders dictated he slink away with his tail between his legs. He raised the glasses, located the faint trace of bow wave and reluctantly let it go. There'd be other opportunities, and in the meantime he'd get a signal off to Harwich. He'd have to be careful with the wording. There was no verification that it was a convoy, he had only suspicions. But he could give his position, their bearing and theoretical speed. He turned to the bridge, determined to set a course for Terschelling and get visual confirmation of their position.

'Starboard ten, steer oh-eight-oh degrees. Stand down from the torpedo tubes.' The voice-pipe relayed his order and he waited topside while *Trophy* gradually came round astern of the enemy shipping and resumed her journey. In a couple of hours the Telegraphist could transmit to his hearts content.

Trophy's wake boiled down the saddle tanks, foaming astern, receding into the night, and Lieutenant-Commander Craig Mitchell stared east over the bows, impatient for landfall.

Just past midnight he gave the order to stop diesels, engage the electric motors and submerge. With hatches secured the submarine nosed stealthily beneath the waves, levelled off at sixty feet and at four knots, began to close the coast. After a twenty minute run he ordered the boat up to periscope depth and this time found their first sighting of land. He made a prolonged inspection of the island. A long strip of white beach loomed bright, two thousand yards ahead of the bows, and before completing his visual check he made certain of their position by identifying two landmarks.

He pulled away from the eye pieces and snapped the handles.

'Down periscope.' The tube sank into its well and he turned to the chart where Crawford stood with dividers poised. He touched the point to the paper.

'From your sightings, sir, we're here. That's five hundred yards east of our estimate. There must be a fair sea running for us to be so far out.'

'Mmm,' Mitchell mouthed, non-committal. Navigation was not an exact science beneath the waves, hence the necessity to get a visual fix to confirm their position.

'How are we for trim?'

Crawford checked the gauges and raised an eyebrow to the Cox'n on the forward planes.

'Trim is level, sir.'

'Very well. Stop engines.'

The faint murmur of the electric motors died away and *Trophy* fell silent, drifting with the underwater currents, hanging beneath the waves.

Mitchell glanced at the time and removed his cap. '*Trophy* will remain at periscope depth and we'll repeat visuals at ten minute intervals. An hour from now we'll surface, maintain observations of the area for another fifteen minutes and then move south with main engines. When we do surface I want gun crews at action stations.' He paused and gave the control room a wry grin. 'Can't be too careful.'

Crawford met his eyes and nodded. 'Aye aye, sir.'

An hour later, Lieutenant Jeremy Crawford waited for the clock's minute hand to coincide with quarter to the hour and passed the order.

'Up periscope.'

The tube hissed and he met the handles as they rose, flicked them into position and pressed his eye to the rubber socket. He swept the horizon, what little could be seen through the darkness, and returned his gaze to the coast. This would be the final short check before he called the captain. *Trophy* had drifted north, not by much, and he made a note of the two landmarks. The narrow strip of beach glimmered under the stars, and from this distance he didn't expect to pick up on any detail.

Satisfied with their positioning, he took a final look round the horizon and snapped up the handles.

'Down periscope.'

He walked across to the log, entered his findings, then moved to the chart and noted their position. He took a careful look at the boat's trim; all seemed well. A glance at the time and he nodded to himself. In three minutes he would call the Commander.

Mitchell heard the call, 'Captain to the Control Room,' and walked into *Trophy's* command centre, raising an eyebrow to his First Lieutenant.

Crawford made his report. 'We're three-thousand yards off shore, sir. My last fix had us five-hundred yards north of our previous position. No enemy activity to report.'

Mitchell nodded and glanced at the chart for confirmation.

'Thank you, Number One. Have the gun crews stand by.'

'Aye aye, sir,' Crawford said, and called quietly. 'Gun crews prepare for action.' He turned to the trim gauges, an automatic reaction whenever men moved through the boat. 'Watch her, Cox'n.'

Mitchell smiled to himself. There'd been no need for the warning, but this close to the surface it remained uppermost in the mind.

'Gun crews ready, sir,' came a call from the forward compartment.

Mitchell nodded to Crawford.

'Up periscope.'

The bulk of the tube lifted from its well and Mitchell bent to the eyepiece. He paused for a second to allow his pupil to dilate, focused with the twist grip and found the beach. He traversed carefully through three-hundred and sixty degrees, checking his visible perimeter, and came back to the island.

'Time?' he asked abruptly.

'Oh-one-oh-five hours, sir.'

144

'Slow ahead. Starboard ten,' he ordered. He needed to get *Trophy* back on station, only a few hundred yards to the right, but it would make all the difference to later navigation. The shoreline swung left as the submarine came round to the south and he corrected the steering.

'Wheel amidships.'

'Wheel amidships, aye aye, sir.'

'Steady, steer one-eight-oh degrees.' *Trophy* settled to the bearing and idled south.

Mitchell made himself relax and stared through the lens of the periscope. The manoeuvre had allowed him to run down parallel with the shore. *Trophy* now lay three-thousand yards out. He watched and waited. The minutes ticked by and finally *Trophy* cleared the southern end of Terschelling.

'Time?' he snapped.

'Twelve minutes past one, sir.'

He pulled away from the eyepiece, rubbed his face, and reconnected. They were in open water.

'Surface!' he ordered. 'Down scope, slow ahead together.'

To the hiss of compressed air, a rating undid the lower hatch, stood clear and Mitchell headed up the tower. He unclipped, accepted the splash of seawater down his shoulders and hoisted himself up onto the navigating bridge. A hasty check through his binoculars, fore and aft, port and starboard. All clear, and the gunners briskly set about manning the four-inch on the casing below the conning tower. The bridge swayed unevenly in the long swell and he propped his elbows on the bulwark. He heard a call from the pipe.

'Bridge,' he answered.

'Hydrophone Operator thinks he heard acoustics at three-five-oh degrees, sir. Maximum range.'

Mitchell frowned but kept his binoculars trained ahead. 'Very well,' he said. The acoustics must have been heard just before they surfaced, and that meant anywhere from five to ten nautical miles distant.

'Lookouts, keep an eye on the starboard quarter. We may have company.' To the voice-pipe he said, 'Start main engines,' and the diesels coughed noisily into life. The Cox'n appeared and took the steering and Mitchell took true command of the bridge.

'Obey telegraph,' he ordered and settled down for a stint on watch. In accordance with his orders he made the decision to quarter this sector. It was widely known in the Admiralty that this marked the navigational turning point for southbound shipping, particularly for those accessing Rotterdam. He would give it until dawn and see what transpired. And now, with no fear of a wireless transmission being directly linked to their early brush with the German convoy, he ordered the sighting signal to be sent.

'Gun crew below,' Mitchell called, and within a minute, they had vacated the casing. 'Lookouts below, prepare to dive.'

As they lowered themselves down the tower, he took a last look through the binoculars, slowing his sweep as he came to the port quarter, concentrating on those final acoustic reports. The visible horizon proved to be empty and for a long moment he rested on the steelwork and stared at the dark sea. Mission successful, he thought with a smile, and turned to the pipe.

'Control-room. Dive, dive, dive.' He pulled the hatch down over his head, secured it and swung off the bottom rung. 'Half ahead together, port twenty. Steer two-seven-oh. Fifty-five feet.'

To a flurry of hushed commands and repeats, and the practised expertise of the boat's company, *Trophy* swung west and nosed into the depths.

Mitchell checked the time, gave the submarine a few minutes at five knots and then ordered a reduction in revolutions to three knots. Before doing anything more he wanted the Hydrophone Operator to have a prolonged go at listening for propellers. 'Silence in the boat.'

He took a step closer towards the operator, and raised an eyebrow. The young man met his eyes and held them, his lips compressed into a straight line as he listened intently to the sounds of the sea. His head tilted slightly to the right, and then he dropped his gaze, frowning at the dial. He made an adjustment, swinging the pointer to *Trophy's* starboard bow, slowly turning it back and forth. His chin sunk to his chest, eyes closed in concentration, then finally he looked up and shook his head.

'No H.E., sir.'

Mitchell nodded, no hydrophone effect equated with no propeller noises and they were clear to proceed. 'Well done, better safe than sorry.' He looked at the time and turned towards the chart table. Their current course, due west, clearly marked. Their next patrol area lay to the north-west of Rotterdam.

'Port ten. Steer two-four-oh degrees, depth eighty feet.'

Acknowledgements came and the bow planes dipped, the depth gauge moving to correspond with their descent. At seventy feet the Cox'n reduced the angle of inclination and the submarine levelled off at a precisely eighty feet.

Mitchell leaned over the chart, picked up the dividers and walked the points on a theoretical line towards Amsterdam and beyond. He made a mental note of the distance, calculated estimated time of arrival, and decided to remain submerged.

In silence, *Trophy* continued her journey: thus far, mission accomplished.

In Harwich, at 02.10hrs on Wednesday 29th, the duty Telegraphist acknowledged receipt of a signal from the submarine *Trophy* and passed it across for decoding. Within minutes the cipher room converted it to plain language and handed the slip to the Duty Officer.

The message reached the Admiralty's Operations Room in London shortly thereafter, and having contacted the relevant 'to whom it may concern', at 05.30hrs Captain James Pendleton received word from Commodore Collingwood informing him of a suspected small convoy moving south past the Frisian islands.

At 06.15hrs he strode into the cellar of his Dover headquarters and set about implementing a change to what had become known as 'Operation Harvest'. The duty officer appeared at his summons. 'Morning, sir.'

Pendleton glared up from the desk. 'Morning,' he barked. 'Get a message to *Brackendale*. Ask Lieutenant-Commander Thorburn to join me for 09.00hrs. Then give the Wren's quarters a call and ask if Second Officer Farbrace is fit for duty. If so, I would appreciate it if she would also report here by nine o'clock. Understood?'

'Yes, sir.'

'Well don't just stand there man, I haven't got all day.'

'Right, sir,' the Officer stammered, and backed out of the door.

Pendleton allowed himself the smallest of smiles and turned to his large chart of the North Sea and the English Channel. Smoothing his beard he examined the Dutch coast for possible convoy routings, Rotterdam being the most likely first port of call. And the convoy would shelter there during daylight hours before resuming their journey west. Aerial reconnaissance would give him confirmation; from *Trophy's* report the merchantman was too big to miss.

And Pendleton knew just the man to call on. He reached for the 'phone and dialled the number for Wing Commander Colin Ashworth. Time to call in a favour.

Chapter Fourteen . . . Blue-Five

Jennifer Farbrace had already awoken when someone knocked her door. She'd been sat with her back resting against the plumped up pillows and looking out a dazzling blue sky. A pair of collared doves had caught her interest, fluttering along the ramparts of the castle's walls and cooing softly in the still air.

'Yes?'

A young Wren popped her head round the door. 'Sorry to disturb you, ma'am, but we've had a call from Captain Pendleton's office. They're asking if you're well enough to attend for nine o'clock?'

Jennifer reached a hand up to the bandage round her neck and turned her head from side to side. The sharp pain of the initial damage had backed off, now no more then a throbbing ache at worst. The pain killers took the edge off and she could picture the Captain chomping at the bit for her return. She remembered Richard's words, about not being rushed back before she was ready, but after two days of enforced idleness, she felt ready to give it a go.

'Yes, you can tell them I *will* be in.'

The girl frowned. 'If you're sure, ma'am. I could easily tell them no.'

Jennifer smiled gently. 'No, it's alright, I'm getting bored anyway.'

The woman hesitated.

Giving her an inquisitive stare, Jennifer asked for her name.

'Wendy Stafford, ma'am,' she said, dropping her eyes to the floor.

'Well, Miss Wendy Stafford, thank you for your concern, but I'm sure I'll manage, so please do as I ask.'

'Yes, ma'am, sorry ma'am, but you do look a bit off colour.'

Jennifer threw back the covers and swung her bare feet to the cold floorboards. The sudden movement gave her a moment of light-headedness, but she shook it off and managed a smile.

'And I can't criticise you for that, but please have a driver ready at a quarter to nine.'

Wendy Stafford half bowed, half curtsied, and with a disarming smile nodded and closed the door.

Jennifer breathed in, pushed herself up from the bed and stepped over to the plain wooden table. She wriggled her toes into her slippers, slipped into the dressing gown and collected her wash bag and towel. The corridor lay empty and she walked quietly down to the communal washrooms.

At eight o'clock the cook in the Officer's Mess served her a boiled egg and a slice of thinly buttered toast, and as she sat nursing her mug of tea a number of colleagues wished her well, glad to see she was back on her feet.

With quarter of an hour to spare, she returned to her room, checked her makeup and brushed her hair. The bandage felt uncomfortable under the collar of her blouse and she removed the tie and folded it into a pocket. Undoing the top button relieved the discomfort and she decided that Pendleton would have to accept she was out of uniform. Cap on her head, gas mask slung over her shoulder, she picked up her Parker fountain pen and closed the door behind her.

Outside in the cobbled courtyard a Wren waited with the car ticking over. Jennifer slipped into the front passenger seat and the driver found a gear and eased the Hillman down the slope. Passing under the old archway, they swung left onto the main road and drove down the steep hill.

Five minutes later, the Hillman pulled to a halt outside the headquarters and Jennifer hurried inside and down to the cellar. Pendleton's office door hung ajar and she knocked.

'Morning, sir.'

He looked up from a sheaf of papers and immediately rose to his feet. 'How are you, young lady?' he asked coming round the desk to greet her. 'I hope you've not come back too soon, that wouldn't do at all you know. I probably shouldn't have called.'

She smiled as he fussed round her and pulled out a chair. 'I'm much better, sir. Please excuse me not wearing a tie.'

'Didn't even notice,' he said, and Jennifer raised an eyebrow at the obvious lie. Normally the slightest discrepancy in the wearing of a uniform, something as small as an upside down button, would draw a disparaging remark. She wished he'd stop fussing and spoke through his efforts.

'I would like to know what's going on?'

'Yes, yes of course. Do sit down and I'll run you through the latest.'

Jennifer could see the agitation and so took her seat. She noticed the chart on the wall had been modified with annotations and a row of red pins, up near the Frisian Islands.

Pendleton briefly ran her through all that had transpired during her absence and tugged his beard.

'I've had an update from Collingwood,' he said, his eyes straying towards the chart. 'There's been a sighting off the Dutch coast, a convoy of sorts, headed south. The signal came from a submarine, H.M.S. *Trophy*, carrying out a surveillance operation. There was a positive identification of a large merchantman just after a depth charging from an Elbing destroyer. The captain's orders forbade the use of torpedoes unless he could be certain of the size. He couldn't be certain and avoided contact.' He glanced at his watch. 'Richard will be here shortly for a full briefing and I need you in on it. In the meantime, organise the shore staff and get things moving.' He hesitated. 'But only if you feel up to it.'

'I'll manage,' she assured him, and came to her feet. Since arriving from Chatham she'd had no time to arrange her office or anything else and wanted to get things sorted.

Pendleton cleared his throat, a faint smile lighting his eyes. 'Don't try and do everything yourself, for God's sake delegate. Your staff are more than capable of carrying out your instructions.'

'Of course, sir,' she nodded. 'I'll get on then?' She watched, and recognised the moment he reverted to the role of Captain (D).

'Very well. And there's a couple of 'Hunts' arriving. I need to be informed the moment they get in.'

'Yes, sir,' she said, and pulled the door closed. Her own office occupied the room next door, sparsely furnished but complete with her familiar typewriter and filing cabinets. The Wireless/Telegraphy office and switchboard had established itself in a storage room and at the far end of the cellar; Petty Officer Danbridge held sway over the Wrens in the typing pool.

For the first time since the attack on *Brackendale* she began to feel in control. She picked up the telephone receiver and spoke to the switchboard. She had an outside line if needed.

Hauptman Karl Jäeger had taken the decision to make a solo reconnaissance of the Dover Straits. A long frontal system of fair weather cloud had bubbled up over the sea, an ideal opportunity for cloud hopping. He warned Weimar to inform anyone who asked that he was on a test flight, silenced his remonstrations with a curt dismissal, and instructed the ground crew of his intentions. Ten minutes later, fully armed, and with a tank full of fuel he took off and climbed for the clouds. Climbing to three-thousand metres the Messerschmitt slipped inside the damp mist and he set course for Dover. Flitting from cloud to cloud, never too long in clear skies, Jäeger took full advantage of the cover. Closing in on the English coast he turned north-east and looked down on the harbour, disappointed to see the destroyer unharmed.

Ahead and below came the first in a succession of flack bursts and he turned away to duck back in the cloud. Fuel gauge gave him another forty minutes and he took the 109 up to four-thousand metres, arrived at mid-channel, and turned north on the off chance he might find a convoy, anything on which to vent his frustration.

Seven miles to the west of Dover, at the Royal Air Force station of Hawkinge, Pilot Officer 'Teddy' Whitlock tickled the Spitfire's throttle and waved away the chocks. The ground crew obliged and gave him a thumbs up. He taxied out to the end of the airstrip and with judicious use of throttle and rudder brought the aircraft round to the end of the runway. He lowered his goggles, settled them for comfort and glanced at the tower. He could see the Flight Controller watching.

'Hello Control, Blue-Five ready, over.'

'Hello Blue-Five, you are clear for take-off.'

Whitlock nodded, closed the cockpit and throttled up. As the revs climbed he released the brakes and the Spitfire bounded forward. The fighter gathered speed, raced down the grass strip, and hardly registering the moment, rose majestically into the air. Wheels up, he lifted the nose and then angled left to pick up a north-westerly bearing. Gaining altitude he levelled out at eight-thousand and set the air speed at two-hundred miles an hour. Patches of wispy cloud drifted by and far ahead, a long trail of altocumulus formed an intermittent front at what he estimated to be fourteen-thousand feet.

Having established he had the skies to himself he climbed for the cloud base, thankful for the all enveloping fog like barrier. He dodged inside a dense bank of moisture, flitted between two lumps of cotton wool and then dropped out to check below. Clear so far as he could see, and he floated back up into obscurity. He flew on, skimming the underside of cloud, one moment in the open, and the next, hidden from view. Then came the unmistakeable outline of Rotterdam's ragged basin.

Twenty miles from the coast, Whitlock dropped the Spitfire's nose and dived for the sea. He'd already decided that his best option would be to hide in the open, hugging the waves before surprising the German defences. He'd be in and away before they had time to react, and he raced on.

A mile out from the coastline he opened the throttle, powered up to three-hundred miles an hour, and soared into the sky. The pulsing roar of the Rolls Royce vibrated through the controls, pulling him urgently upwards to a thousand feet. To the left, ahead of the port wing, the skeletal cranes and crowded docks sprang into view. A few small ships tied to the wharves, a tug crossing the water.

He tensed and pursed his lips in a silent whistle. Berthed alongside a dock beside a railway track, a large vessel lay quietly at rest. What surprised him was its size, at first glance nigh on four-thousand tons, easily three-hundred feet in length. More like an auxiliary cruiser than a merchantman. And then he glimpsed what appeared to be a large calibre gun muzzle protruding from the afterdeck housing. Pushing the nose down he banked to port and then flicked right, coming in over the ship's stern. At six-hundred feet he could see a dummy enclosure, designed to hide the weapon. He flashed over the funnel and the enclosed bridge, and as he skimmed the sharp end, a huddle of pale faces stared up. Too late, they dragged a canvas tarpaulin over a large calibre cannon, bigger than the one at the stern. Accelerating hard, Whitlock flew on, knowing he needed a second pass to be certain of the detail. He hauled the Spitfire into the sky, banked right into a tight circle south and headed back at right angles to his original bearing. Altimeter showed nine-hundred feet and he levelled out. A fast check of the skies, and he dived for the ship.

Tracer arced up from the quayside, spraying ahead. He concentrated his gaze on the ship's main deck, ignoring the machine-gun bullets. His perseverance paid off. This time he located two pairs of guns tucked either side of the foredeck ahead of the bridge, almost hidden by the ship's sides. In an open ended shelter ahead of the bridge he picked out the dark shape of an Arado seaplane. There were flak guns on the well deck and even a pair of Pak anti-tank guns.

That was enough, time to leave. Wrenching the Spitfire into a hard left roll he headed seawards and braced for a gauntlet of gunfire. He wasn't to be disappointed; the German gunners had woken up.

Streams of multi-coloured tracer criss-crossed the air. The Spitfire jumped, taking hits, and he weaved to throw out their aim. At full throttle he whipped through the lethal blanket of ground fire. Another hit, and the fabric of the port wing erupted into jagged holes.

And then he was clear.

The sweet howl of the engine powered him out to sea and gaining height he tentatively tested the controls, feeling the Spitfire's response. All good. A scan of the surrounding skies; no sign of enemy activity. Time to gain altitude and head for the clouds. A pull on the stick and the aircraft soared upwards, and he allowed himself the faintest of smiles. His luck had held. At thirteen-thousand feet and with the Air Speed Indicator showing three-hundred plus miles an hour he lanced up into the base of the cloud and the welcoming fog. Another thousand feet and he broke through the top into bright sunshine.

Levelling out, he throttled back to cruising speed and checked his compass. A small correction to the west. He glanced at the port wing, at the ragged tears, and frowned with concern. A split in the fabric had linked between holes, flapping hard in the wind. Gritting his teeth he nudged the throttle back to lessen the air flow and prayed it held together. Gently, the Spitfire sank lower. A gap showed itself in the clouds and he slipped through the opening and spiralled slowly down to port. Again he levelled out, but this time with the coast of England in sight. Relieved to see the distant landscape he eased his shoulders and relaxed his grip on the stick.

Richard Thorburn stepped lightly from the motorboat to the quayside. The chill of early morning had been replaced by warming sunlight as the sun rose higher. He exited Granville Dock and paused for a squad of soldiers to march past, acknowledging the corporal's shouted 'Eyes left!' with his own salute. When they'd gone he crossed over and cut through an alleyway that opened into the next street. A hundred yards to his left on the opposite side of the road he saw the sandbagged entrance to Pendleton's new headquarters. Striding over to the far pavement he looked about in surprise, stunned by the amount of damage to the surrounding buildings. As opposed to the other night when he'd walked the streets in the blackout, daylight revealed the true extent of Dover's suffering. The unjust scars of war were all too evident, in stark contrast to when he'd first visited the town in 1940.

A pair of Marines guarding the entranceway snapped. to attention and he climbed the steps to find himself confronted by a small reception desk manned by a Petty Officer.

'Where do I find Captain Pendleton?' he asked.

'In the cellar, sir,' the man said, pointing to the top of a flight of stairs. 'Down those, turn left, and his office is third door along, sir.'

Thorburn nodded his thanks, followed the man's advice, and found himself in a poorly lit corridor. He counted doorways and as he walked past the second open door, glanced inside and stopped. There at a desk sat Jennifer Farbrace, rifling through a stack of paperwork. He tapped on the door frame and grinned.

She looked up with a frown, took a moment to realise who it was, and then he watched her face soften into a warm smile.

'Richard,' she said happily, dropped the papers and stood to come round the desk. He noticed her familiar habit of smoothing down the skirt, spotted the absence of a tie, and lost his grin, concerned by the bandage round her neck.

'How's the wound? You're not over doing it are you?'

She came close and he caught the delicate fragrance of her perfume. She laid a hand on his chest, stretched up and kissed his cheek. This near, her eyes sparkled with warmth.

'I'm not over doing it and his 'Lordship' told me to make sure I delegate.' She laughed and turned away, sat down behind her desk and gestured to the room next door. 'You'll be late, he's waiting.'

'Then he'll just have to wait. You haven't told me how the wound is.'

A deep base voice cut in from behind. 'Waiting for junior officers is not something to which I'm accustomed, Commander.'

Thorburn swallowed, regretting the unguarded remark, and turned to face justified anger.

'Sorry, sir . . . ,' he began, and stopped short. Pendleton stood there grinning broadly, the heavy beard shaking with suppressed laughter before he managed to control himself.

'Just this once, my boy, I'll excuse the insubordination, and I can assure you, Miss Farbrace is not here under duress.' He walked to her desk and slid a manila folder across to her in-tray. 'You'll need that. It's a list of captains joining the flotilla.' He turned back to face Thorburn and touched his shoulder.

'Come along, Richard, we've work to do,' and with that he strode out.

Thorburn threw an embarrassed glance at Jennifer, raised his eyebrows and shrugged. 'Oops,' he said, and followed Pendleton out into the corridor.

When he entered the office he chose to stand respectfully to one side, waiting while Pendleton swivelled his chair and sat.

'Close the door, Richard. Don't want too many eavesdropping on this.'

Thorburn closed it gently and Pendleton pointed to a chair. He indicated a large chart on the wall.

'North Sea, the Frisian Islands,' he said, waving a hand to encompass the Dutch coast. 'This morning at 02.10hrs we received a signal from one of our submarines. They reported a German convoy bearing south, south-west, probably headed for Rotterdam.' He paused staring at the chart. 'That sounds to me as if the Commodore wasn't too far off the mark and those are the ships he spoke of. I've asked the R.A.F. for confirmation by having a look at Rotterdam's waterways. If the report was correct, there should be a big fat merchantman waiting to make the next leg west.'

Thorburn let him talk. No doubt he would get to the point in his own good time.

Pendleton leaned forward and planted his elbows on the desk, lowering his voice. 'Your new flotilla, if it ever gets here, will sail to intercept that ship as it takes passage down the coast. As yet, we're unclear about its next destination.'

'Ostend, sir?'

'That's our best guess as the next port of call.' He stood and moved to the chart. Pointing to the Belgian coast he tapped the area north of Ostend. 'That's where

I'd want to make an interception.' The sharp eyes narrowed. 'I'm not sure this is as straight forward as it appears. My gut instinct says there's something special about that ship.' He turned back to his desk with a flash of irritability, glancing at his wristwatch, and Thorburn hid a smile.

'I wish to God the R.A.F. would get on with things. I expected some news by now.'

Chapter Fifteen . . . Bandit

Pilot Officer Teddy Whitlock brought the Spitfire down to nine-thousand feet, lined up with the South Foreland, and checked his instruments. Oil pressure, engine temperature, speed and altimeter; all as they should be and he made a check of the sky. Clear. He flexed the fingers of his gloved hands, looked again at the damage to the port wing, saw that it held for now and wondered what else had been damaged, hidden from sight.

His earphones crackled. 'Hello Blue Five . . . , Control, over.'

He flicked the button. 'Blue Five receiving, over?'

'We have a lone bandit to the west of you, angels fourteen.'

Whitlock made another check without seeing anything. At fourteen-thousand feet that bogey had height advantage. 'Roger, Control. No sign yet.'

He shot a glance at the holes in the port wing and shook his head. This wasn't the time to be timid, drop the natural instinct to nurse her home and take a chance. The comforting band of cloud had dropped behind, only clear skies between him and the coast. A push on the throttle to increase speed and he yawed left and right watching for the Hun.

'Blue Five, bandit closing from the west, angels twelve.'

'Roger,' he said, and swivelled his head. Nothing. Time to take action. He banked right and then rolled left twisting through the air, all the while scanning the sky behind. That Hun had dropped altitude so he'd probably seen the Spitfire, but would be wary of being bounced by another flight.

He dropped the nose slightly, turned towards the east and peered at the mirror. A speck slid across the glass and he corrected the turn. There it was again, a fast moving dot, growing in size. Whitlock gripped the stick, holding his nerve.

'Hello Control, our friend is with me now.'

'Roger, Blue Five. Red section on their way.'

He pursed his lips in thought. So Jimmy, Andy and Rob were coming to help. He turned over his options, limited with the damage to the wing. Run for home, or fight it out? He'd been a fighter pilot long enough to have fought a few battles, knew he had what it took to engage in a dogfight.

The dark silhouette transformed itself into a solid shape and he recognised it as a Messerschmitt. In normal circumstances the Spit could out manoeuvre the ME109, tighter turns, and beneath the oxygen mask he smiled tightly. He would hold straight and level, as might a rookie, wait to the last moment and then break right and let him overshoot. He moved his thumb to the fire button, reflector sight on and airscrew pitch set.

Karl Jäeger latched on to the single Spitfire, closing from above and behind, an ideal firing solution. At first sight he'd hesitated, searching the sky, certain there'd be more British fighters waiting to pounce. But having waited for a full minute he knew he'd struck lucky, an isolated dummkopf waiting to be picked off. He'd taken the Messerschmitt in a wide turn to the south before leaving the cloud. He dropped a wing, peeled down and held back before throttling up and winging in for the attack. A sitting duck. His thumb caressed the firing button, sights on, inside five-hundred metres, could not miss.

He punched the button.

Whitlock saw the moment the front of the Messerschmitt flashed with gunfire and slammed the Spitfire into a tight turn. He heard hits on the fuselage. Tracer slashed past the cockpit. He fought to bring her round, desperate to get behind, lifting his eyes to the top of the canopy, tracking the 109. The ME stopped firing, banked left and swept down.

He grimaced in triumph; wrong move you bastard. It allowed him to shorten the turn, to pull out onto the Hun's tail. He flicked left, levelled out and swooped onto the black crossed target. A hundred yards and he pressed the button. The Spit jumped as the four guns hammered. He saw strikes on the tail, driving forward along the fuselage. In seconds bullets tore into the port wing, shredding the skin, flaying the spars. The Messerschmitt staggered and dropped, flew on.

Whitlock pulled left and watched as the fighter went into a dive. A fine wisp of smoke trailed behind, thickening as the aircraft lost altitude. He peeled the Spitfire down in a chase to the sea, closed from the port quarter and fired a long burst. Smoking tracer pummelled the cockpit and he pulled up parallel with the port side. The ME109 careered on down towards the sea and then, very gently, came out of the headlong dive to glide low and level, drifting down to the waves.

Jäeger sagged in the cockpit of his Messerschmitt, fighting to keep it in the air. His situation had become hopeless. Pulling out of the attack his fighter had been severely mauled by machine-gun bullets. One had smashed his left elbow, scythed through bone and tendons, and left him bleeding heavily. The blood poured freely down his useless forearm, his gloved hand hanging limp. In the same instance the engine had coughed and lost power, and the joystick became erratic, sluggish in response.

A nauseating weakness flooded through him and he involuntarily screwed his eyes shut; forced them open again. The Messerschmitt yawed, lost altitude and he instinctively pulled on the stick to gain height. The 109 lifted into a stall, staggered and slipped sideways. The engine hesitated, spluttered and recovered, still down on power. He put the nose down to gain speed, but his altimeter showed three-hundred metres, too low.

Jäeger knew it was only a matter of time. Surprisingly, the agonising pain in his arm eased, and he guessed shock had set in. He reached up with his good hand and pushed the goggles up from his eyes and then unclipped his oxygen mask, letting it fall to the side.

The engine grumbled and died, the propeller grinding to a halt. He resigned himself to the inevitable, heard the rush of wind over the cockpit and watched the sea come to meet him.

With a violent impact his fighter hit the waves. In a moment of frightful clarity, Jäeger felt the full impact. His body slammed forward against the harness and the force smashed his ribs, lungs punctured. An explosion of water engulfed the cockpit, bright sunlight gone, the dark sea swirling in. As the wings tore apart, his lungs filled and his chest heaved in a reflex spasm, to no avail. The weight of the engine took him deeper, and unable to breath, his heart fluttered and stopped, and last of all his brain began to shut down. Death came as he drowned in the cockpit, dragged to a watery grave.

'Bastard!' Whitlock mouthed into his mask, elated by his success, and turned away in a climb for the Kent coast. Overhead, the three Spitfires of Red section arrived and turned with him, drifting down to take up a loose formation. He raised a hand in salute, received a waggle of wings in reply, and together the fighters flew in over Deal's shingle beach.

In minutes, Hawkinge airstrip came into view, in itself a welcome sight. But for Whitlock, seeing the damage to his port wing, knowing he'd taken multiple hits to the fuselage, this was a moment of concern. Only when he activated the landing gear would he find out if the hydraulics were damaged. He made it happen and waited for the green lights. After what seemed an interminable delay they both lit to show the wheels locked in place. He breathed out gently, lined up the Spit with the runway and adjusted the throttle to take him in on the glide path. Crossing the airfield perimeter he coaxed the revs down, deployed the flaps, and at ninety miles an hour, gratefully touched the wheels onto the grass. A small bounce and he taxied the aircraft along to dispersal. Red Section followed him in.

The ground crew helped him out and he dropped to the ground, turning to inspect the damage. Holes and tears disrupted the smooth surface of the fuselage, and a section of the tail plane had been shot away. He bent to look under the port wing and grimaced; it was a mess and Whitlock realised for the first time how close he'd come to ending up in the drink.

Jimmy from Red Section ducked under the wing and slapped him on the flying jacket. 'Chalk one up, Teddy,' he laughed gleefully. 'We'll confirm.'

'Thanks,' he said, and pointed to the damage. 'Close call.'

For a moment, as the others joined them, the two men surveyed the aircraft and nodded in sombre contemplation. Those who flew theses wonderful machines also understood the fine line between success and failure. As tough as the Spitfires were, the wrong bullet in the wrong place, and your chances of survival hung on the end of a parachute.

Whitlock grinned. 'I'd better find the C.O, he'll be waiting.'

At Dover, the newly established switchboard in Pendleton's underground headquarters received a call from Hawkinge and the Wren patched it through to Second Officer Jennifer Farbrace.

She picked up the handset, listened briefly and transferred the call to the Old Man's desk.

In his office the Captain answered the telephone. 'Pendleton speaking.'

'Morning, James, Ashworth here. I have news.'

Pendleton raised a hand to interrupt Thorburn, sat forward and reached for a cigarette. 'Good morning, Colin. Good news I hope?'

A chuckle came down the line. 'All depends what you expect to hear. My chap found your merchantman alright, tied up at the quayside in Rotterdam. The thing is, he initially thought he might be mistaken, the ship was a lot bigger than he imagined. It had so many big guns on board he reckons it has to be some sort of commerce raider. Too small for an auxiliary cruiser but definitely an armed merchantman. He estimated three to four-thousand tons, at least three-hundred feet long. What do you make of that, eh?'

Pendleton slowly sat back, the cigarette forgotten, pulling distractedly at his beard. 'Did he say exactly how many guns?'

'He counted four at around the five-inch mark, two of them disguised. A pair of Pak anti-tank guns and a lot of anti-aircraft stuff. He had no doubt it was a converted merchantman. He managed two passes before he had to clear out, things got a bit hot. A Messerschmitt bounced him just off our coast. In the end we chalked up one for the R.A.F.'

Pendleton was silent for a moment while he digested the news. 'Thank you, Colin,' he said, 'I couldn't have asked for better, and I'd appreciate it if you'd pass on my thanks to the pilot. First class job.'

'Of course,' Ashworth said cheerily. 'Glad to be of service, I'll tell him.'

'Good,' Pendleton said, 'I owe you,' and he thoughtfully replaced the receiver. He looked up, lit the forgotten cigarette, and smiled at Thorburn's quizzical expression.

'Seems like we hit the jackpot. That so called freighter is armed to the teeth; five-inch guns, all sorts of stuff. The question is . . . , how soon can we move?'

Thorburn smiled ruefully. 'When do the others get here, sir? Sooner the better now.'

There was a discreet tap on the door and Pendleton looked over. 'Come,' he said, and his expression softened as Jennifer entered.

'Two signals, sir. *Cranbrook* estimates arrival by 10.00hrs, *Darrow* 10.20.'

'Well . . . , that's part of the answer,' Pendleton said, and he wondered if all the boats would make it on time. 'Anything on the Gunboats or M.T.B.s?'

Jennifer glanced down at her pad. 'As far as I can see here, they're all on their way. The last to arrive will be from Portsmouth Coastal Command.' She looked up. 'Depends on the weather down there, sir.'

'Yes,' Pendleton said, tapped the desk and peered at his watch. 'In that case we'll reconvene at soon as they're all in.' He stared for a long moment at Thorburn's passive features. 'I suggest you decide on a plan of action, Richard. Try and speak with the captains as they come in. The most senior of the M.T.B.s is a Charles Holloway, Lieutenant. He has a lot of experience.'

'Right, sir,' Thorburn said, and came to his feet. 'Are you expecting us to sail tonight?'

The Captain shook his head. 'I doubt it. I'll have another word with Collingwood, see what he says, but I wouldn't have thought so.'

Lieutenant Robert Armstrong dropped down the ladder from the fo'c'sle and walked slowly aft along *Brackendale's* starboard side. When he reached the Jacob's ladder he paused and leaned his elbows on the guardrail, studying the harbour. Close inshore a Motor Torpedo Boat turned away to the Eastern Arm and he watched her cruise quietly out towards the Southern Breakwater. She then veered to starboard and peeled off to the west, wending her way between the moored cargo ships. The boat swung in around the far side of the Price of Wales pier and disappeared from view.

Armstrong straightened and continued down the side, subconsciously inspecting fittings and equipment. He glanced at the Carley floats, checking their ties, and then reached out for a turnbuckle that tensioned a steel wire brace.

But his thoughts wandered, and for the umpteenth time he wondered about the make up of the new flotilla and what Pendleton had wanted with the skipper? The last time Thorburn had become involved with senior staff, *Brackendale* had ended up fighting a major engagement. It was only the captain's extraordinary skills that had brought them through, more or less in one piece. The newspapers classed these things as 'special operations', Armstrong preferred his own definition, 'dangerous' operations.

His walk took him past the galley housing and he found himself standing beneath the four-inch gun barrels of the quarterdeck mounting, and he stopped to stare out beyond the breakwater and that narrow strip of sea. His dark eyes roamed across the gently breaking waves and as he reflected on his captain, a small, tight-lipped smile broke his sombre mood. Lieutenant-Commander Richard Thorburn, oft times known as the 'rebel' when dealing with senior staff, had more than proved himself in combat. An unorthodox maverick Thorburn might well be, but Robert Armstrong had long since sworn allegiance to a man that deserved his unswerving loyalty.

He heard the sound of engines overhead and watched a flight of Hurricanes power into the blue haze, watched until they became dots, and then wandered around to the depth charge rails. A check on the time told him lunch would soon be served, and he turned to make his way forward up the portside. The cook might actually have something decent on the menu and he rubbed his hands at the prospect.

Word of a Spitfire's intrusion over Rotterdam's secure harbour reached Wilhelmshaven shortly before midday and Admiral Mathias Krause found himself wondering to what extent *Holstein's* presence had been reported. The fact that the fighter had made two passes over the ship indicated a deliberate reconnaissance and that seemed to signify the plan to draw in the British might well be achieved. Krause had personal experience of the Royal Navy's belligerence, and he knew they wouldn't leave this alone. Having thought it through he picked up the telephone and placed a call to Großadmiral Erich Raeder's headquarters.

Raeder answered with his customary politeness and listened attentively while Krause explained the situation and put forward a proposal that would add an additional safeguard to the mission. When he finished, Raeder asked him to wait while he consulted.

After a lengthy hold Krause stiffened as the line came back to life.

'Are you still there, Mathias?'

'Here, sir.'

'It is approved. You may proceed.'

It was mid afternoon before the last of the little boats entered Dover harbour, by which time Thorburn had gone to the bridge to see for himself. The weather had taken a turn for the worse with a threatening sky and a keen westerly making for choppy seas. The two M.G.B.s approached bows up and dancing in the waves, white water spraying from the 'V' shaped hulls, their White Ensigns whipping firmly in the wind.

Armstrong was taking his turn as Officer-of-the-Day and Thorburn stepped across to join him at the screen.

'That's it, Number One, those are the boats from Portsmouth, completes the flotilla. Get a signal off to all captains, "Report *Brackendale* at 17.00hrs." And warn the stewards, we'll make this informal.'

Armstrong nodded and they watched the boats turn in between the breakwaters, dwarfed by the solid bluffs. In line astern they burbled quietly into the harbour, throttled down to a mere two or three knots and headed along inside the Eastern breakwater towards the so called 'submarine pens'. Once under the protection of the thick reinforced canopies their safety was assured.

'Right, sir, I'll see to the signal,' Armstrong said, and walked off towards the back of the bridge.

Thorburn moved to the forebridge and rested his elbows on the folded down screen, letting his gaze drift over the two 'Hunts'. They were both Type I and very similar in layout to his own but markedly different in their camouflage schemes, visually striking disruptive patterns. The most significant variation was *Cranbrook's* radar installation, an advantage he hoped would prove significant.

'Captain, sir?'

He turned to find Telegraphist Smith waiting, and took the offered slip. He read it and smiled. Pendleton might be out of sight in a cellar but his lookouts were on the ball and had obviously seen the last of the arrivals. He wanted a briefing for all captains at 19.00hrs.

'Right,' he nodded. 'Acknowledge, and let the First Lieutenant know.'

'Aye aye, sir,' Smith said, and moved off.

Thorburn watched him go, took a last look round the harbour and then gazed out at the Channel. On the other side the Germans assumed they were relatively safe from major interference as they convoyed up and down between ports. It might well be that this little flotilla would put a severe dent in that confidence.

He turned and made for the ladder, there was much to be done.

Jennifer Farbrace watched with a critical eye as two tables from the first floor were brought to Pendleton's office and placed side by side to form a single rectangular surface. She then asked the senior rating to roll out the chart of the English Channel and checked to ensure the Captain would be satisfied.

'That's fine.' She said, and dismissed them with a, 'thank you.' She moved to the steel cabinet in the corner behind his desk, opened a drawer and pulled out a box of plain red and blue ship models. Distributing them strategically round the chart for easy access, she retreated to her office wondering, not for the first time, why Richard was again chosen for such a hazardous mission. Without dwelling on it, she instinctively knew the answer. Richard Thorburn attracted the attention of those in need, his devotion to duty never in doubt.

Jennifer sighed and inwardly smiled. There was also that disarming, devil-may-care grin that hid a natural modesty. Even so, she thought, the hand of fate was dealing him another card from the bottom of the pack.

Chapter Sixteen . . . Flotilla Born

At precisely a minute to five, Thorburn entered *Brackendale's* wardroom amidst the general hubbub of small talk, and moved across to stand beneath a plaque of the Ship's Crest. The heraldic artwork depicted a pony's head, which in this case was a symbolic representation of the New Forest, and that in itself was half framed by a gold hunting horn of the local 'Brackendale' foxhunt. It had been with them, watching over them, ever since the destroyer had been commissioned.

He turned away to face the wardroom.

'Gentlemen,' he began, 'for those of you who don't know, I'm Lieutenant-Commander Richard Thorburn, and I've been given the dubious honour of commanding this new flotilla.'

There were smiling nods from the destroyer captains and some nervous chuckles amongst the younger skippers.

'I've asked you here for an informal get together before we're called to see Captain (D), give us all a chance to get to know one another.' He looked across their heads and nodded towards Armstrong. 'My Number One is opening the bar and the stewards will take your orders, feel free to take advantage, doesn't happen very often.'

Someone clapped his hands and another gave a small cheer, and there was a general move towards the serving hatch. A young Sub-Lieutenant standing alone by the door seemed uncertain of the protocol and Thorburn walked over.

'Alright, Sub?' he asked casually, attempting to put the man at ease.

He hesitated before replying. 'Yes thank you, sir,' he said, lowering his voice, 'but this is all a bit new to me.'

Thorburn grinned at his honesty. 'It was the same for all of us once, what's your name?'

'Kenneth Stokesley, sir.'

'And how long have you been in command?'

'Four months tomorrow, sir.'

'Seen any action?'

The young man's face lit up in a broad grin. 'Yes, quite a lot really. We sank an 'R' boat on our last outing, up near the Dutch coast.'

'Good man,' Thorburn said sincerely. Young he might be but he'd been in the thick of it, and combat experience counted for a lot when it came down to the nitty-gritty. He laid a hand on his shoulder and turned him towards the hatch. 'Let's have that drink, what'll you have?'

He felt Stokesley straighten under his touch, more self-assured now he'd had a personal introduction. 'A gin and a splash, please,' he said brightly, and Thorburn ushered him through the crowd to place the order.

At the serving hatch Armstrong interrupted. 'Captain, sir? May I introduce Lieutenant Charles Holloway, M.T.B. *Forty-Nine.*'

Thorburn turned to meet the commander of his small boats and offered his hand to a tall well built officer.

'Glad to have you aboard. I'm told you have a knack of killing Germans.'

The man laughed, an easy deep-throated chuckle. 'It's mostly stupid bloody Krauts throwing themselves in front of my torpedoes,' he answered, accepting Thorburn's hand with a firm shake.

Thorburn held his eyes, and in that brief moment felt a kindred spirit, the rebel of his early days.

'I suspect there might be a bit more to it than that,' he said, unable to avoid a smile. 'Have you worked with destroyers before?'

'Never,' came the quick reply, and then said mysteriously, 'only as targets.'

Thorburn gave him a small nod, recognising the irony. 'And I've not worked with your lot either, we've got a lot to learn to make this work. I'll probably have a few questions.'

Holloway stuck out his jaw and nodded. 'Fire away, whatever you need to know.'

Thorburn glanced at Armstrong. 'Thank Christ for that, I think we've found someone who knows what they're doing. Might be quite useful really.' As the laughter subsided a short squat man with a boxer's nose and dark, bushy eyebrows stepped forward. His jacket cuffs displayed a set of wavy gold stripes.

'Name's Sullivan, *Cranbrook*. And this,' he gestured behind him, 'is one of our Aussie cousins, Geoff Hudson, in command of *Darrow*. At your disposal.'

Thorburn shook hands and nodded respectfully, after all they were of equal rank. 'Thank you,' he said, 'hope you don't mind my being in command of this flotilla?' If there were going to be any issues, best clear the air now.

'Not in the slightest,' Hudson said, his pale eyes glinting out of a leathery face, 'you have my undying gratitude. No more East Coast convoys.'

Thorburn smiled. 'Well I can't guarantee for how long, but certainly not for the immediate future.'

'Suits me,' the Australian beamed, and rubbed his hands with pleasure. 'Scuse me but I'm gonna take advantage of your kind offer,' and he squeezed his way to the hatch.

Richard Thorburn allowed himself to relax slightly. So far so good, his biggest concerns alleviated. He had the willing co-operation of his equals and Holloway had already shown he was ready to help. Hopefully, everything else would fall into place. He looked at his watch, wouldn't do to be late for Pendleton's briefing. Plenty of time yet and he set about getting to know some of the other skippers.

By seven o'clock that evening, Pendleton's below stairs office had filled with the captains of the new flotilla. Thorburn counted ten beside himself, eleven all told, two of which were from the spare Coastal Forces boats. They stood talking quietly while waiting for Captain (D) to make his appearance, and as the minute hand of the wall clock ticked round to the hour, Thorburn detached himself from their company to stand near Pendleton's desk. He noted young Stokesley confidently mingling with his peers.

The open door swung ajar and Second Officer Jennifer Farbrace entered, all eyes following as she walked elegantly to a chair by the desk. She glanced briefly at Thorburn and he blinked in answer to her secretive smile, and then she deposited two substantial buff coloured files on the table. Clutching both her notepad and fountain pen in one hand, she turned to face the door.

And in swept the stocky figure of Captain James Pendleton, striding along in full dress uniform, gold braid gleaming on his cap and the soft sheen of four broad bands on the cuffs of his double breasted jacket.

A silence fell across the assembled officers as they straightened to attention and Pendleton took his place at the head of the room, behind his desk. For a moment he looked down at the two manila files before addressing his audience.

'Gentlemen,' he said, 'let me begin by saying time is short. You've been selected to take part in an offensive sweep that will encompass the French and Belgian coastline. The aim of this mission is to find and attack a German convoy that includes an armed merchantman by the name of *Holstein*. That ship has already sailed from Wilhelmshaven to Rotterdam on the first leg of what we believe is a passage to Brest.' He paused and Thorburn watched him smooth his beard as he found the next phrase.

'The Admiralty, under Churchill's guidance, has taken the decision to eliminate this vessel before it can be let loose in the Bay of Biscay. I'm sure you're all well aware of the ongoing support our convoys provide to our forces in North Africa. Malta too has major issues with provisions; we cannot afford an armed raider interfering with our supply lines.'

Pendleton glanced at Jennifer, poised with her notepad for the inevitable questions that would arise. He turned for a moment and Thorburn met his eyes, before he looked back at the hushed assembly.

'I know you've all met Lieutenant-Commander Thorburn. He's been chosen as Commanding Officer for the duration and will implement his own tactics according to the overall strategy. I should tell you that this officer has previously been awarded the Distinguished Service Order. Whilst carrying out a dangerous mission off the Cherbourg Peninsula he sank a Zerstorer class German destroyer. His experience of fighting in enemy coastal waters will, I am sure, benefit all of us in the next few days.'

Thorburn squirmed with embarrassment at being singled out for praise and lowered his eyes.

Pendleton grinned and then stepped forward towards the chart Jennifer had so meticulously laid out.

'Now,' he said, leaning his fists on the table, 'this is our expected area of operations.' He looked up as they shuffled round. A number of heads peered over between shoulders.

'Up here to the north, Rotterdam,' he said, pointing to the fissured coastline, 'where the *Holstein* waits right now.' He waved a hand down the coast. 'Next stop, probably Ostend, then more than likey, Calais, but possibly straight past to Bolougne. Those calculations are an educated guess on the regular pattern currently being used. Each stop is dependant on prevailing weather conditions and duration of darkness.'

Thorburn managed to catch a glimpse of the chart from behind the Australian and watched Pendleton raise his head to his audience.

'Our theoretical point of interception is somewhere between Ostend and Dunkirk, giving us a thirty mile stretch of the shoreline. We know there are two minefields to avoid, one guarding each of the approaches to those harbours. Shore defences are radar controlled 88s, worth bearing in mind if you're closing the shore. They're lethal at six miles. Hopefully they won't fire for fear of hitting their own.' He straightened up and stood back. 'That is the broad outline of what you will encounter, so at this point I'll let Commander Thorburn take over.'

He returned to his desk and Thorburn moved back opposite Jennifer.

'As Captain Pendleton is aware, it is my intention to deploy the flotilla to search in line abreast with the three 'Hunts' ahead of the M.T.B.s and Gunboats. We have the advantage of radar aboard *Cranbrook*. Initial contact by whatever means will be signalled by starshell to illuminate the target. *Cranbrook* and *Darrow* will veer to starboard and draw their fire, while *Brackendale* exploits the inshore flank. That should give the M.T.B.s the chance to attack the *Holstein*. That way the enemy are faced with three separate divisions to split their firepower.' He paused to watch their reactions. It seemed positive, a few nods and smiles.

'One thing we destroyers need to bear in mind is the latest enemy tactics. Of recent times, when the destroyers and E-boats make contact in a night action the enemy immediately close to within torpedo range and fire a full spread, everything they've got. Then while we take emergency avoiding action by combing their tracks, the enemy withdraw at high speed to regroup as a diversion, allowing the prime target to escape.' He took a breath and collected his thoughts, then stared directly at Holloway.

'With your shallow draught I'm assuming those torpedoes are not an issue?'

'That is correct, sir.'

'So you don't have a problem with attacking at that juncture?'

'No . . . ,' Holloway said slowly. 'Providing we locate the target,' and he met Thorburn's eyes with a tight grin. 'We'll be in there like ferrets up a drainpipe.'

'Good,' Thorburn said, pleased with the man's response. He looked round the faces, paused on young Stokesley, and then found *Cranbrook's* C.O.

'Any questions?'

Sullivan nodded and spoke up.

'The *Holstein*, what's her armament?'

Thorburn pursed his lips, annoyed for not giving the detail earlier; remiss of him.

'From the intelligence reports, there are four five-inch, at least two anti-tank guns, and a whole bunch of secondary armament, the usual small calibre anti-aircraft stuff.'

Sullivan nodded as he digested the information. He glanced sideways at a brother officer, raised an eyebrow and shrugged his shoulders, hands spread wide. 'Shouldn't be a problem then.' A ripple of laughter went round the room and despite the seriousness of the subject matter, Thorburn caught the infectious mood and found himself grinning along with Pendleton.

When the laughter died away and before he could say more, Lieutenant Holloway raised a finger. 'A suggestion, sir.'

'Of course,' Thorburn agreed.

'We have a spare Torpedo Boat. In light of what you've told us, we're out to sink the *Holstein* with only three M.T.B.s on the sweep. That gives us a maximum of six torpedoes, I'd be a lot happier with another M.T.B. It'd give us a total of eight shots.'

Thorburn nodded at the practical implications, saw how it made sense, and turned to face Pendleton. 'Sir?'

The Captain tugged at an earlobe and then smoothed his beard. He looked at Jennifer and waited for her to stop scribbling.

'What say you, Miss Farbrace? Do we forget about holding onto the spare, put all our eggs in one basket so to speak?

Thorburn saw Jennifer blush, her cheeks a crimson glow at being dragged into the limelight, but she wasn't to be flustered.

'In this instance, sir, I believe Lieutenant Holloway has an extremely valid point. None of the destroyers has provision for tubes and whereas the initial plan was to make nightly sweeps of the enemy coast, it now seems a case of all our nothing. I would take the spare boat.'

Pendleton clapped his hands. 'Bravo!' he grinned, 'well said, my thoughts exactly. Mister Holloway, you have your extra boat.'

Thorburn glanced round the room and spotted an officer smiling in the background. At first sight he looked capable, an aura of confidence about him.

'Are there any more questions?' he asked.

Silence greeted his query and he breathed in. 'Very well,' he said. 'We will exercise my tactics this evening with what's left of the daylight and transfer that into two evolutions during the dark hours.' He looked at his watch and then over to Pendleton.

'With your permission, sir, I should like to start manoeuvres within the hour?'

The Captain nodded and came to the front of his desk. 'One thing more, gentlemen. I know you've all seen action before but this is somewhat out of the ordinary. Be under no illusions as to the German willingness to fight. He'll be in his own waters and under the protection of his shore guns. I have no doubts as to your proficiency, but I remind you of why you're going. *Holstein* could wreak havoc on our merchant seamen. Your primary role is to eliminate it from proceedings.'

Thorburn nodded at Pendleton's succinct reminder and spoke for them all.

'Thank you, sir. Permission to carry on?'

'Granted,' said Pendleton, 'and good luck to you all.'

Jennifer came to her feet and the officers began filing out. The Captain found his chair and settled down with the folders. Thorburn caught Jennifer's elbow as she made for the door and they walked round to her office.

'How's the neck?' he smiled.

She turned her head gently from side to side and met his eyes. 'It would benefit from a long massage,' she said pointedly, and he grinned.

'I'm sure it would, but although I have the inclination, unfortunately, I don't have the time.'

'Any excuse,' she laughed, stretched up and kissed him lightly on the cheek. 'Go on, I'm sure your officers are waiting.'

Thorburn caught the delicate aroma of her perfume, avoided taking her in his arms, and turned away. 'See you soon,' he said lightly, 'and see that no one else gets to massage that lovely neck.' He heard her giggle as he went out into the corridor, took the steps two at a time, and with a smile on his face, headed for the harbour. Time to put things in motion.

In his office, Pendleton picked up the phone to the main switchboard and asked to be connected with Commodore Collingwood. The operator got a line and he heard a barked announcement in his ear.

'Collingwood.'

'James Pendleton, sir. Thought you'd like to know we're up and running. All the captains joined today and I've briefed them alongside Thorburn. He's just about to put them through their paces. We'll be ready by eleven tonight.'

'Glad to hear it, James. Took a bit of arguing to get *Darrow,* but Thorburn was right about the V&W taking her place. Captain (D) at Sheerness wasn't happy but we managed to get an extension on that detachment. If all goes according to plan *Trophy* should let us know when *Holstein* makes a move. She's on station off Rotterdam and given half a chance she'll have a crack at it. I doubt she'll have much luck, but either way she'll let us know.'

'Thank you, sir. I'll await your signal.'

'Hopefully not too long . . . . Goodbye,' Collingwood said, terminating the call, and Pendleton dropped the receiver onto the cradle. He leant back in the chair and looked down the room at the chart. How long before all these plans became reality?

Korvettenkapitän Wolfgang Schulze departed Calais at 23.00hrs and led the second destroyer north for Dunkirk. Trailing in their wake two Schnellboats maintained station in line astern, torpedo tubes armed and guns ready. They were to rendezvous with a minesweeper and five more Schnellboats at Dunkirk before being released whenever *Holstein* cleared Rotterdam's outer delta. He would avoid joining the escort screen to seaward and instead, remain hidden inshore as reinforcement when required.

Schulze relished the prospect of coming to grips with the enemy. The Royal Navy believed they were invincible but recent events had shown that the Kriegsmarine, given the right opportunity, could outwit their naval counterparts. He thought suddenly of that last big battle, what the British now called the 'Channel Dash'. He'd been screening *Gneisenau* when the bi-planes attacked with their torpedoes, and he'd watched in amazement at their lumbering approach, at the suicidal courage of the pilots. And all to no avail.

And then later it had been a flotilla of old V&W destroyers, veterans of the Great War, with the same result. The engagement had proved to be short and sharp with far too much firepower for the British warships. Schulze had personally overseen the bringing down of an attacking bomber. The Kriegsmarine's battle squadron had sailed on unharmed, the entire flotilla escaping the Royal Navy's belated attempt to destroy them.

In the aftermath, every German ship involved in the breakout had been personally mentioned and congratulated by the Führer, and Korvettenkapitän Wolfgang Schulze remembered it with pride.

He gripped the rail and smiled thinly. On this occasion it might not be battle cruisers, but *Holstein's* journey would be just as dangerous. And possibly just as exciting. He crossed to the chart table and peered over his navigator's shoulder. As leader it was crucial to ensure they didn't get lost and made a timely arrival at the designated berth. His navigating officer's dividers hovered over the previously identified plot and Schulze turned away with a satisfied nod. All was proceeding according to plan.

For Lieutenant-Commander Richard Thorburn and his fledgling Flotilla the exercises off Dover's southern coastline did not immediately go according to plan. It took time to synchronise such a wide discrepancy in the size and speed of his force, and it was gone midnight before he felt they'd achieved a semblance of uniformity.

When he finally turned in for what remained of the night, he found it difficult to sleep. Would his tactics stand up to the reality of combat? Would the commanders under his leadership find the courage to prevail? He yawned and turned over. They would all find answers when battle commenced.

Approximately fifty kilometres west-south-west of Wilhelmshaven, at the German port of Emden, a vessel of the Kriegsmarine put to sea in accordance with very specific instructions from Admiral Mathias Krause. It was a dark night as it pushed out of the channel and north into the wide expanse of the North Sea. There'd been a high degree of secrecy surrounding the vessel's departure, a move deliberately designed to coincide with *Holstein's* predicted course and position the following night. The commander had seen maritime warfare close to hand, an experienced, well taught Officer of the Third Reich, and his crew were all veterans.

In the early hours of Thursday morning, Wolfgang Schulze stood on the bridge of his destroyer and led the small flotilla into Dunkirk's inner harbour. The passage up from Boulogne had been without incident and he congratulated himself on their timely arrival. Shrouded by the blanket of darkness, each vessel drifted slowly across to the designated wharf and tied up to the quayside.

Refuelling began almost immediately, and leaving the process in the hands of his officers, he marched off to find the Kriegsmarine's Duty Officer.

Outside a pre-war shipping office fronting the basin he was challenged to produce his identity papers. He did so and then asked for directions. The soldier indicated a side alley with a personnel door to his right, and Schulze stepped inside. A Lieutenant sitting behind a dimly lit desk looked up sharply.

'Shut the door!' he snapped angrily, and waved a hand at the blacked out windows. 'No lights!'

Schulze fumed at being spoken to in such a manner, about to shout him down, but bit back his frustration and obliged, closing the door quietly. He walked forward and glared down at the man's frown.

'Korvettenkapitän Schulze,' he offered, 'I must inform Marine-Oberkommando Nordsee of our arrival. Admiral Krause waits for news.'

The Lieutnant sighed, unimpressed. 'Ja, so we were informed.' He pointed to a man at the other desk behind the door in the corner. 'Use that phone, he'll ring the number,' and totally disinterested, resumed the reading of his magazine.

Schulze waited while the man made a connection, spoke to an Oberleutnant in the communications centre and was told he would be signalled when to commence operations. He dropped the phone to the desk, sauntered to the door and looked back at the Lieutnant, still engrossed in his magazine. He smirked, opened the door wide and walked out into the alley. A string of verbal abuse followed and he strode off, leaving them to close it themselves. Korvettenkapitän Wolfgang Schulze was not to be demeaned by an inferior officer and he whistled in time with his footsteps.

Soon now, the Englanders would be tested to the full.

Chapter Seventeen . . . Deployment

In Wilhelmshaven, as the wall clock ticked over to midday, Admiral Mathias Krause studied the giant chart of the Channel and smiled thinly. The British were in for a shock. Always the Royal Navy thought attack the best method of defence, and he had ensured this convoy would be too tempting to ignore. And the final nail in their coffin had been his own masterly moment of inspiration, with his late proposal to Großadmiral Raeder instantly seen as a brilliant addition to the overall strategy.

He wandered thoughtfully back to his desk and flicked open the file of operational signals. All the small delays had been well managed, the extra time gained put to good use, and he nodded his approval at the likely outcome. The one outstanding issue that he wished to resolve was that of a certain Wolfgang Schulze, a relatively unknown quantity for Krause himself. He was reputed to be a forceful young officer, well capable of his current role.

The Admiral frowned and glanced at the time. He'd already been informed that the two Flottentorpedoboots had made the safe anchorage of Dunkirk harbour, and Krause closed the file and strode to the interconnecting door.

'Hauptman!' he barked, 'get me Dunkirk, I will talk with this Kapitän Schulze.'

The officer reached for the handset. 'Jawohl, Herr Admiral.'

Krause left him to it and retreated to his desk, sinking his frame into the comfort of his chair. After what seemed an interminable delay the telephone rang and he grabbed the receiver.

'Schulze? He demanded.

'Yes, sir, this is Korvettenkapitän Wolfgang Schulze.'

'So,' Krause began, marshalling his thoughts. 'You are aware of my requirements?'

'I am, yes sir.'

'Good . . . , is there anything you need?'

'No, everything is in order, sir.'

Krause thought for a moment, liking what he heard. The man was obviously no fool and certainly not cowed by speaking with higher authority.

'Tell me, Schulze, what battle experience have you had?'

'I was in the escort for *Gneisenau* when we came out from Brest.'

The answer was brief, without elaboration, and the Admiral narrowed his eyes knowing full well what that implied.

'This operation may prove very similar, Schulze. I trust you know how much we rely on you?'

'Of course, sir. I have read your battle orders, the Englanders will be decimated.'

Krause smiled into the mouthpiece. 'In that case, Kapitän, I will not keep you longer, I am sure you are a busy man. I just wanted you to know the Kriegsmarine is with you. Do your duty and victory is ours.'

'Yes, sir. Thank you, sir,' Schulze said, and Krause slipped the receiver back on the cradle. If there'd been any lingering doubts as to the man's capabilities he felt that conversation had dispelled them. His informants had been correct, Wolfgang Schulze sounded just the man for the job.

In the ex shipping office on Dunkirk's quayside, Schulze thoughtfully replaced the receiver, and ignoring the inquiring glances of a now respectful officer, made his way back to the ship. Before boarding he paused, hands on his hips to look down the length of the dock. There were another five Schnellboats tied to the jetty; his flotilla grew larger by the hour. He would finalise preparations during the afternoon.

As the sun sank towards the horizon, Kapitän-zur-See Baumgartner watched carefully as he conned the *Holstein* out from Rotterdam's harbour entrance. Two minesweepers cleared the way, with the first of the new Elbing destroyers between them and the *Holstein*. And then consecutively, in line astern, came the second of the Elbings, followed by the 'R' boats and lastly the Schnellboats. It was some time since he'd been involved with so many vessels; Norwegian waters were sparsely populated by freighters and an Armed Merchantman deliberately journeyed alone, an apparently harmless friend on the open sea. He watched as the minesweepers turned south of west and began the passage down towards Calais, and he recalled the various ports, the distances involved.

The nearest harbour of Ostend lay just over a hundred kilometres away, followed by Dunkirk, another fifty kilometres, and lastly Calais, almost two-hundred kilometres in total.

Baumgartner sat in his padded chair and doubted Calais was a plausible target for this sortie. Certainly it could not be achieved overnight. It would be well into daylight hours before *Holstein* could make a sighting of that port.

'Konrad?' he called. 'Have the crew disperse from Harbour Stations and bring the ship to Defence Watch One.'

'Jawohl, Herr Kapitän,' and Baumgartner heard him pass the order. And then came the moment for *Holstein* to make the turn.

'We will come left ten degrees,' he ordered, and the helmsman spun the wheel. Slowly, laboriously, the big ship made its turn into the westerly breeze, rising and falling to the underlying swell.

Chapter Eighteen . . . The Warning

In the semi-darkness of Thursday night Paul Wingham crouched behind the damaged parapet of an abandoned warehouse and cautiously raised his head to peer out towards the nearby repair basins. The nearest dock held the remains of Hitler's once threatened invasion, a dozen or so wrecked barges, bombed by the R.A.F. Beyond that the water stretched away to his right towards Dunkirk's outer harbour. But what drew his attention were the two recently arrived destroyers berthed alongside the opposite quay. Although he didn't pretend to be an authority on types, he believed they were 'T' class, or Flottentorpedoboot, a pre-war design easily identified by their raked prow and single funnel. Ahead of them, further along the quayside was what appeared to be a minesweeper, and he counted seven E-boats tied up at a long low jetty. All the vessels were in varying stages of preparing for sea.

If they had any intention of leaving he needed to change location, to the seaward end of the roof. He lowered himself below the parapet and crawled to his right over a mess of broken bricks. He winced as his knees met jagged bits of mortar and cursed the sharp edges. It took him another full minute to reach the new vantage point and find a spot free of debris. Lifting to one knee he slowly came up to view the harbour.

The outer seaway lay before him protected by the arm of the distant mole, and nearby were the new piers rebuilt since the evacuation of the British Expeditionary Force. Now two years on, there was little evidence of that desperate withdrawal, even the infamous beaches had been cleared and mined. He shook his head at the thought and glanced back at the minesweeper. If those ships really were about to leave, that vessel would be the first to depart.

The sound of voices drifted up from below, and he froze. With great care he leaned to look down. Two steel helmeted soldiers of the Wehrmacht ambled towards the warehouse, rifles slung casually over their shoulders, and seemingly in some sort of heated argument.

A few more paces and they came to a halt, surveying the far side of the harbour in the darkness.

Wingham dodged back from the edge and ducked out of sight. He regulated his breathing and listened. The conversation resumed, quieter this time, the argument possibly resolved, and their voices slowly receded as they strolled off along the cobbles. He gave them time before easing up to take another look.

At the quayside, activity amongst the E-boats had increased, and even at this distance he heard an engine start, a subdued growl in the clear night air. Ropes were thrown and men hopped aboard from the jetty. Wisps of smoke coiled up from the destroyers and the minesweeper drifted out from the side. An E-boat swung into mid harbour and made for the exit, closely followed by the remainder, the grumbling noise of their engines echoing from the dock. They turned left inside the mole, line astern, and the minesweeper slowly edged into their wake. The destroyers manoeuvred out from the quayside and joined the column, taking station behind the minesweeper.

A few barked commands from nearby made him start and he risked a look down across the railway lines at the basin with the damaged barges. From the inner wall a pair of 'R' boats came to life and peeled away towards the inlet.

Wingham cursed, surprised by their appearance, annoyed at his lack of awareness. But now it was simply a case of waiting, which way would they turn? Staring into the distant gloom he watched as the E-boats met open water, their white wake increasing in width. But the expected turn failed to materialise. They fanned out slightly and commenced circling offshore, idling in the waves. He turned his attention back to the minesweeper, watching closely as it met the sea. It too initially steamed straight out to the circling boats, passed between them and only then made a turn. It curved right, parallel with the coast and headed for Ostend. Straining to focus through the darkness he saw the ship begin to sweep for mines.

The two destroyers, in what must have been a pre-planned move, slowed to join the E-boats before they too, turned north-east, holding station well back from the sweeper. Last to exit, the 'R' boats joined the rear of the flotilla.

Wingham watched for a while longer until the night swallowed them from view, and squinted at his watch. It showed ten to midnight.

Bent double he moved back from the parapet and crunched across the rubble strewn roof, reached the top of the damaged stairwell and quietly began to descend. Between each floor was a half-landing where the interior darkness lightened a little from the long since shot away windows. During his many climbs to the roof he'd cleared the broken glass and knew where to place his feet to avoid excess noise.

He made it to the ground floor and crept into the corridor, turning for the rear of the building away from the harbour. A door from the ransacked storeroom led him out to a miniature courtyard surrounded by a six foot wall. Sometime in the past the solid wooden gate had been nailed shut with a large wooden joist, but in the far corner he'd stacked a few bricks to give himself easy access to look over the wall. He hopped up, made a careful check of the street and with no one in sight, hauled himself over the top. He landed lightly in the deserted road, straightened and paused again to examine the dark streets. Here in Dunkirk, as in cities all over Britain, the authorities enforced a blackout against possible bombing. The unlit streets now worked in his favour and he made quick progress through the alleyways.

In a matter of minutes Wingham turned into the top of Marianne's road, and stopped short. A German soldier stood between him and the door, leaning against the nearer house, surreptitiously smoking a cigarette. He tensed and swore softly, already too many paces into the road to turn back without making it obvious he was in the wrong place at the wrong time. He frowned with annoyance, not wanting to afford the delay, the signal to England needed to go now. He would try and bluff his way through.

Sliding his hands into his pockets, he put his head down and ambled towards the soldier, each stride longer than it appeared. The pistol under the finger of his right hand leant a feeling of security to his gamble, not that he wanted the sound of gunfire. He managed seven long paces before the soldier realised he was there, just six paces short. The cigarette spun glowing into the road and the rifle came up in a rush.

'Halt!' he demanded forcefully, and took a step closer. 'Where do you go?'

Wingham raised his head slowly, stealing two more steps and stopped a few feet away. He'd given himself a chance.

The soldier nervously jabbed the muzzle of the rifle, extending it almost to within reach.

Wingham mumbled something in reply, deliberately incomprehensible, and the man leaned closer.

'Speak up, what is wrong?'

It was enough. Wingham lashed out with his right forearm and the rifle went spinning. In the same moment he lunged forward, barrelling into the man's midriff. They hit the cobbles hard, half in and half out of the gutter. The rifle clattered against the wall, and the man heaved himself out from under, freeing himself from the tangle.

Wingham aimed a punch at his head and connected, but a powerful arm clamped round his neck, twisting him down on his back. He tried prising it away and failed, so chopped backwards with an elbow. The man gasped and the arm hold slackened. With a violent twist, Wingham smashed a fist into the vulnerable nose. The man gasped and whimpered, face contorted in pain, and turned away.

Wingham gritted his teeth, threw his left arm round the man's neck and slammed his right arm up to interlock with his left hand, a stranglehold. He pulled with all his strength, the man struggling desperately, arms flailing. And then Wingham delivered the coup de grâce. He cupped his right hand behind the steel helmet, tore sideways, and with a crunch of bone, snapped his neck.

Breathing hard he lowered the body and let it be, stealing a glance up and down the street. Empty . . . , as were the windows and doors. No one bothered with a disturbance outside, better to mind your own business.

For a moment he hesitated, caught in a quandary. Should he leave the body out in the open or hide it?' Marianne's door was only three away and he knew how the Germans would react, any excuse to launch a house to house search and they'd swarm through the buildings looking for a culprit, even if there was little prospect of a positive result. No, he thought, the dead man had to be hidden. Mind made up, Wingham bent and grabbed the man under the armpits and dragged him to the door. He let the body slump, unlocked, and pulled the dead weight off the street. He returned and retrieved the rifle, took a last look up and down the cobbles, and thankfully closed the door. The body at his feet had now become a 'missing' soldier, absent without leave. At the far end of the hall beneath the stairwell was the cleaner's cubby-hole, big enough to conceal a body. Since the bombing of early April the cleaner had not been seen, presumed dead, no one had been sent to take his place.

Wingham felt for the wrists, took hold of the corpse and dragged it to the small room, bundling it unceremoniously in amongst the mops and buckets. The rifle followed, propped in a corner behind a caretaker's brown coat. He closed the door with a grimace and made for the stairs. Things had conspired against him and it would no longer be safe to stay in the apartment, now he and Marianne would have to make their escape. In the meantime, first and foremost, he had to get a signal off to England.

In the apartment, Wingham briefly explained what had happened with the soldier downstairs, and what he'd seen in the dockyard.

Marianne raised an eyebrow and pursed her lips. 'Then we must leave, it is no longer safe.'

He nodded, thankful she understood their predicament. 'Yes, there's not much time. I'll contact London and then we must go.'

He went for the bedroom and made certain the blackout drapes were fully drawn. He lit the remnants of a candle, unearthed the wireless, and pieced together the component parts on the dressing table. Connecting the makeshift antenna he opened the window and dangled the aerial outside in the dark, before returning to the set. He transcribed his message into code, checked it thoroughly and put the book to one side. At the flick of the switch the wireless hummed into life and he brought the Morse key closer. A few taps to call London and he waited. Thirty seconds later his earphone responded and he began to tap out the signal; the number of vessels involved, time of departure and direction of travel.

Twenty seconds after sending the last batch of letters, London confirmed and he signed off.

Wingham leaned back, and in the flickering light of the feeble flame, turned the wireless off and began dismantling the equipment. Transmitting module isolated, receiver broken down into its constituent parts, the Morse key disconnected along with the antenna. Quickly, thoroughly, he hid the separate units, this time in pre-prepared cavities under the floorboards. When all was done he stood for a moment and surveyed his work. Picking up the book he placed it with three other run-of-the-mill novels on the bedside table, collected his notepad and hesitated for one final check of the room.

Satisfied, he snuffed out the candle and joined Marianne in the kitchenette.

She stood dressed in a leather jacket and an outsize pair of trousers, all finished off with a stout pair of shoes. A small woven bag hung from her shoulder.

'Ready?' she asked.

'Sorry,' he said, and stared at her, struggling to find the right words. He'd not really had an option with the soldier, wanted to explain his actions, but she saw the emotions in his face and shook her head.

'There's nothing to say, Paul. These things happen, it is not what we wish but we know there is always the possibility. This time our luck runs out.' She tossed her head in defiance. 'Come, there is nothing here now.'

Wingham nodded, no regrets, and he stepped closer. He stooped and kissed her, lingered, and she responded for that moment, then drew back and held him with those dark eyes. They both knew it might be the last time they would see one another. He eased past her. 'You know the rendezvous?'

She looked away, turning for the door. 'Of course, Armbouts-Cappel, at the house of Philippe Gueta.'

'And don't forget, if either one of us is not there by tomorrow night, do not wait.' He saw the minimal nod of her head, the reluctance to agree, but it was enough that she accepted the importance, and he pinched out the candle.

Downstairs he opened the main door and peered into the street. It was empty and he stood back to let her go. She squeezed his arm and went without looking back, walking quickly down the street, hurried but measured, and he waited, giving her time to get clear. Better not to be caught together, the Gestapo were only too adept at extracting information from travelling 'companions'. He peered at his wristwatch. It showed quarter past eleven.

Five minutes of patience and he too stepped out into the night, closed the door, locked it, and headed south. Only about six or so miles to the commune of Armbouts-Cappel, but Paul Wingham was only too aware that those few miles were full of the enemy. He caressed the gun in his pocket and walked on. Whatever happened now, he'd warned London those ships were at sea, and that was good enough, duty done.

Chapter Nineteen . . . Shallow Waters

In *Trophy's* Control Room, Lieutenant-Commander Craig Mitchell looked at the time, brought the crew to readiness, and having completed all preliminary checks, ordered the submarine to the surface. He emerged from the hatch to find the bridge bathed in a soft grey light, a half moon glinting in an almost cloudless sky. The conning tower swayed to a short choppy sea, with enough of a wind to make it feel cold. The bridge-watch squeezed up and took their positions and once he was satisfied the sea lay empty, he gave the order.

'Start main engines.'

His first priority was to take a star fix and re-establish their position, and having made his celestial computations, waited for the Navigating Officer to finally confirm they were thirty-three miles south-west of Rotterdam.

'Starboard ten. Half ahead both, make revolutions for twelve knots.'

He waited as the bearing came on. 'Steady . . . , steer one-one-oh degrees.'

'One-one-oh degrees, aye, sir.'

Trophy steadied on a south-east heading to close the Dutch coastline halfway between Rotterdam and Ostend, and a long roller undercut the choppy waves to rock the bridge in a gentle arc. Mitchell braced against it, a pertinent reminder of the shallow depths below the boat.

If they had to dive *Trophy* might be in no more than sixty to seventy feet of water, a dangerous place in which to be depth charged. And like waves crossing a sandbar, the Channel waters behaved in a more volatile manner in shoaling seas.

He put it to the back of his mind and concentrated on the mission. In these moonlit waters he should be able to acquire a visual sighting at five miles, with luck six or seven . . . , maybe. And because the Germans normally stayed within three miles of the coast, his initial plan was to close to within ten miles of the shore.

For Richard Thorburn, the time had come to leave harbour and with it the relief of knowing the waiting was over. As Senior Officer, he took *Brackendale* out of Dover's eastern exit, beneath the silent guns of the breakwater, and then stepped to the port bridge-wing to watch the remainder of the flotilla file out in line astern. *Cranbrook* and *Darrow* led the way, closely followed by the seven boats swaying and weaving through the wake of the destroyers.

He turned away to the screen and heard Armstrong at the voice-pipes.

'Port ten.'

The ship canted to starboard as the bows came round to the north-east, lifting to the open sea. A small light flickered far ahead and he heard the signalman's lamp clatter in acknowledgement.

'Signal, from *Cramer*, sir. "Channel swept, good hunting." End of message, sir.'

Thorburn narrowed his eyes in the semi-darkness; that would be the minesweeper, an unsung hero of the Channel, daily risking life and limb to carry out the thankless task of clearing the underwater hazards.

'Make, "Thank you and goodnight," and no more Aldis lamp for the duration.'

The 'Aye aye, sir,' preceded another sharp chatter of the hand operated lamp, and the bridge fell silent.

'Starboard watch to defence stations, Number One.'

'Aye aye, sir,' Armstrong said, and passed the order via the pipe.

Thorburn moved to the bridge-chair and settled down to wait for the North Foreland to come into view, their point of departure for the enemy coast. He glanced to his left across the port wing, at the dark bluffs of St Margaret's at Cliffe, with Deal, Ramsgate and Broadstairs yet to come. This stretch of the coast had become all too familiar to the patrolling warships of the Channel; he himself had navigated it on numerous occasions. One of his first patrols in *Brackendale* had taken him up past these headlands and into the Thames Estuary, and he smiled at the memory. A fairly young captain in those days, entrusted with command of what was then a recently built £400,000 destroyer. It had been a fraught time of learning, a case of adapt or die, culminating in a major battle. They'd all grown up pretty quickly in those early days.

Thorburn shifted position in the bridge chair and eased the pins and needles in his right leg. He thought of Pendleton poring over the charts, worrying over his hurried improvisation, whether it would prove successful. A lot of lives hung in the balance. He rubbed his face. Much of that responsibility now rested on his own shoulders. These people looked to him for leadership, he hoped he had the wherewithal to carry it through. His leg went numb and he stood and stamped his feet for circulation. Must be getting old, he thought and leant forward against the screen. Not long now.

By the time *Trophy* arrived on station it was 11.20hrs and Mitchell called for a change of course.

'Starboard ten.'

The submarine swung towards the west and he steadied her onto a bearing of two-two-oh degrees. Searching cautiously down the Channel, he held her on that course for forty minutes before turning back up the coast on a reciprocal course. The night remained clear, a strong breeze imparting a distinct chop to the long swell, short waves breaking into tumbling crests.

For the umpteenth time he checked their bearing and then leaned against the starboard side of the bridge, binoculars poised for yet another scan of the sea.

'Ship!' called a lookout. 'Bearing, Green four-five. Range six-thousand.'

Mitchell focussed quickly and almost immediately found the target. Clearly visible in the moonlight he judged it to be a German minesweeper cruising slowly down Channel, not making more than ten or twelve knots.

He held his breath. Was this the convoy? Where were the rest? And what about *Holstein*? Only one way to be sure.

'Starboard thirty,' he snapped. 'Revolutions for ten knots.' *Trophy* turned towards the enemy, reducing the distance. After a minute he established a fresh course, on a line that would angle his boat in towards the head of the possible convoy.

'Steady . . . , steer one-hundred degrees.'

'One-hundred, aye, sir.'

'Ship! Red three-oh, sir.'

Mitchell swung left with his binoculars, training them across the port bow. A glint of bow wave and he had it. Some sort of destroyer, which made it more than likely this was the convoy. But did that include an Armed Raider? He lowered the binoculars and studied the sea ahead, giving the area a quick once over. Should he take the gamble and get in closer?

'E-boats dead ahead, sir.'

He found them straight away through the glasses, three in number, passing from roughly north to south across the lens, and keeping pace with the destroyer. Frowning at this new sighting, knowing how quickly they could turn to attack, he decided not to take a chance.

'Slow ahead together, two-hundred revolutions.'

Trophy slowed, reducing her foaming wake and Mitchell tried to piece together the parts of the jigsaw. Were those ships leading the convoy or did they constitute an escort stationed on the right flank?

'Sir!' called a lookout. 'Red five-oh, a freighter, sir.'

He lifted the binoculars and spread his feet against the conning tower's swaying movement, standing clear of the steelwork, knees bent to retain his balance. He searched for only a few seconds along the line of sight, and breathed again. There could be no mistaking that ship's profile. A tall mast fore and aft, a single squat funnel amidships and from the look of it, easily displacing in excess of four-thousand tons. Question was, could he make an attack? He figured out the range and swore softly. Too far away to make it worth his while, those escorts were doing too good a job of keeping him at bay. No, he thought, err on the side of caution, his priority must be to get off a signal. But firstly he needed to get *Trophy* out of harm's way.

'Port thirty,' he ordered. 'What depth have we got, Number One?'

'Eighty-five feet, sir.'

Mitchell managed a grim smile, Crawford must have been watching the sounder closely.

'Very well,' he said, and added, 'get a fix on our position.' At the same time he thought about using the Radar to get a better understanding of the convoy's disposition, but immediately discarded the idea. If the radio waves were detected *Trophy* would still be highly vulnerable, he must ensure they were well clear of possible retaliation.

The boat came south and round away from the coast and he settled due west as an interim heading, pushing out into deep water. In the meantime he needed to compile that sighting report.

He gave *Trophy* a thirty minute run and decided his mission had been accomplished. It was time to set a true course home for Harwich.

'Starboard five, steer two-nine-oh degrees.'

The submarine swung right across the waves for Harwich and Mitchell raised his glasses over the stern casing. A few small clouds interrupted the moon's grey light, giving an intermittent shadowing of the sea's surface. After a long minute of scanning the waters he dropped them to his chest, watching *Trophy's* iridescent wake curving aft into the night. He peered at his watch, made a swift calculation on how far they'd travelled and moved to the voice-pipe.

'Number One?'

'Sir.'

'Send the sighting signal,' he said, and lounged with his back against the periscope standard.

'Object at Green one-hundred, sir!'

Mitchell twisted round to starboard. 'Range?'

'Difficult to say, sir. Two-thousand yards?'

Aligning the glasses down the starboard after casing, Mitchell searched carefully along the line of sight.

'Object moving across our stern, sir.'

He shifted the binoculars to dead astern. Something glinted in the pale light, a faint reflection on the sea.

'I have it,' he said, suppressing his excitement. He adjusted focus to clarify the image, and there it was, the unmistakeable shape of the hated enemy, the conning tower of a U-boat cruising on the surface.

'Clear the bridge!' he barked, and the watch keepers tumbled below. He snatched another glance through the glasses, hoping against hope that the U-boat's lookouts had not spotted the British submarine. It held its course, no sign of alarm. He lowered the binoculars, his mind racing. This was a chance in a million, an opportunity to kill a U-boat, and he wasn't about to let it pass.

He bent to the pipe. 'Dive, dive, dive' he ordered calmly, and sealed the voice-pipe's cover. Dropping into the tower he pulled down the hatch and made it secure, then clambered below to the Control Room.

'Fifty feet,' he ordered, and then added, 'Group-up,' to warn Engineering to switch the batteries into 'parallel' for more power. He called to the radio room. 'Did we get that signal off?'

'Yes, sir.'

'Very well. Number One, stand by. We have a U-boat on the surface,' he added, and then; 'Port thirty, full ahead both.'

The helmsman confirmed. 'Thirty of port wheel on, sir.' And the telegraph rang for the change of speed.

Mitchell watched the depth-gauge needles swing and at forty-five feet the hydroplane operators eased the dive and the boat levelled off at fifty feet. The compass showed *Trophy* turning through west, and on through south-west, and he intervened.

'Midships, steady . . . , steer two-one-five.'

'Steer two-one-five, aye aye, sir.' The assembled crew waited, and the helmsman reported. 'Course two-one-five, sir.'

'Very well,' Mitchell said, and nodded to Crawford. 'How's the trim?'

His First Officer gave him a thumbs up, a strained smile on his face. 'Trim is satisfactory, sir.'

'In that case, Number One, take us up to periscope depth.'

Fore and aft, the planes rotated to their required angles and *Trophy* rose up towards thirty-two feet. Crawford read out the decrease in depth and at twenty-eight feet, Mitchell went into action.

'Up periscope,' he ordered, and before the tube had risen to full height, bent and sighted through the socket. His view was initially obscured by the sea before the lens broke clear of the waves and he caught the pale light of the moon's ambient glow. He swept the periscope round through one-hundred and eighty degrees; all clear. The U-boat's tower came into the lens and he cleared his throat.

'Start the attack,' he said, and gave his Sub-Lieutenant time to prepare the plot ready to feed the readings into the 'fruit machine'.

'Attack table ready, sir.'

'Stand by all bow tubes.'

A short pause before Crawford spoke. 'Bow tubes one to six ready, sir.'

Mitchell, glued to the eye piece, could see he needed to come right of the target, give himself some leeway.

'Starboard twenty,'

'Starboard twenty, aye, sir.'

Trophy's bows swung away and Mitchell stayed with the U-boat through the periscope, traversing left to hold focus. The seconds ticked by as he let the angle open, and then countermanded the order.

'Midships . . . , steady.'

'Wheel's amidships, course, two-four-oh, sir.'

Mitchell took note, almost west-south-west, that would do.

He carefully cantered the lens on the unsuspecting U-boat and reeled off the numbers; range, bearing, speed of target.

'Down scope,' he said, and stood back while those at the table saw that the information was logged and transferred to the 'fruit machine'.

'Up periscope.' It hissed from the well and he grabbed the handles.

Again he swept it round the waves, briefly hesitating as he came across the stern, and with no sign of danger, brought it onto the target. A cloud flitted past the moon and he lost the U-boat, but only for a moment. When the pale light returned he realised the point of intersection was fast approaching, no time for the usual procedure.

'Flood tubes,' he snapped, and then passed the fresh set of readings to the plot.

'Number One,' he said from the corner of his mouth. 'No time for any more, we'll go with what we've got. Set for shallow running.'

'Aye aye, sir. Tubes flooded.'

Mitchell twisted the handle, enlarging the image. The U-boat maintained course and speed, oblivious to *Trophy's* presence off its starboard side.

'Stand by,' he warned.

'Standing by, sir.'

Trophy's hull shifted under a swell, a wave foaming across the lens, and Mitchell waited for it to clear. He made one last rapid calculation. If the 'fruit machine' had calibrated correctly then a well aimed spread of six torpedoes must surely find the target.

'Ready?'

'Ready, sir.'

'Fire one!'

A pause. 'One fired, sir.'

'Fire two!'

'Two fired, sir.'

And now Crawford concentrated exclusively on pumping ballast forward to compensate for the loss of weight in the bow compartment.

Mitchell held back a moment, and then said; 'continuing firing by stopwatch.'

During the next few seconds, four more fish ejected from their tubes and streaked off towards the target.

'All torpedoes running, sir,' said the Sub-Lieutenant.

'Very well,' he acknowledged. 'How long?'

'Forty-two seconds, sir.'

Mitchell watched and waited. He'd amassed a fair tonnage since becoming the captain of his own boat, but enemy warships were not easy to come by and he had only two anti-submarine trawlers to his credit. But a U-boat, that was an altogether different animal.

'Thirty-eight seconds.'

Then he gave a sharp intake of breath. The U-boat was diving. That meant a reduction in speed, and would it get deep enough to avoid the torpedoes? Had a lookout seen Trophy? If so, he must take avoiding action.

'The bloody U-boat's diving,' he snapped, voicing his disbelief. The conning tower was sliding beneath the waves, almost underwater.

'God's teeth,' he said, and screwed his eyes shut. When he next looked, the U-boat had gone and he straightened from the periscope.

'Forty-two . . . . forty-three . . . . forty-four . . . . forty-five . . .'

The explosion came late, a deep, muffled underwater rumble resonating on *Trophy's* steel shell.

Mitchell grabbed for the handles, focussed through the lens, but found only a dark expanse of water. No . . . , wait, there was something, a possible disturbance where the U-boat might have been. Then a bubbling gout of boiling water came to the surface.

With a caution deeply ingrained from all his time in submarines, he turned the periscope in a sweep to all four points of the compass, and only then gave his next order.

'Down periscope, surface the boat.'

On a controlled ascent, *Trophy* broke the waves bow first, and Mitchell clambered from the hatch and stepped forward. The pungent reek of diesel oil met his nostrils, the cloying stink assailing the senses.

'Slow ahead, two knots,' he said to the pipe, and made a quick check of the lookouts; both in position and watching their sectors. *Trophy* nosed forwards, the stench of oil growing stronger, and then something knocked against the saddle tanks and came bobbing down the side. He saw that it was part of a wooden crate, and beyond that, almost hidden in the inky blackness, he detected the body of a man face down in the water. Even in what little light there was to see by, he knew it was a uniformed German.

'Stop engines, Number One to the bridge.'

Crawford's head appeared from the hatch and he hauled himself out to stand at Mitchell's elbow.

'Slow astern.'

'Slow astern, aye, sir,' Mitchell heard repeated, and pointed at the water for Crawford's benefit. 'What do you see?'

His First Lieutenant squinted, staring at the sea, then as his eyes accustomed themselves to the relative darkness, he nodded slowly.

'I would say I'm looking at a dead German submariner, sir,' he said very formally.

Mitchell gave a smile. 'Thank you, number One, I just needed your confirmation.

Crawford grinned. 'Congratulations, sir. I'll let the crew know.'

'Yes,' Mitchell said, 'and have a couple of men with boathooks salvage anything useful, we might find ourselves a souvenir.'

Still grinning, Crawford gave the customary, 'Aye aye, sir,' and went below calling for volunteers.

When the two seamen appeared on the after casing, Mitchell spent fifteen minutes conning *Trophy* slowly through the ever widening circle of oil, and when there was nothing more to find, he ordered 'Start main engines' and set a course for home. The sum total of recoverable items included two oil soaked sailor's caps, a half bottle of Schnapps and an oilskin jacket. With *Trophy* pushing on at twelve knots, he ordered an extra tot of rum for all hands, and thanked them for an outstanding night's work.

He ordered the destruction of a U-boat to be signalled to Admiralty and copied to Harwich and then retreated to his cabin. Alone, he sat back on his bunk and closed his eyes in thought. *Trophy* had achieved a rare feat of arms. With the sinking of that U-boat she would become a 'name' within the proud service of submarine operations.

Content in that knowledge, he poured himself a small gin and toasted their victory.

In the German port of Wilhelmshaven, Admiral Mathias Krause sat at his desk and waited for news of Operation Triton. Three of his senior executive officers had joined him and they whiled away the time with a bottle of Cognac and a game of cards. Convinced it wouldn't be long before battle commenced and anticipating a speedy victory, they chatted amiably as the game progressed.

Krause himself had his own reasons to be confident of success, a secret mission he'd instigated for a Type VII U-boat to shadow the *Holstein's* convoy and add its own lethal presence to ensure a positive outcome for the Kriegsmarine. Blissfully unaware that the boat had been blown apart and now lay at the bottom of the sea, he savoured another mouthful of Cognac and smiled with satisfaction. The antique clock on the walnut sideboard ticked on, and every now and then his eyes strayed to the Roman numerals. Soon, he thought, soon the Royal Navy would pay the price for its naked aggression.

Chapter Twenty . . . Hunter's Moon

At the designated time, as Margate's headland came up on their port beam, the three 'Hunts' made the turn north-east and Thorburn increased speed to twenty-two knots. The last report had been a bit sketchy with the German convoy leaving Rotterdam at dusk and turning west. The actual makeup of the warships involved varied between five and ten, but he was assured the *Holstein* had definitely sailed with that convoy. The assumed destination was Calais and the Admiralty had no reason to believe the Kriegsmarine would break their normal pattern of behaviour.

Thorburn's bigger concern was the almost cloudless sky and a half moon; in one aspect good for station keeping, on the other hand, not the best conditions with which to make an attack. The best he could hope for would be to make an approach from the north as the moon passed its zenith and travelled west, silhouetting the Germans against the light.

'Signal, sir.'

He turned to the Chief Yeoman. 'Operational?'

'Yes, sir.'

He took the slip and moved to the chart table, and bending to the feeble light of the bulkhead lamp, he peered at the message.

"Confirmed sighting at 01.15hrs Friday 31st. *Holstein* plus destroyers and minesweepers. E-boats attached."

He stared at the words for a moment longer before handing the slip back to the Yeoman.

'Acknowledge,' he said, and turned to an expectant Armstrong. Thorburn grinned in the gloom. 'Seems like half the German navy are on the move,' he said by way of an explanation.

Armstrong chuckled. 'I'd be disappointed if they weren't.'

Thorburn nodded, still smiling. 'Yes,' he said, 'wouldn't do to have the odds in our favour, would it?' He glanced round at the compass platform. 'What's our position, Pilot?'

Martin peered closely at his watch before answering.

'Should be three miles from the North Foreland, sir.'

'Very well,' Thorburn said, making a few rapid calculations. 'We'll bring the ship to Action Stations, Number One. No need for the alarm, just pipe it through.'

'Aye aye, sir,' Armstrong said, and moved off to the rear of the bridge. A moment later the pipe shrilled as the order went out to the Ship's company. She came alive to the pounding of boots, controlled pandemonium as the crew made for their stations. Men clambered up ladders, others slid down. Hatches banged shut, watertight doors sealed. It all happened as expected, as it had so many times before, and yet Thorburn never failed to be surprised by the smooth transition from 'defence stations' to *Brackendale* becoming a ship ready for war.

The reports began filtering in to Armstrong on the bridge telephone.

And so the ship steamed on under Lieutenant Martin's direction, only the occasional correction quietly spoken to the wheelhouse voice-pipe. In line astern, almost hidden in the darkness, *Cranbrook* and *Darrow* followed in *Brackendale's* wake. Three of His Majesty's warships, the smallest destroyers in the fleet.

On the Pompom platform, Taff Williams swivelled in his seat and felt for the trigger, settling his eye to the rear sight and finding the rings of the outer. Happy with his position he adjusted the strap of his helmet and relaxed in the pale grey of the moon. He glanced round and caught sight of Ordinary Seaman Terry Shepherd, not yet nineteen years old and still wet behind the ears. He'd only joined ship two hours before *Brackendale* had left Dover, and 'Guns' had assigned him to the Pompom as a loading number. He looked a little lost so Williams gave him a wink. He had a soft spot for newcomers to his crew, had never forgotten what it was like to join your first ship.

The young man smiled uncertainly and ventured a question.

'What's it like when we make contact, Taff?'

In the faint light of the half moon, Williams studied his innocent face and wondered how best to explain.

'Well, boyo,' he said patiently, 'the first thing is you ignore everything but what you're here for. You *do* know what that is?'

Shepherd looked round the others of the gun crew before answering.

'To load the ammo,' he said, hesitant.

'That's right,' Williams reassured him. 'When the battle begins all you have to do is load . . . , and load, and load. There'll be smoke, a lot of smoke, and noise like you've never heard. Ships shooting at us, and us firing at them, and you won't know if we're winning or losing.'

'Oh,' Shepherd said, his face puckered in thought. 'But what will the skipper do if there's too many of 'em?'

Williams gave a short laugh and rubbed his jaw.

'No such thing, not for *Brackendale*, and the skipper will do what he does best . . . , he'll fight! Give him half a chance and the bloody Germans won't know what hit 'em.'

The young seaman forced a half hearted smile. 'Is that why he's got a medal?'

Williams grinned in the darkness. 'It is, I seen it all, that's *exactly* why he's got a medal.'

At the bridge-screen Thorburn hunched his shoulders inside the duffel coat. Clouds flitted across the moon, a wind rising from the west. But the fleeting moments of darkness shrouded them from prying eyes and he relaxed and let Pilot continue to navigate them across the narrow sea.

'Port ten,' said Martin quietly on the compass platform.

Brackendale nosed to the left, lifting her bows to the gently rolling waves.

Thorburn crossed to the port bridge-wing and looked aft across the stern quarter, watching the small flotilla of boats managing the deeper waters, each in turn riding the long swells.

'Time?' he inquired.

Armstrong answered. 'Oh-one fifty-six, sir.'

Thorburn nodded in the darkness, satisfied with their timely arrival at mid channel. 'Thank you, Number One,' he said, and returned to the forebridge. *Brackendale* twisted slowly and pitched into a shallow trough, the fo'c'sle encased in a fine sheet of spray.

Richard Thorburn bared his teeth in a broad grin and tasted that familiar tang of salt. The hunt was on and woe betide any German who crossed his path this night.

'How long on this leg, Pilot?' he asked.

'Two minutes, sir,' Martin replied promptly.

'And the run to Ostend?'

'Fifteen minutes at twenty knots, sir.'

Thorburn nibbled his bottom lip. 'Very well,' he said, and raised his binoculars. The darkness of the night ahead defeated him and he dropped the glasses to his chest. He crossed to the starboard wing to check on the destroyers, found them surging along in *Brackendale's* wake, pale moonlight glinting on flowing bow waves, holding station in perfect line astern. He moved back to port for the M.T.B.s and Gunboats, and watched them skipping over the waves. For *Brackendale* the seas made no real impact; for the wooden hulls of the power boats, it looked to be a lively encounter. But they powered on in arrow formation, seven boats parallel to the destroyer's midships, and Thorburn felt a humbling pride for the young men that manned these vulnerable craft.

Lieutenant Martin straightened from the chart table. 'One minute to the turn, sir.'

'Very well,' Thorburn acknowledged, and raised his binoculars in search of the coast. The faintest of blurred outlines met his vision, but try as he might to correct the focus it wouldn't improve.

'Thirty seconds, sir.'

Thorburn lowered the glasses and moved to the platform, waiting. The compass showed oh-eight-oh degrees, due east.

'Time, sir.'

He leaned to the voice-pipe and gave the order. 'Starboard ten.'

'Starboard ten, aye aye, sir.'

Brackendale heeled gently to port, cutting round to the south, riding the long swell. He watched the bearing come through to the south-west and pre-empted the moment to catch her swing.

'Midships . . . , steer two-four-oh degrees,' he said, following Martin's plot to run parallel with the coast.

Falconer's firm acknowledgement echoed up the pipe. 'Steady on two-four-oh degrees, sir.'

Thorburn stepped down from the platform, moved to the starboard wing and found *Cranbrook* peeling away to take station line abreast. Beyond her, *Darrow* followed suit pushing out to the right flank, her camouflaged outline merging with the dark sea. He glanced astern and picked out the four M.T.B.s, Holloway leading them on in a staggered 'V', their hulls creaming easily across the rollers. And the three Gunboats veering away to take position in the void between *Cranbrook* and *Darrow*. He allowed himself a tight smile of appreciation at their well defined deployment.

Armstrong came and stood at his side. 'Exactly as we rehearsed.'

'Yes,' Thorburn said, for the first time feeling the full weight of command. 'One might say, the die is cast.'

Armstrong replied quietly. 'In for a penny, in for a pound.'

Thorburn grinned and reached a hand up to his First Lieutenant's shoulder. 'Let's hope the gamble pays off.'

He turned and crossed to the bridge-screen, eying the seas ahead, the half moon partially obscured by fleeting black cloud. He paused to look again, staring with narrowed eyes at the pewter grey sky, at the sharp contrast between that and the dark, undulating sea. A smile teased his lips and he straightened to his full height above the screen, suppressing a chuckle. He turned his head to call over his shoulder.

'Gentlemen, a good omen. We have ourselves a hunter's moon.'

Wolfgang Schulze, at the head of his flotilla, pushed cautiously up the coast from Ostend, squeezing his ship as close to the shore as he thought prudent. In places he was less than six-hundred metres from the foreshore, risky, but given the circumstances, he felt it more than justified. He had ordered the ship to Battle Stations shortly after leaving Dunkirk, and the lookouts were at their posts scanning the seas around their sectors.

He lifted the binoculars to train on the shoreline ahead and focussed on a spit of land projecting into the sea. Flecks of pale surf shone in the moonlight where sea tumbled on the sand and he decided to give it a wide berth.

'Left by ten degrees,' he ordered, and waited for the ship to veer away. When he felt sufficient clearance had been achieved he brought them back parallel with the coast.

'Right five degrees, course east by north-east.'

He'd deliberately positioned his ship closest to that French shoreline knowing any move he made would be followed by the remainder of the flotilla.

His Second-in-Command came to his side and saluted.

'The flotilla has changed course also, Herr Kapitän.'

Schulze spared him a glance.

'Good. Are the Schnellboats to seaward?'

'One half kilometre off our flank, yes sir.'

Schulze nodded his approval. 'Then all is well, you may attend to your duties.'

'Jawohl, Herr Kapitän,' said the man, threw up a salute and strode off.

Ignoring the departing footsteps, Schulze raised the glasses and studied the darkness in a broad search to the north. Any time now they should catch sight of *Holstein's* outlying escort. He managed to quell the excitement coursing through his body and forced himself to concentrate on navigating their passage.

After all, was he not the Admiral's chosen man?

On *Brackendale's* bridge Thorburn stood bellied up the fore-screen, binoculars trained steadily over the port bow. If his calculations were correct, and with the moon lowering in the west, this must surely be the ideal situation. He winced at a spasm from his shoulder blade, the old wound reminding him of its presence, and it tailed off to leave a manageable ache. His stomach fluttered as always before battle and he took an extra intake of air. He'd lived with that low level of pre-battle nerves for so long it hardly registered, and anyway, never to be disclosed to others. The man in command was the strength of the ship, any visible weakness abhorrent to the process. The ship's company looked to him for strong leadership.

'Captain, sir?'

He turned to find the Chief Yeoman holding a message slip.

'Signal, sir.'

Thorburn took it and leaned into the dim light of the chart table. The words did not make for good reading. "Report of second flotilla moving north-east from Dunkirk. Mixed units. Destroyers and R boats." He frowned at the message, there was no time of departure. 'Is that all,' he asked.

'Yes, sir.'

He rubbed his jaw in frustration. If that flotilla joined up with *Holstein's* group then that would mean a serious escalation of numbers, putting Thorburn's group at a major disadvantage.

'Very well, acknowledge,' he said to the Yeoman, and returned to the fore-bridge, thinking over the problem. On the other hand the German flotillas might not join forces at all, remain as two separate units. That could prove the worst of all possible outcomes, a second force roaming around unseen. He frowned. So many ifs and buts.

He glanced round in the darkness. 'Number One?' he called softly.

Armstrong stepped forward from behind the compass housing.

'Yes, sir?'

'Bad news, I'm afraid. A second German flotilla has been reported leaving Dunkirk and heading this way. Didn't get a time of departure but it can't be co-incidence. They must be joining forces.'

For a long moment Armstrong remained silent, and then Thorburn saw him turn his head to speak. 'Could be a trap, an ambush?'

Thorburn stared at his silhouette, caught by the simplicity of the statement. Of course, why not? If the Germans were aware of British interest then they would be angling to take advantage.

'I think,' he said slowly, 'you've hit the nail on the head. We'll have to rely on *Cranbrook's* radar, hopefully they'll pick them up early.'

Armstrong lowered his voice. 'We could give ourselves a bit of leeway. Get a lookout up the mast.'

Thorburn turned and looked up at the crosstree. There was no provision for a crow's nest up there, so the man would have to wrap himself into the ladder and the masthead. But the sea was relatively calm, it had to be worth asking for a volunteer. He walked across to the port wing.

'Jones,' he said to the lookout's back. 'Fancy a spell up the mast?'

Lowering his binoculars, Jones turned in surprise. In the pale light Thorburn felt the eyes querying his Captain's sincerity. But there was only a second of hesitation before his teeth glistened with a grin.

'Change is as good as a rest, sir.'

'Good man,' Thorburn said. 'Now listen. We've had a signal to say there could be another German flotilla operating in this area. Whatever happens when we make contact with the convoy, I need you to concentrate on other sectors. Don't be distracted by the battle ahead of us, it could be a ruse to divert our attention away from a more serious threat. Understood?'

Jones nodded. 'Avoid the battle and watch the shadows, sir.'

'Exactly that. Think you'll manage up there?' he asked, gesturing at the mast.

The grin returned. 'Not a problem, sir.'

Thorburn stared at him for a second. Jones had a proven track record, honest and hardworking with the sharpest pair of eyes aboard.

'Very well then,' he said. 'Carry on.'

'Aye aye, sir,' Jones said, and headed for the flag deck and the masthead ladder.

Thorburn returned to Armstrong. 'Here's hoping,' he said, and once more raised his glasses.

Armstrong stepped away and called for another lookout to take over from Jones. In the meantime he temporarily filled the port wing and brought up his binoculars.

'Masthead closed up, sir!'

Thorburn heard the call from above and glanced up over his shoulder. Jones had sat himself astride the crosstree with a leg locked round the mast and an arm entwined in the rigging. His binoculars were already trained at the inshore waters.

'Number One?' he called quietly.

Armstrong looked round and Thorburn gestured with his chin. 'We have ourselves a man in the crow's nest.'

His First Lieutenant smiled and gave a small nod. 'You'll be wanting us to set the mainsail next,' he said and chuckled.

Thorburn laughed and returned to scanning the sea. They were as ready as they could be, now it was all in the lap of the Gods.

Chapter Twenty One. . . Night Action

In *Forty-Nine*, Holloway snatched a glance at 'Ginger' Lambert's M.G.B. and watched the hull keening over the waves, a powerful beauty in the thrust of her hull. He switched back to stare at the blackness ahead, the never ending strain of peering into the depths of danger. As they'd done the other night, the usual routine would be to have had the boats motor out to a predetermined destination, to where the enemy had already engaged in surface combat, or to a known patrol line. This business of pushing forward at speed to find trouble gave him an unnerving tingle down his spine.

And the noise of the roaring engines took away one of the vital senses. A prominent tool in finding the enemy at night was that of hearing. Given the right circumstances a skipper would cut engines and listen; but this time, on this night, Holloway didn't have the option.

The boat danced sideways and skipped back on course, the hull thumping a wave.

'On the starboard bow, sir!' McCallum called in warning.

Holloway focussed his binoculars, searching the impenetrable darkness. A shimmer of white water swam across the lens. A bow wave? Propeller wake? He couldn't be certain.

'Starboard wheel, Cox'n.'

'Starboard wheel, aye, sir.'

The M.T.B. skidded away to the right, and Holloway checked the swing.

'Midships.'

'Wheel's amidships, sir,' the Cox'n affirmed.

Through the glasses again, and this time he found white water immediately, the phosphorescent wake of a warship. Undoubtedly the enemy, it was about to get interesting.

'We have contact,' he said loudly to let the crew know, and prepared for battle.

At 02.06hrs on Friday the 31st of July, battle commenced with a flash of gunfire, and a magnesium flare from *Cranbrook* burst high in the night sky. On *Brackendale's* bridge Thorburn tensed as it swayed, drifting, a white light in the wind. Under the harsh brilliance the sea came alive with enemy craft. Silhouetted in the distance he could clearly make out the shape of a large vessel, but between himself and that ship were the enemy escorts.

'Full ahead both! Hard-a-port!' He snatched a glance to his right. *Cranbrook* and *Darrow* were on the move, sheering away to starboard.

Brackendale drove forward and heeled over to head inshore, the bridge swaying with the momentum of her turn. The power of the engines surged through the deck plates, bow wave flaying the fo'c'sle. A second starshell flashed white and illuminated a wide swathe of sea.

The crash of guns sounded as *Cranbrook* and *Darrow* opened fire, the first broadside of the engagement.

Thorburn found himself leaning towards the port side, left knee bent to compensate for the little ship's wicked incline. She charged round in the darkness, beyond the light of the flares.

'Midships!' he snapped at the voice-pipe, and the ship swung violently upright, throwing the crew off balance. There were exclamations of surprise and men cursed the Cox'n.

Thorburn grinned . . . , always the Cox'n, never the Captain.

'Steady!' he ordered, and *Brackendale* centred to a new course, powering through the waves. Thorburn let her run. Off the starboard quarter the night lit up with tracer, the secondary armament coming into range. Main weapons from both sides hammered out salvoes, plumes of water exploding with hits. But there was no time to admire the pyrotechnics.

'Hard-a-starboard,' he called to the pipe, and the agile little ship responded to the helm, dipping her portside guardrail under a welter of swirling foam. Her sharp stem cleaved the waves, fighting to turn onto the new course.

Thorburn waited, watching the enemy warships reappear off the starboard bow.

'Midships . . . , steady . . . , steer oh-seven-five degrees.'

'Oh-seven-five degrees. Aye aye, sir.' It was the Cox'n's voice echoing up the pipe.

'Half ahead both,' Thorburn said, 'twenty knots.' this time with more control to his command.

'Half ahead, speed twenty knots, aye aye, sir.'

An enemy flare arced high over *Cranbrook* and lit the sky, and Thorburn spotted Holloway's *Forty-Nine* leading the power boats into an attack.

So far undetected, *Brackendale* had pushed away into the gap between the enemy's left flank and that still partially obscured shoreline, and for the first time Thorburn felt the forward planning had been worth the effort. He lifted the glasses and picked out the bulky shape of what he assumed had to be the *Holstein*. Another two or three minutes and the enemy would be in broadside territory at the mercy of his guns.

He picked up a bulkhead handset. 'Guns?'

'Guns, sir?'

'Stand by.'

'Aye aye, sir.'

A wave slapped the bow and sprayed the upperworks, tossing a fine mist over the bridge-screen. Thorburn licked salt rimmed lips and wiped the lens of his binoculars. Another starshell glared brightly, well to starboard, the dark outline of warships showing in the light.

Kapitän-zur-See Gerhard Baumgartner squinted into the dazzling glare of bursting starshell and called to Konrad.

'Man the weapons!'

The men of *Holstein* were waiting and the ship quickly changed from Defence Watch One to Battle Stations, crowding round the guns.

Baumgartner was only too aware of his limitations in mounting any serious opposition against a flotilla of warships. Unlike a normal cruiser, each gun had an Officer-in-Command with no central Control. Overall direction was passed from the spotting platform via handsets, the Senior Gunnery Officer prioritising what he judged to be the greatest threat.

Shouted orders rang through the decks and Baumgartner impatiently strode out onto the starboard wing. After the warmth of the enclosed bridge the cool night air fanned his cheeks, a bracing caress, and he tugged his cap down over his forehead. Through the glasses he found the British ships, a twinge of trepidation reflected in his frown. Even now, the enemy turned seawards, the two destroyers deploying at speed, bringing their guns to bear. A flicker of foam grabbed his attention and he focussed again, and found the fast moving Royal Navy torpedo boats swarming to attack, bows up and powering over the waves.

An enemy salvo ripped across the sea, a broadside from the pair of destroyers. A second flare burst ahead of *Holstein* and he knew how much the incandescent light would silhouette his ship's bridge. In that instant, the two Elbings sped past firing their forward guns, the Schnellboats fanning out in line abreast.

He turned and re-entered the warmth of the inner bridge; time to teach the British a lesson. 'Make ready with our prime weapons,' he ordered.

Neuman picked up a handset. 'Clear the hatchways!'

To port and starboard, the gun crews dropped the steel doors that concealed the main armament, wire cables allowing them to fold out and down on their hinges. The large calibre guns traversed round to point out from the ship's side.

Neuman looked up. 'Ready, sir.'

Baumgartner straightened to his full height and glared at his young Second-in-Command, and smiled.

'Now, Konrad,' he said, his voice strident with emotion, 'now we fight. Tell the spotters to concentrate on the destroyers.' He glanced at the navigating compass, and then towards his quartermaster at the wheel.

'Hard right, full speed.'

The man spun the wheel and the seaman standing at the telegraph rang down for maximum revolutions.

Holstein quivered as the big four-bladed bronze propeller bit into the dark waters, pushing four-thousand tons of Armed Raider away from the shore.

Baumgartner moved to starboard and raised his glasses to the enemy. Their turrets rippled with gunfire and his face hardened into a taut smile. The British concentrated on the Elbings, giving the advantage to *Holstein*. And as his ship stood out from shore, directly across the path of the Englander's destroyers, he centred the course.

'Steady. Hold your bearing.' And he gave the command to engage.

Richard Thorburn spotted the moment *Holstein* began to turn, and cursed aloud. He'd assumed the ship would make an escape while the escort took the brunt of the Royal Navy's bombardment. This was not what he'd been told to expect, the Kriegsmarine were not conforming. He swept his binoculars to the starboard beam and selected the German destroyers. Tracer cut through the night, shells and bullets streaking between the two flotillas. And joining the Elbings at speed he caught sight of the E-boats charging forward to complete their line of attack.

A lookout yelled. 'Enemy opening gun ports, sir!'

Thorburn swung the glasses onto *Holstein* and found the openings, gun muzzles appearing, the lethal weapons that had surprised so many innocent seamen. What were they, six inch equivalent? They could make a mess of a Hunt. He frowned, rapidly sifting through his options and settled on the one thing *Brackendale* was well positioned for; she could make herself known to the *Holstein's* captain by opening fire. And unlike a capital ship, this cruiser was thin skinned, no armoured belt. Yes, he thought, *Cranbrook* and *Darrow* had enough on their plate with the threat of torpedoes. Time to intervene.

Wolfgang Schulze stiffened to the sight of a brilliant light bursting in the night sky, well ahead of the port bow. The sound of heavy gunfire rolled down the coast and he trained his binoculars on the distant glare of drifting light.

'Emergency full ahead!' he barked, and followed the command with a string of obscenities. This was not good, his flotilla lay too far to the west. The best he could do now was to close the distance and hope they were not seen.

He stepped across to the port side and looked at Vogel's ship, its bow wave growing rapidly in size as the vessel accelerated in response. He caught a glimpse of Schnellboats powering forward to push ahead, dispersing into line abreast. More heavy gunfire reached his ears, a sustained salvo, and a second starshell lit the heavens, and then for the first time a splash of multi-coloured tracer flashing over the sea. He returned to the main bridge, raised his binoculars and scoured the scene ahead. His ship rose and fell to the waves and he braced for the moment to engage.

Leading Seaman Allun Jones was doing exactly as he'd been ordered; ignoring the din of battle and concentrating on the darkness off the port beam. With one foot hooked securely in the ladder and an elbow crooked round a rigging line, he sat on the crosstree and swept his binoculars methodically from midships to bow. He'd twice been forced to momentarily suspend the lookout and grab hold as *Brackendale* turned hard on a change of course, one way and then the other, leaving him dangling precariously over the foaming sea.

But his diligence brought reward. At the end of a sweep towards the bows, he lowered the glasses to release the tension in his arms. When he resumed his search something swam across the lens, a vague shadow, darker than the surrounding sea, a solid object.

Jones stopped his movement and then swung the glasses slowly back to the right. The experienced discipline of a determined lookout paid off. Unflustered by all that was taking place around him, and needing to be certain of his sighting, he steadied on the blurred image. He focussed the magnified lens and settled on the shape of a fast approaching warship, and he recognised the flared bows of a 'T' class German destroyer. And there to the right, another, coming on at speed.

'Bridge?' he shouted over the noise of battle. 'Enemy destroyers at Red three-oh! Range five-thousand.'

On the navigating platform below he saw the Captain look up and wave a hand in acknowledgement, and Jones deliberately stretched out an arm to point at the new found enemy. He watched the skipper lift his binoculars, and only then did he rest for a moment to ease the cramp in the muscles of his right arm.

A stray bullet whipped through the shrouds and he flinched; it was all beginning to get a bit too lively.

At Dover, in Pendleton's underground office, Second Officer Jennifer Farbrace fretted over *Brackendale's* exact whereabouts. *Trophy's* signal had been received and the German convoy pinpointed. And in conjunction with Trophy's signal, a clandestine message had been passed from Combined Operations warning of a second German flotilla sailing from Dunkirk

As she stood staring down at the chart, surveying the little blue and red models, she couldn't help but be fearful of the forthcoming engagement. Richard's flotilla was clearly outnumbered, vulnerable to an ambush. She found herself gripped by a sense of foreboding, but at a loss as to how to explain her feelings.

Pendleton's deep base voice broke into her thoughts.

'Well, young lady,' he said from behind his desk, 'if we're right, *Brackendale* should be almost on top of *Holstein*.'

Jennifer turned to see him shrouded in a fog of cigarette smoke and she nibbled at her bottom lip. That cloud of blue smoke did nothing to boost her confidence because she knew from past experience that when the Captain chain-smoked he tended to be a worried man. So she voiced her thoughts.

'What about that second flotilla from Dunkirk, sir?'

'Mmm,' he mouthed, bushy eyebrows coming together in a heavy frown, tugging at his beard. 'Not the best of situations, I grant you.' He scraped back the chair and came to his feet, then walked ponderously up to the chart table. A smile briefly flickered across his lips, although in her opinion, Jennifer thought it more resembled a grimace. She could see he was trying to size up the situation.

Her most recent positioning of the ten blue 'friendlies' placed Thorburn's flotilla running down to the east, towards Ostend. Ahead of his position she's moved the red convoy pieces to within thirty miles of the port, but the unknown factor was the location of the Dunkirk ships. In the end, making a guess as to their speed, Jennifer had stationed them a little west of Ostend.

A sharp knock on the door made them look round and a Telegraphist hurried in with a pink slip in his hand.

'Excuse me, sir, signal from *Brackendale*.'

'Well, now, there's a thing,' Pendleton said reaching for the message.

Jennifer waited while he read it through, impatient to hear what it said. He rubbed his nose and pursed his lips before finally looking up.

'Have you acknowledged?' he asked the man.

'Not yet, sir.'

'Please do,' Pendleton said, staring at the chart, and the Telegraphist closed the door behind him.

'Well? Jennifer demanded.

'Well, young lady,' he said, this time with a genuine smile, 'we have ourselves a longitude and latitude. Perhaps you'd like to transfer these coordinates to our chart.' He handed her the slip of paper.

She scanned through the words which in themselves signalled nothing more than what they'd been expecting. "Enemy in sight," and a set of grid coordinates. Glancing down at the chart she hesitated, not because there were any doubts as to the stated position, but because she couldn't be sure whether the signal meant the convoy or the flotilla from Dunkirk.

'Do we assume they mean *Holstein's* group, sir?'

Pendleton nodded slowly. 'Until we know more, that is my assumption.'

Jennifer leaned across the chart and slid the opposing forces together, being careful to position Thorburn's marker on the precise coordinate. At least she knew the 'where', now she could worry about whether he'd get hurt. She sighed and stood back, the blue and red models appearing deceptively peaceful on the chart. She felt Pendleton's eyes watching her and looked at him.

'Always the same,' he said, 'it's the waiting, not knowing. Not easy is it?'

She shook her head in agreement and wandered towards his desk. The ash tray needed emptying and then she tidied a few pieces of discarded paperwork.

'Leave that,' Pendleton barked suddenly, 'we'll get some fresh air.'

Jennifer stared at him in surprise. Did he really want to walk out of the office at such a critical moment?

'Come on,' he insisted, 'do us both good. A few minutes outside won't make a blind bit of difference one way or the other.'

Reluctantly, and with a last look back at the chart table, Jennifer followed him out into the corridor and up the steps. The pair of sentries on duty at the main door, momentarily taken unawares by the Captain's appearance, snapped to attention.

In the cool darkness of the night, James Pendleton and Jennifer Farbrace walked side by side along the pavement, the half moon hanging low in the western sky. Somewhere down towards Portsmouth the stiffening breeze brought with it the buzzing drone of bombers and she wondered how many had made the return journey? But after the stuffy confines of the cellar, that same breeze had an invigorating freshness, and she filled her lungs with air.

Pendleton stopped and turned to face the south-east, standing with hands on hips and peering at the sky beyond the nearby rooftops. She joined him and took another deep breath.

Then faintly, as the gentle wind fell away, the distant echo of gunfire reached her ears.

Beside her Pendleton ran a hand down his beard and nodded.

'I think,' he said softly, 'battle has commenced.'

Chapter Twenty-Two . . . Exposed

Thorburn had to make a decision. Either attack *Holstein* or meet the new threat. He dropped the glasses to his chest and snatched a quick glance across the stern beyond the starboard quarter. *Cranbrook* and *Darrow* were still in one piece, firing steadily. The M.T.B.s had split up in search of an angle to release their torpedoes, and the Gunboats were blasting their way through the E-boats. Tracer flew from every angle, the heavier guns thumping out round after round.

Enough dithering, he thought, the rest of the flotilla would have to manage, and he grinned into the night. To hell with it, this lot want a fight, then that's what he'd give 'em.

'Hard-a-port!' he yelled at the voice-pipe, heard a faint acknowledgement and grabbed a handset.

'Guns?'

'Sir?'

'Change of target, look inshore. At least two destroyers, fire when ready.'

'Aye aye, sir,' Carling said.

Thorburn slipped the handset back on its bracket and watched the compass revolve until he had the bearing.

'Midships,' he ordered. The ship came back onto an even keel and he remembered Jones clinging to the masthead. He looked up and called.

'Jones! That's enough, come down.'

The forward turret cracked off a pair of shells and he raised his binoculars to focus all his attention on the inshore flotilla. The German destroyers had parted company, moving swiftly left and right. And there, hugging the waves he found E-boats, line abreast and powering in for the kill.

An enemy flare erupted overhead to leave *Brackendale* fully exposed to their gunnery, and Thorburn winced under the blinding light. A shell whistled past the bridge, columns of water thumping high into the air off the port beam. Still the forward turret spat out an unrelenting salvo of high explosive.

But why no torpedoes? The enemy had *Brackendale* at their mercy, but for some reason held their fire. Amidst the cacophony of gunfire he risked a glance around, and then it dawned on him. By sheer good fortune *Brackendale* had come round bow on to the German flotilla leaving *Holstein* immediately astern. His mouth turned down at the corners in a wry smile . . . , they were afraid to hit the raider. But if that was a momentary respite, it would soon be nullified as he took the ship ever closer to the enemy.

Bullets ricocheted, flashing off steel panels and he instinctively hunched his shoulders. Peering at the destroyers it dawned on him that steaming straight between them might achieve exactly the same result, opposing ships unable to fire for fear of striking their own.

Snatching up the bulkhead handset he turned and looked at the Tower. 'Guns?'

'Sir!'

'I'm taking her through the middle, you'll have targets port and starboard.'

'Understood, sir.'

Thorburn replaced the hand piece and straightened to his full height, time to run the gauntlet.

The range decreased rapidly.

Lieutenant Charles Holloway had his hands full. The amount of incoming tracer reached a crescendo, a torrent of scything machine-gun fire lancing in at his boat. Miniature yellow and green fireballs whipped past his head, yet more striking the hull. And through the intense volume of fire he desperately sought to con *Forty-Nine* into a firing position.

'Port wheel!'

The boat turned, bouncing on a wave.

'Steady!'

A vivid flash and an explosion rocked the boat. Ginger Lambert's M.G.B. disintegrated under a direct hit. He grimaced. No time to dwell on it, concentrate on the attack. Shells whined over the bridge, heard above the noise of the engines. Binoculars to hand he found the *Holstein* and for a moment hesitated, not able to believe his eyes. The ship was actually turning across his path.

'Starboard wheel!'

Forty-Nine veered right.

'Steady,' he called, and waited while the firing angle improved, but he needed to close the range.

He shot a glance to his right, only one M.T.B. in sight.

'Where's our other boat?' he shouted.

'Dropped astern, sir!' someone yelled.

He shook his head . . . , so now it was just the two of them, from eight torpedoes down to four.

Bullets slammed into the foredeck and he felt them striking home. An 'R' boat sped across in front of *Holstein* and he watched it turn head on. An E-boat zig-zagged at high speed to his right, careering wildly out of

238

control. A Gunboat took evasive action and then bracketed the E-boat with everything it had. At close range the Gunboat's Pompom tore the enemy apart, punching great holes in the hull. In the next moment it blew apart, disintegrating in an orange flash.

'Stand by torpedoes!' he yelled over the noise of the exhausts.

And then *Holstein* opened fire, the starboard guns hammering a pair of shells at *Darrow*. The Hunt was hit amidships on the boat deck and flames licked up along her side.

'Port wheel!' he ordered, and *Forty-Nine* slewed hard left. A huge column of water lifted dead ahead, submerging Holloway in a heavy deluge.

'Starboard,' he managed, and she jinked right and he caught her swing. 'Steady . . . , hold her there, Cox'n!'

A stream of tracer latched on to them and destroyed the anti-shrapnel matting round the cockpit.

Then came a rumbling bark from an exhaust as an engine coughed, caught, coughed again, and died. *Forty-Nine* slowed with an immediate loss of power and Holloway prayed the boat retained enough speed to complete the attack. He gripped the rail and steeled himself for a final lunge.

Brackendale vibrated to the power of her engines and raced into the midst of the enemy. Thorburn narrowed his eyes to the blinding light of tracer, trying to navigate right through the middle of chaos. The fo'c'sle gun mounting traversed left, paused, and the twin muzzles exploded with gunfire, hurling shells at the nearest destroyer. The quarterdeck pairing swivelled to starboard and let rip on the opposite side. And the Germans returned fire with a will. Twenty-millimetre enemy shells raked the flag deck and a signaller tumbled off the platform to the boat deck, his left arm missing. A shell found the whaler and reduced it to splinters.

Thorburn stood glued to the forebridge, guiding his ship through the melee. An E-boat came in too close to the bows and *Brackendale* hit it a glancing blow. The German helmsman lost control; it swerved, bounced, and turned turtle. Thorburn nodded, one down. The noise had become intense, a mind-numbing wave of ferocious gunfire, and it seemed that every weapon of *Brackendale's* armament had joined the fight. The acrid taste of cordite filled the bridge space, the Lewis machine-guns hammering short bursts at fast moving targets.

The Bow-chaser pumped a torrent of two-pound shells at the German's stern gun mount, sparks glowing under the hits.

'Torpedo! Red seven-oh!'

'Hard-a-port!' Thorburn yelled, and heard the Cox'n acknowledge. *Brackendale* heeled hard to starboard, white water coursing down her main deck, foaming astern. Men lost their footing and cursed, recovered, and swore at anyone who'd listen. She clawed her way round through the blast of guns and Thorburn held his breath. From the forebridge he could see no sign of the lethal cylinder but knew their best chance was to turn head on, minimise the surface area presented to the torpedo.

He concentrated on the compass, waited to correct the swing, and gave the order.

'Midships . . . , steady.'

The Cox'n acknowledged. 'Wheel's amidships, course one-six-four, sir.'

A twenty-millimetre cannon shell ripped into the wheelhouse, ricocheted off a stanchion and impacted human flesh.

The Cox'n gasped in anguish, the breath driven from his lungs. The shell hit his left side, splintered two of his ribs and tore its way out of his back. He sagged on the wheel, the pain flooding his brain, and dragged himself upright. The wheel tugged violently to starboard and he fought to bring it under control, wincing in agony. Blood flowed freely, wet and warm down his waist. Somehow he managed to stabilise the steering. He held on, forcing his knees to support his waist, pain lancing through his chest.

On the bridge Jones called, 'Torpedo to port!' and it swept harmlessly down the side.

Thorburn momentarily shut his eyes at the close call and then saw the ship's bearing would take them out beyond the stern of the German destroyer. An 'R' boat swung in and opened up with all its weapons, bullets smashing the bridge upperworks, stitching a row of holes in the steel plating.

The starboard Oerlikon thumped out a reply, orange tracer seeking the target.

Thorburn ignored the chaos and concentrated his thoughts on the enemy destroyer. Should he follow it round? If he let it get away it could cause havoc with Holloway's boats. The forward guns bellowed and another salvo winged away, but Thorburn was intent on intercepting that German destroyer.

'Port twenty,' he ordered into the voice-pipe and straightened, expecting to hear the formal repeat. When there was no reply he barked at the pipe.

'Port twenty, Cox'n!'

A wheezing gasp came to his ears. 'Aye aye, sir . . . , port twenty.'

Thorburn heard the tremor in Falconer's voice and frowned. 'You alright, Cox'n?'

The answer came weakly, hardly audible. 'Wounded, having trouble, need another helmsman down here.'

'Hang on,' Thorburn said, and turned to look for the bridge messenger. 'Ingram?' he called, 'get someone on the wheel. The Cox'n's hit.'

Ingram scurried down the ladder and after a few moments Thorburn heard a new voice from the pipe. 'Bridge . . . , wheelhouse, Leading Seaman Atkins, sir.'

'Well done, Atkins. Port twenty.'

'Port twenty, aye aye, sir.'

And this time *Brackendale* heeled over to begin the turn.

Thorburn trained his glasses on the fast moving destroyer, hoping the delay could be made up.

Ingram returned to the bridge, came to his shoulder and saluted. 'Cox'n's pretty bad, sir, but he refused to leave the wheelhouse. Said he wasn't going to sick bay.'

Thorburn allowed himself a moment to smile. Typical Cox'n. If there was one place on the ship he didn't like it was Doc Waverley's berth.

'Very well, carry on.'

On *Forty-Nine's* tiny bridge, Holloway felt his boat taking hits. He glanced at the tubes sitting either side of the cockpit, two torpedoes waiting for the firing mechanism to be activated. Each torpedo with a massive five-hundred pound warhead, and it would only take one hit to sink a ship, almost any ship, if aimed correctly.

And Holloway was experienced enough to know his ideal approach should be slightly forward of *Holstein's* midships, beam on to the enemy bow. He bent to set the aim, backsight and foresight in line. A correction was needed in the boat's alignment.

'Port a little.'

'Now starboard . . . , hold her there!'

Incendiary bullets flashed in from ahead, crisscrossing the waves to converge on *Forty-Nine's* bows. He blinked at the dazzling array. Now he must slow the boat, bring her down to launch speed, so the torpedoes would find their correct depth.

'Twelve knots!'

The boat came down from her bow up plane, instantly, as if they'd stopped. He ran through the procedure. Range . . below fourteen-hundred. Angle on the bow . . on. Aim . . as good as he could achieve under the circumstances.

Baumgartner watched the torpedo boats converging on *Holstein*. His main armament engaged the British destroyers, leaving only his small calibre weapons to tackle these fast moving boats. The sea sparkled under the lurid glow of dancing tracer and starshells hovered, their white lights giving no hiding place, but somehow the boats kept on coming. A gunboat disintegrated in an orange flash as a pair of boats could be seen lining up on his starboard bow. It seemed unbelievable that they could survive that amount of machine-gun fire.

Holstein shuddered to a shell ripping into the bows, and again as another exploded on the main deck.

But Baumgartner couldn't drag his eyes from the two boats. They held their bearing, running in for the kill.

Holloway gave it a few more seconds, ducked below a line of tracer, and pulled the triggers. Two small explosions and the torpedoes launched, plunging ponderously from the tubes, propellers spinning. They splashed heavily into the sea, lunged to the surface and dived to their set depth. Twin tracks appeared briefly, and then as they accelerated to thirty-five knots, he lost them to the dark water. He glanced at his watch.

'Hard-a-starboard,' he snapped; time to get clear. Another glance at his wrist watch, how long? Eight seconds already . . . , nine, ten, eleven . . . . What was the running time? Thirty seconds?

A shell hit the water off the port bow, a column of water thrown high and drenching the bridge, throwing *Forty-Nine* off course.

'Full ahead!' he shouted above the racket, and her remaining two engines lifted the bows clear of the water. At twenty-eight knots they ran for safety.

On *Holstein's* bridge, Baumgartner detected the launch, two torpedoes splashing heavily into the waves.

'Hard right!' he shouted above the din, and clenched his teeth. Twin tracks glistened in the waves, and there could be no mistaking the accuracy. His ship's slow, lumbering turn would never be enough.

Kapitän-zur-See Gerhard Erich Baumgartner took a deep breath and waited for the inevitable. His long career as a naval officer appeared to be ending in ignominious defeat.

Then came the detonation. The torpedo struck *Holstein* forward of the bridge, eight feet below the surface. The five-hundred pound warhead exploded on contact, ripped through the thin steel plate and found the ammunition hold. The concussive impact of high explosive slammed into the storage compartment and set off a chain reaction. *Holstein* erupted in a thunderous roar, an enormous orange fireball rolling skywards, a seething flash of billowing flame.

Holloway turned to look, shielding his eyes, mouth open in amazement.

'My God,' he muttered, 'look at that.'

What remained of *Holstein's* bows sheered off, sinking fast. The entire aft section listed to port, floundering with the inrush of water. A high-pitched shriek of escaping steam rent the air, and from out of the billowing smoke burning men tumbled for the side. The waves smothered their frantic cries for help, flailing arms splashed helplessly and men slipped below the surface. And dominating the awful sight, the fireball rose high above the wrecked ship, growing briefly in size, a turmoil of white, yellow and red flames, curling and boiling in the oxygen rich air.

For a long moment a strange unexpected silence gripped friend and foe alike, the spectacle of a violent end overwhelming the senses.

Thorburn squinted, hiding from the intense glare. The shockwave hit, a blast of scorched air whipping through the bridge space, throat and lungs struggling. He coughed and looked for the German destroyer. It was pushing after *Darrow* and deploying its portside torpedo tubes. The brief cessation of gunfire was ended with warships on both sides bathed in an orange glow, and gunners took advantage.

He wiped his mouth with the back of his hand, how best to make this work to his benefit? The German destroyer slowed into a starboard turn, readying itself for the attack. Thorburn needed *Brackendale's* next move to be significant, a major threat to the enemy's numerical superiority. A forgotten phrase came to the fore, an edict from Nelson to his captains at Trafalgar.

"No Captain can do very wrong if he places his ship alongside that of an enemy." He grinned; that old reckless streak of maverick commander gaining the upper hand. Thorburn stared hard at the German destroyer, turning it over in his mind. Maybe not hull to hull but turn in along the enemy's starboard side, point-blank range.

'Full ahead together!' he snapped at the pipe.

Atkins repeated. 'Full ahead both, aye aye, sir.'

Holstein's glaring fireball faded, and but for a few pockets of flame, darkness returned. *Brackendale's* forward guns banged off another pair of shells and Thorburn saw a corresponding flash on the German's after gun housing.

'Bloody marvellous,' he said to those within earshot, and balanced himself as the ship lifted to the waves. He raised the binoculars to focus on *Darrow*, seemingly oblivious to the threat, but with all guns blazing at a target off the port bow. He trained left and steadied onto an Elbing destroyer, its guns replying shot for shot with *Darrow's* salvoes. *Brackendale* corkscrewed unevenly, and then another starshell burst and lifted the gloom.

Thorburn dropped the glasses, willing his small 'Hunt' to fly. He knew Dawkins would be squeezing the engines for every last drop of power and he tensed as the gap closed.

Holloway flinched to a burst of machine-gun fire and found himself caught in crossfire. An Elbing and an 'R' boat converging from opposite directions, out for revenge. And *Forty-Nine* took a mauling from their firepower. Splinters flew as shells struck the fragile boat.

Seaman Gunner Jenkins screamed in agony as a burst of tracer decimated his gun tub. The twin weapons stopped firing and he collapsed from sight. In the radio compartment, Leading Telegraphist Stoppard died as shrapnel scythed through the wooden hull, ripped his neck and severed the artery. He fell forward onto the small table. Blood pumped across the radio.

Holloway felt the boat shudder under the combined assault of the crossfire. Incendiary rounds fizzed into the foredeck and flames took hold, fanning back across the bridge. A lazy arc of tracer floated in from the port side, and then whipped by the bridge. Gilman crumpled clutching his stomach, doubled over, and Holloway grabbed the wheel. The 'R' boat had closed in on the starboard side and he took evasive action, aiming for a gap between ships and the safety of the dark Channel.

But a thirty-seven millimetre gun opened up from the German boat, smashed *Forty-Nine's* cockpit and battered the bridge into fragments. Two shells hit Holloway simultaneously, tore him from the wheel, and slammed him across the splintered remains.

Ripped apart by the impact, he died as the boat careered headlong into the night, his bloodied torso draped over the shattered screen.

Chapter Twenty-Three . . Forge Ahead

In Dover, on the pavement outside Pendleton's headquarters, Jennifer Farbrace stood rooted to the spot. An awful, distant orange glow lit the night beyond the harbour, and the dull, prolonged rumble of an explosion reached her ears. She involuntarily put a hand to her mouth and glanced up at the pugnacious thrust of the Captain's bearded chin, his eyes lit by the fiery radiance. She saw him make a slight nod, lips pursed, and waited for him to speak. Her breathing came in short gasps behind the hand.

'I do believe that battle is joined,' he growled, and turned his head to meet her eyes. 'Chin up young lady, if anybody knows how to win a fight, Richard's the man.' He looked back at the pulsing light, a faint smile lifting the corners of his mouth.

'Come on, let's get back to business,' and he motioned for her to make a move.

Jennifer turned and walked toward the entrance, fighting back the bile of nausea that had risen to the back of her throat. She swallowed hard and lifted her chin, determined not to let Pendleton see her fear. But she couldn't shake the feeling that Richard was in grave danger.

They entered his office to find a Petty Officer repositioning the models away from the coastline, and he looked over as they appeared.

'Latest situation, sir.'

Pendleton advanced to the table and hovered over the chart, surveying the new configuration, and Jennifer moved round to the far side, holding onto her private thoughts.

The Captain pointed to the increased number of red models, muttering under his breath. 'That second German flotilla has made contact,' he said finally, 'but at least Thorburn has them engaged.'

Jennifer felt her spirits lift, the relief of knowing all was not lost, and she managed a tentative smile. 'Can they really do this, sir?'

Pendleton laughed, a big warm rumble rising from his chest. 'Have faith, young lady. The Royal Navy has overcome much greater odds than these.'

She smiled again, a tremulous attempt at making light of a desperate situation. But the more she looked at the plot, the less confident she felt.

The Petty Officer reappeared. 'Signal from *Cranbrook*, sir. *Holstein* destroyed.'

'Ha!' Pendleton beamed, and slapped a fist into a palm. 'Just as I thought. Pound to a penny we witnessed that ourselves.'

Jennifer Farbrace nodded and passed her tongue over dry lips. One down, but how many more to go?

Twenty-five miles to the north-west of Thorburn's Flotilla, H.M.S. *Trophy* continued her push towards the security of deeper water. *Trophy's* Telegraphist had deciphered enough intercepted signals to indicate a major battle taking place. And Craig Mitchell, leaning against the port side of the bridge, studied the sea to the south, watching the distant array of pyrotechnics with professional curiosity. It was a grim reminder of what a surface action in the dark was all about and he yearned to close in and lend a hand. But the boat now lay at the south-western extremity of his patrol area; any further down channel and he risked being attacked by the Royal Navy, who would have every right to assume they were in the presence of U-boats. So, knowing there was little more that he could do to help, he turned his binoculars across the bows.

A lookout shouted in alarm. 'Sir! Red one-fifty.'

Mitchell spun round ready with his glasses, but stopped to leave them hanging from his neck. He watched in awe as the night sky lit up with a pulsing orange glow. The focus of the detonation lay below the visual horizon and he could only guess at the circumstances. It was certainly an enormous explosion, somewhere in the vicinity of Ostend. Seconds passed as the four men on the bridge stared at the throbbing light, mesmerised by the sight before them.

Then Lieutenant-Commander Mitchell recovered from his astonishment.

'Watch your sectors,' he snapped, reminding them of their responsibilities. He waited for a moment, secure in the knowledge they'd resumed their lookout, and raised his binoculars for one last glimpse. He found the glowing centre and squinted against the brightness, fading even as he watched. He lowered the glasses and shook his head, returning to the fore-bridge. At least *Trophy* had been able to warn others of the German convoy's movements. He again looked across the bows at the dark sea, allowing time for his pupils to adjust from the brightness of the explosion. Foam surged aft along the saddle tanks, curving away to melt into the night, and he steadied himself to raise the binoculars. Beneath his feet *Trophy* pushed on for Harwich and her rendezvous with a Royal

Navy minesweeper assigned to escort them safely into Parkstone Quay. Mitchell relaxed the glasses to his chest and gripped the periscope standard. It had been an intriguing mission and his thoughts turned to the next patrol and where it might take *Trophy* and her crew in the near future. The Mediterranean might make a pleasant change.

What he had failed to see, and what none of the lookouts were able to focus on, was a spherical black object oscillating in the waves, its deadly array of lethal prongs riding the peaks and troughs, primed to catch the unwary.

Fourteen-hundred yards out from the enemy destroyer *Brackendale* forged ahead and Thorburn prepared to engage. This, he thought, was one of those rare moments when a man had to take his chances, make it count. He very deliberately bent to the voice-pipe.

'Starboard thirty!'

'Starboard thirty, aye aye, sir,' came the acknowledgement, and the small 'Hunt' swept into the attack, her wonderful agility coming to the fore. She heeled hard over into the tightest of turns, seawater creaming down her port side. The Battle Ensign crackled, whipping in the wind, heavy spray lifting from the bows.

Below the bridge, the forward guns traversed to port, coming to rest on the enemy's upperworks.

'Midships!' Thorburn called, 'steady as you go.' He breathed out, slowly. Luck was on their side, the German lookouts too intent on *Darrow* to notice a King's Ship closing their starboard beam. At a point blank range of twelve-hundred yards he gave the order.

'Open fire!'

'Shoot!' Carling snapped.

And from fore and aft, *Brackendale's* main armament roared, and a lethal broadside whipped across the intervening divide.

A shell hit the German's wheelhouse, and thirty-five pounds of high explosive incinerated the confined space, the helmsman obliterated, and the destroyer veered wildly off course. A second shell struck simultaneously and detonated on thin armour plating. Men died horribly, shards of steel slicing through fragile flesh.

The German captain, Oberleutnant Heinrich Vogel, decapitated by red hot shrapnel, somersaulted violently across the bridge.

The Officer in charge of torpedoes, feeling the ship swinging off course, fired in desperation. They plunged into the sea in sequential pattern, but he knew it was all a wasted effort.

And *Brackendale's* guns hammered on, battering the enemy warship with everything Carling could throw at it, only the starboard Oerlikons unable to join in.

Thorburn flicked a glance round the bridge, only too aware of the need for vigilance. The lookouts hadn't been distracted, still concentrating on their sectors. And now *Brackendale* was overtaking the German as he slewed uncontrollably away towards *Darrow*. A final flurry of the four-inch guns and *Brackendale* ran clear. The lethal array of torpedoes meant for *Darrow* sped harmlessly out to sea.

Thorburn nodded with satisfaction; he could see the enemy ship had taken a pounding and looked round for another, more urgent target.

'Hard-a-starboard,' he ordered.

'*Cranbrook* signalling, sir.'

Thorburn peered out against the flying tracer and found the glint of a signal lamp.

'What's she saying?'

The Aldis lamp clattered, and he waited.

'Message reads, "No Y gun. No Radar. Ten knots, steering damaged." End of message, sir.'

Thorburn raised his glasses and focussed on *Cranbrook's* silhouette. Through spiralling smoke he could see flames burning where the after-deck gun mounting should have been visible. Now only distorted fragments of twisted steel marked the spot. Abaft the funnel, billowing steam escaped from a gaping hole in the side plates, and the mast had sheered off level with the flag-deck. She was in a sorry state, and there must have been significant casualties.

He turned to Smith. 'Make . . . "Can you reach Dover?" and tell me what she says.'

'Aye aye, sir,' the man said, and Thorburn returned to the needs of *Brackendale*. She was still heeled over on the starboard turn.

The Signaller flashed the query and moments later *Cranbrook's* lamp flickered.

'Message reads, "If ordered," sir.'

Thorburn compressed his lips in a tight smile. That reply showed a commendable reluctance to leave the field of battle and he agreed with the sentiment. But their prime target had been destroyed and he felt that the remains of his Flotilla could yet overcome the rest of the Kriegsmarine's forces. If *Cranbrook* could make it back then better to save the ship and her crew.

'Send . . . "Proceed Dover. Good luck," that's all.'

The lamp shuttered, and in his glasses Thorburn picked out *Cranbrook's* flickered acknowledgement, and then frowned as she turned away. Right or wrong, he'd made a decision, time to move on, and he put it to the back of his mind. *Brackendale* held the hard turn to starboard and it was time to establish a new bearing.

'Midships,' he said to the pipe, and the destroyer regained the upright, ploughing ahead through a torrent of spray, steadying onto the reverse of her previous course. Half a dozen starshells lit the sky and a flurry of multi-coloured tracer zipped back and forth across the sea. Guns stabbed from every direction, plumes of spray lifting as shells thumped the waves. An Elbing appeared through a swirl of smoke to port, firing as it came, and a shell shrieked past amidships.

Lieutenant Carling recognised the new danger, brought the main armament to bear, and once again the gun captains unleashed their weapons. *Brackendale's* full salvo straddled the enemy and Thorburn watched as a red glow flared and died on the enemy's port bow.

'Ship! Green four-oh!' came a shout from Jones, and Thorburn caught sight of the other 'T' class German destroyer deploying for a torpedo strike. He gripped the bridge rail and took a moment to collect his thoughts. To his right, *Cranbrook's* stern was disappearing into the darkness, and further round off *Brackendale's* starboard quarter, *Darrow* was engaging the German warship whose bridge and wheelhouse had been destroyed. And between and around their bigger consorts, the E-boats and Gunboats fought their own private battles, engrossed in the effort to survive. He sifted quickly through his options and let instinct guide his choice.

'Stop engines!'

There was a hesitation from the wheelhouse before he got the reply. 'Stop engines, aye aye, sir.'

Beneath his feet, *Brackendale* lost momentum, her onward rush stilled. As the speed came off he felt the waves pitch her up and down, no longer the sleek driving warship. A salvo from the Elbing plummeted into the sea ahead, in exactly the spot where *Brackendale* would have been, and Thorburn gritted his teeth at the luck. A check on the 'T' boat and he tightened his grip on the handrail.

Wolfgang Schulze had brought his ship into the heart of the action. *Holstein* was gone, there was nothing he could do about its demise, but he could exact revenge on the Royal Navy. And he had his eyes on a particular destroyer, a 'Hunt' that had charged at Vogel and himself when he was about to engage. And it had been Vogel who'd suffered under the guns of the Britisher, the bridge and wheelhouse pounded.

He'd watched as the 'Hunt' turned hard right and reversed course, and had deliberately come round on her starboard side, using his extra speed to close for a strike. All six torpedo tubes now pointed at the British destroyer and with his ship perfectly poised for maximum effect, he gave the order to fire. Raising his binoculars he refocused on the Englander, which at a range of three-thousand metres must surely be doomed.

Too late, he clearly recognised the distant outline of an Elbing from *Holstein's* flotilla attacking the destroyer from her opposite side. He tried rescinding the order to fire but heard the torpedoes launching, splashing down over the side.

And then, unbelievably, the Royal Navy warship slowed and appeared to stop, and Schulze, astonished, cursed angrily. What was the Englander thinking? No one stopped a ship in mid battle, it was unheard of. Or maybe it had suffered engine failure, taken damage. He shook his head with frustration and watched the torpedo tracks head for a target that was no longer there to be hit. The Elbing had become the next available target, the realisation only serving to incense him further, and he slammed a fist onto the bridge screen. How could he have foreseen the Englander stopping? Why did the Elbing not turn after the 'Hunt' and move out of harm's way? It was the worst possible situation and he could do nothing to stop it.

On *Brackendale* a lookout shouted in alarm. 'Torpedoes on the starboard bow!' The forward turret cracked off another salvo and in the midst of the noise Thorburn acknowledged the report.

'I have them,' he said, swallowing to clear his ears. He blinked, dry eyed from cordite smoke, and rubbed his lids. He strained to pick up the track of the nearest torpedo, unsure of their spread, and all the while *Brackendale* drifted to a swaying halt.

'Torpedoes passing ahead, sir,' Jones said, pointing across the port bow, and Thorburn nodded, twisting round to the voice-pipe.

'Half ahead together, twenty knots.' He heard the telegraph ring, echoing up the pipe and felt the kick of power flood through the grating.

'Starboard thirty.' A calmness spread over him as he determined to battle it out, that bloody-minded rebellious streak of old returning to drive him on.

Sub-Lieutenant Kenneth Stokesley had lost track of *Forty-Nine*, too busy battling an E-boat, and in the last exchange of machine-gun fire he'd been stunned as a bullet hit his arm. Shocked by an unimaginable amount of pain, the searing torture of it coursed through his young body. He refused to look at the wound, clamped his teeth to prevent himself from crying out and forced himself to concentrate on the E-boat.

'Port five,' he gasped through the agony, and the Cox'n nudged the wheel left. The boat responded, dodging to port, and Stokesley countered.

'Starboard a little.'

The Cox'n turned the wheel.

'Steady,' he managed to say, and grinned faintly as the alteration proved positive and they intercepted the E-boat on its starboard side. The fore-deck Pompom thumped into action and either side of the bridge the twin Lewis machine-guns hammered, spraying the target, empty shell cases bouncing clear.

The E-boat again returned fire, glowing tracer converging at head height. Stokesley flinched but remained upright, in command.

'Come right . . . steady now, hold her there.'

The boat skipped sideways and then weaved as the Cox'n tugged her back on course across the waves. Bullets smacked the hull and left a row of holes along the side.

Stokesley clung on, weak with pain, willing the gunners to finish it. A massive geyser of spray erupted to starboard and lifted the M.G.B., blinding Stokesley and swamping the bridge.

'Christ!' he muttered aloud, wiping his eyes. If only . . .

A ragged cheer rang out from the Pompom and it vaguely crossed his mind that the German tracer had stopped. He looked again at the E-boat, slowing now and on fire abaft the cockpit. The flames spread quickly, fanned by the forward movement, highlighting three bodies sprawled round the afterdeck guns

The Pompom blasted again, punching holes in the stern along the waterline. The E-boat lost all forward movement and wallowed to a standstill, a floating wreck.

'Port, hard over!' Stokesley urged, and with but a few yards to spare, they powered past on the turn. He immediately began searching for another target. But the loss of blood proved to be too much and he sagged at the knees, unable to shake off the weakness.

'Skipper's hit!' the Cox'n shouted, middling the wheel.

The port Lewis gunner leapt from the tub and Stokesley felt a hand come round his shoulder in support. He accepted the help and the gunner lowered him gently to the deck. He heard the Cox'n call for Petty Officer Dixon, navigator and Second-in-Command. As consciousness slipped away he closed his eyes to the pain.

He'd done his best.

Wolfgang Schulze stood and waited for the inevitable destruction of the Elbing. Any second now, one of his torpedoes would be the catalyst that caused the death of many comrades. Schulze closed his eyes, afraid to look, and a muffled explosion billowed across the waves. He opened them to see the Elbing veering off course, the bows no longer visible, wrecked by the detonation. From forward of the bridge, what remained of the fo'c'sle had become a twisted shell, a tangle of crumpled steel, a gun turret hanging in the void.

He looked away, unable to constrain his anger. The Britisher had out foxed him and he swore.

'Enemy is moving, Herr Kapitän, turning for us,' a lookout called in alarm.

Schulze stared at the destroyer, not wanting to believe his eyes. It was true, the 'Hunt' came round under her own power, accelerating, the bow wave clearly defined.

'Verdammt!' he cursed. 'Come left, bring us round to meet him.' At that moment the last of the starshells faded to leave them in relative darkness, the light of the moon a poor substitute. He made a grab for the bulkhead telephone and the Gunnery Officer answered.

Schulze shouted his orders. 'Off the starboard bow, the British destroyer! Fire!'

'Jawohl, Herr Kapitän!' the man yelled, and the ship's guns blasted out the first salvo.

Chapter Twenty-Four . . The Crash of Guns

Richard Thorburn caught the flash of enemy guns and braced himself. *Brackendale* held her turn, moving quickly right, gathering pace. Water erupted off the port side, fifty yards short. An enemy shell hit the port side abaft the bow compartment, detonating on impact, and Thorburn almost lost his footing. He recovered quickly and tried to guess exactly where the shell had struck, somewhere between the Asdic space and the Cable Locker. Flame belched briefly alongside, then faded to wisps of wind driven smoke, and he hoped the lamp and paint store had escaped the fire. It wouldn't take much for that room to catch alight. He turned his head for a spare body and saw Labatt hunched into the port wing.

'Sub!' he called. 'Get Damage Control to take a look up for'ard, see what they can do.'

'Aye aye, sir,' Labatt answered, and headed for the ladder.

Thorburn watched him go before turning back to the screen, and the forward guns cracked off another pair of shells. The enemy destroyer was coming about, at speed, gunfire rippling along the main deck. But *Brackendale* was giving the German more than enough in reply and he nodded in appreciation of Carling's gunnery. Even without starshell he was finding the target and at less than three-thousand yards the ship's gun crews were making it count.

He lifted the binoculars in readiness to alter course and waited for the right moment.

On the quarterdeck, Lieutenant Patrick Hardcastle stood at the port depth charge thrower with three of his ratings, ready to give a hand whenever he might be called upon. Number One had taken the majority of his crew to tackle a blaze in the gland compartment and with the afterdeck turret shooting over the stern it was prudent to remain to one side, away from the muzzles of the guns.

He spotted Labatt coming along the well deck obviously searching for someone.

'What's up, Sub?'

'Captain wants Mister Armstrong and the Damage Control party up for'ard.'

'He's down in the gland space seeing to a fire.' He turned and gestured to the three ratings to join him. 'C'mon, it's us now.' Running forward along the starboard guardrail, they skirted the motor boat, ducked under the flag deck Oerlikon station and barged their way into the fo'c'sle flats. Two of the seamen switched on their torches, the beams cutting through the black interior. They found the ladder down to the Stokers Mess and pushed ahead into the Provisions room. Eye watering smoke funnelled back from a door to the next compartment, loosely entitled 'Naval Stores' and Hardcastle paused. Above their heads was the crew space where a majority of the seamen lived when off duty, and beyond the storeroom ahead lay the Cable Locker containing the hand forged links of the anchor chains. And that smoke indicated what? Naval stores consisted of a multitude of items for maintaining the ship; spare ropes and lines, canvas, timber props for supports, extra lifebuoys in case of damage, and a number of replacement fenders for coming alongside. Everything he could think of was liable to catch alight . . . , behind that door there might well be a roaring inferno.

He looked at the steel door and reached for the handle. The steel had become hot to the touch and he wished he'd worn gauntlets, but ignoring the heat he forced it open. A blast of flame leapt through the opening, searing his face, burning his eyebrows. He fell back and a rating grabbed him under the arms to pull him clear.

'We have to get in there, put that fire out,' he urged, and coughed violently. He staggered forward but Labatt intervened with an order to one of the ratings.

'Quick, in the Stokers Mess, the fire hose. Get it connected.'

Two of them nodded and turned away, and Hardcastle covered his face with an arm. The heat from the storeroom had become intense, white hot in places, and he feared the worst. Grabbing the open door he slammed it closed, shutting off the heat, and they waited, desperate for water.

It arrived in the form of a canvas hose being rolled along by a rating and a seaman moved to help him, clipping on the tapered nozzle.

'Turn on!' shouted the man, and as water powered from the nozzle, Hardcastle hauled open the door.

Water hit flame and boiled into scalding steam, swirling up and over and round and down, filling the compartment with a dense cloud. They directed the jet of water on the visible heart of a fiery cauldron. But the red heart refused to die and the lead rating holding the nozzle pushed forward through the doorway. The powerful stream found the phosphorescent core, and a secondary explosion engulfed the room.

Hardcastle saw the rating fall, his uniform smouldering, hands blackened, choking in the super heated steam. His mate made a grab for the nozzle, tripped and collapsed, and the power of water in the canvas hose made it whip and snake in the confined space. Labatt threw himself at the nozzle end and trapped it, redirecting the jet into the room.

Hardcastle forced himself through the door and bent to the two ratings, determined to save them from the fire. He caught the ankles of one and dragged him out, leaving him to recover. But the first rating to fall was in a bad way, unconscious and lying prone. He turned him over and grimaced at the burnt face, the charred skin peeling away from raw flesh. Hardcastle reached for his legs and breathed in the toxic fumes, a lethal combination of gases. He gasped for air and with the last of his strength, tugged hard at the man's ankles and succeeded in pulling him halfway to safety, then found he was tangled in a fender line.

Labatt played the hose on the man's head and torso, dousing him with cold water, and Hardcastle held his breath to go back in. He made it to the rating's shoulders, fumbled to free the line from around the left arm but couldn't release it. Eyes streaming, breathing ragged, he tried again and struggled on.

And then came another small explosion, and Hardcastle felt a jarring impact as a shard of steel sliced through his chest. Blood pulsed from the wound, pumping in time with his heart beat, and his head fell forward onto his chest. Light headed, vision blurred he sucked in a lungful of air, and coughed on a throat full of blood.

In that moment Lieutenant Patrick Hardcastle knew he was about to die. He thought briefly of his wife, the children they'd planned, the life they would have lived together. Then slowly, very slowly, he sagged on his knees and toppled over beside the man he'd tried to help. His blood mingled in the water, swilling back and forth, and a blackness descended on the inert figure. Patrick Hardcastle's life had been extinguished.

Labatt fought on and finally brought the entire compartment under control. Ninety percent of the stores had succumbed to the explosion and resultant fire. One rating and one officer had died, and another rating awaited the ministrations of Doc Waverley.

He called for the water to be turned off and surveyed the sodden wreckage of a once carefully itemised and neatly presented storeroom. He dropped the nozzle and made a futile attempt to smarten his uniform, and then retraced his steps to the main deck before clambering up to the bridge. The battle was still very much ongoing and he waited for the skipper to acknowledge his presence. The news he brought wasn't routine but it didn't warrant interrupting a captain's command.

The crash of guns smothered the senses, a pair of shells winging their way towards the enemy. *Brackendale* was hitting hard.

Schulze ducked his head as the ship jolted to an explosion. Shrapnel rattled steel plates, screams of injured men reaching the bridge. Shells whined overhead and the mast's latticework took a glancing blow, severing wires. A blinding flash lit the forward turret, and burning men tumbled out from behind the shield, running frantically from the scalding heat. The muzzle sagged, useless.

'Hard right!' he yelled, unnerved by British accuracy. This head on attack could not be sustained, his ship taking too much punishment. But as they turned to the south shells burst along the port side and Schulze realised he was vulnerable. With empty tubes and no reloads, a third of his firepower destroyed, he knew there could only be one outcome to this madness, and he wasn't yet ready to make the ultimate sacrifice.

'Smoke!' he demanded. 'Make smoke!' His afterdeck guns fired in unison, a futile gesture . . . , and missed, a hurried salvo wasted.

Wolfgang Schulze sighed and cursed, shaking his head in bitter resignation. So much for the Admiral's grandly named 'Operation Triton'. In Schulze's opinion Krause had made a grave error of judgement. Yes, the Royal Navy had taken the bait, but he couldn't believe the tenacity with which they carried out the attack. The Kriegsmarine would be lucky to survive this mayhem. From the stern he heard secondary armament stammer into action, watched tracer disappear out through the smoke at the enemy, and grunted his approval. At least some of his crew knew their duty.

Chapter Twenty-Five . . Cold Fury

A stream of twenty-millimetre shells slammed into *Brackendale's* port wing and the Oerlikon gunner sagged, blood spraying from his neck. The harness held him against the shoulder rests but his loader knew he was dead. He struggled to free the gunner from the bindings, cursing at the fastenings before hauling him roughly to the deck. He slapped on a fresh drum of sixty rounds and grabbed the gun, snugging himself into the curved rests. Pulling the foresight onto the smokescreen he clamped the trigger and let go a fusillade, kept firing until the breech clanged empty. He discarded the empty drum, replaced it with a full one, and again hit the trigger.

Then enemy tracer split the darkness, whining around his ears, ricocheting and tearing into steel. Sweating and cursing, the loader glimpsed the sparkle of machine-gun fire from the enemy's port quarter, aimed for the heart of the flashes, and the gun juddered through his chest. The flashes stopped but he held his aim, pulverising the target into unseen fragments.

When the drum emptied he glanced down at the man he'd known for the best part of two years, two good years of laughter shared, of drinking and whores, narrow escapes and life. All snuffed out in an instance, and he deliberately loaded another canister, settled himself at the gun sight and waited for his opportunity. In the midst of this battle, he wouldn't have long to wait.

Thorburn winced as a shell whipped overhead, fired blind through the smokescreen, but close enough to make him react. He cursed, anger welling inside, and then forced himself to be calm. It would do no good to allow the situation to rule his emotions, a Captain had to remain detached from emotion, retain control, even in the most difficult circumstances. But the memory of the Luftwaffe's unexpected attack on Dover came unbidden, the way Jennifer had almost been killed, and a cold fury settled over him.

'Hard-a-port,' he snapped at the voice-pipe, and *Brackendale* heeled to the helm. He clasped his hands behind his back and braced against the sloping deck, one knee bent to maintain equilibrium. Reaching forward he unhooked a handset.

'Guns?'

'Carling here, sir.'

Thorburn steadied his racing thoughts. 'I'm about to take us into the smokescreen. When the enemy appears it will be at close range, very close. I want all guns concentrated on that ship. Understood?'

'All guns, aye aye, sir.'

'Very well, watch and wait,' Thorburn said, slipped the handset back to its bracket and leaned to the pipe.

'Midships!'

'Midships, aye, sir.'

'Steady as you go.'

'Course is one-nine-five, sir.'

Thorburn waited until *Brackendale* was straight and level. 'Emergency full ahead together!'

'Full ahead both, aye aye, sir!' The repeat was followed by the faint ring of the telegraph, and no longer constrained by any limitations from Dawkins, the ship powered up and thrust her bows into the swirling smoke. Enemy tracer lashed in over the starboard bow, twin arcs, dazzling in the darkness of the dense smoke. A man screamed and someone shouted for assistance, and all the while *Brackendale* careered ahead into a man made fog.

'Keep your eyes peeled,' he called, and emphasised the warning. 'We'll be on top of 'em.'

The smokescreen thickened, a caustic, biting sting to eyes and throat. Men coughed and retched, blinking through tears. Bullets bounced off steelwork, fizzing and whining as they expended energy.

But Thorburn knew they must be drawing closer by the very thickness of that smoke coming off the enemy's stern. And then the first glimpse of something solid, the sheen of steel from across the starboard bow, hidden again by a swirl of smoke. He rubbed at his eyes, desperate to establish a clear contact. The pair of forward guns traversed right, not by much, but pointing out towards that elusive target. Did Carling have a better view?

Brackendale rolled, first to port then to starboard, dipped her stem and rolled back to an even keel, and with that movement, small though it was, Thorburn guessed they were riding the enemy's port side trailing wave. The light of the moon broke through and Thorburn clenched a fist, nails biting into his palm.

There it was.

No more than a cable's length to starboard the German warship appeared from under its own billowing smoke.

'Open fire!' he yelled.

And the guns crashed out their broadside, hurling shells at the Swastika flagged vessel. A deafening crescendo of gunfire reverberated through the little 'Hunt', every sighted weapon joining the fight. A maelstrom of high explosive swept across the dark waters, bullets and missiles finding their mark, bursting with terrible ferocity at such short range. A four-inch shell hit the enemy fo'c'sle plates, penetrated and exploded, a fire raging deep inside.

The Pompom unleashed a torrent of shells, the staccato thump of the four barrels chiming with the noise of the Oerlikons. The main armament roared again, the gun crews working to maximum efficiency, up to twenty rounds a minute each, and all four guns blasting in unison.

On the starboard Oerlikon the loader found a target, German sailors scurrying towards the fo'c'sle.

'Cop this you bastards!' he shouted, and hit the trigger. The gun stammered into life, vibrating to the chatter of its recoil. Twenty millimetre tracer raced through the darkness and he raked the enemy deck, left and right. Bodies tumbled, a man thrown clean over the side. He released the trigger and watched. No one moved, and he looked down at the body at his side in a moment of sorrow.

'That was for you, mate,' he muttered, and braced himself for another target, a furious grimace lining his jaw.

Thorburn grinned amongst the smoke and noise and saw shells detonate on the enemy's bridge. 'Bloody marvellous!' he yelled at the ensuing burst of orange flame. Then to his dismay he caught an unexpected shift in the German's bearing, its port side veering towards *Brackendale*, an attempt at ramming. A collision seemed inevitable unless he acted quickly, and this called for precise control.

'Port thirty,' he barked to the wheelhouse pipe.

Brackendale heeled, turning left away from the enemy's bows. The guns went quiet at the sudden change of direction and Thorburn could clearly see the German's sharply flared stem was about to strike *Brackendale's* trailing starboard quarter. The damage inflicted could be fatal to the ship, he must avoid a collision. Time to wriggle clear.

'Hard-a-starboard!'

The ship swayed upright, leaning wildly to the left, fighting for leverage as she turned in the waves. Thorburn gritted his teeth, watching from the back of the bridge.

And then came the crunching grind of steel as the German's bow caught the stern side plates. Metal squealed under the impact, crushed by momentum, the scraping rasp of hull against hull.

But the turn to starboard was gaining strength, slewing *Brackendale* round, pulling her stern off the sharp prow, breaking free. The after turret moved under Carling's order, aimed at the enemy's upperworks, and settled on the navigating bridge. Twin blasts, both barrels, devastating at such close range, obliterating both men and structure.

Thorburn breathed out through clenched teeth. 'Midships,' he ordered, 'half ahead both, speed ten knots.' He frowned, concerned. Was that a glancing blow or had the side been ruptured? Slowing the ship would give Dawkins a chance to shore the bulkheads, stop any flooding.

But what of the German destroyer? When he turned to look it was peeling away towards the French coast, almost invisible behind its smoking cloak, and Carling still had *Brackendale's* main armament throwing salvos at the fleeing target.

A starshell cracked high overhead and bathed the sea in a harsh glare, and he looked around at the carnage, stunned by what lay before him. E-boats and Gunboats littered the waves, half submerged or upside down. Wreckage of every conceivable shape and size floated past, and here and there a life jacket supporting a man's body on the surface. Of the *Holstein* there was little left to see, the odd flickering embers, oil covered flotsam, barrels and splintered beams. He could just make out the shape of *Darrow* chasing south, her forward guns firing into the distance, but to his way of thinking he felt the battle had run its course. It might be prudent to recall the remnants of his Flotilla.

A bulkhead telephone buzzed. 'Bridge,' he answered.

'Engine room, sir.'

'Go ahead, Chief.'

'It's that starboard collision, sir. There's a fair bit of damage to the side plates and she's leaking water in the tiller flat. I've got a Stoker keeping an eye on it and I'm hoping the pumps'll cope.'

'Right,' Thorburn said, 'let me know if it gets any worse.'

'Aye aye, sir,' Dawkins said, and disconnected. The starshell blinked out and darkness descended once more. The guns banged off another salvo and Thorburn peered out at the fleeing German destroyer, the main body of the ship shrouded in a dense smokescreen. He wasn't about to instigate a chase, not after the Chief's report. So there was little to be gained by continuing the engagement and he bent to a voice-pipe. 'Cease fire, Guns. They've had enough.'

And *Brackendale* lapsed into stillness.

Wolfgang Schulze lay propped against the wireless room partition. Blood seeped from a bandage round his head and the wound throbbed painfully. But Schulze still had his wits about him, and one thing was startlingly clear. He knew Krause would be looking for a scapegoat and he needed to make certain the blame did not attach itself to him. If anything he must elaborate on Baumgartner's failure to comply with procedure. Instead of tactically slipping away from battle the man had actually turned to fight. From that point on the ambush had failed and *Holstein* had sealed its own death warrant. It was no fault of his that Baumgartner had chosen to disobey orders.

He smiled through the pain. His own withdrawal could be explained away as a tactical manoeuvre. There would be more than enough witnesses to substantiate his report.

Leading Seaman Allun Jones called from the port wing. 'Sir, one of our Gunboats. Looks like she's sinking.'

Thorburn stepped across and looked towards the port bow. What was left of the moonlight showed the boat wallowing in the waves, with the crew gathered precariously on the up tilted bridge and foredeck. He squinted, rubbing his jaw, and looked around for other boats. There were none close by so it became an easy decision to make.

'Stop engines.'

'Stop engines, aye, sir.'

Brackendale slowed, drifting forward and drawing the Gunboat closer. There was a bump as the steel bows caught the half submerged remains, and it dragged along the plates until it arrived level with the boat deck. He watched Armstrong take charge, nets going over the side, and Doc Waverley appeared with a sick berth attendant.

'The skipper's in a bad way!' came a shout from the boat.

'We'll have him up first then,' Armstrong called. 'Bring him nearer.'

Thorburn looked away, the base of his scalp tingling at the chance of an unseen threat. After what seemed an inordinate amount of time, the noise of men clambering aboard or being helped over the side fell away to silence and he glanced at the boat deck.

Armstrong waved vigorously in the gloom. 'All aboard, sir,' he called in what seemed a very loud voice, and Thorburn bent to the wheelhouse pipe.

'Half ahead, revs for ten knots.'

And below the waterline in the confines of the engine room, Bryn Dawkins obeyed the telegraph, releasing pent up steam from the boilers to drive the turbines, and once again propel *Brackendale* on her way.

On the bridge, Thorburn shivered; lying stopped in open waters was not something to recommend.

Armstrong came up and stood by him at the bridge-screen. 'Doc's giving them the once over, sir.'

'Good,' Thorburn said, and *Brackendale* twisted gently beneath their feet. He turned to his First Lieutenant. 'I'm calling it off, Robert. I think the German's have had their fill.'

Armstrong met his gaze. 'You'll not get any argument from me, sir.'

Thorburn smiled. 'In that case, get the wireless room to call *Darrow*, tell them to break off and rendezvous here. We'll wait and round up the power boats.' He looked out at the dark waters. 'What's left of them anyway.'

It took the best part of forty minutes to gather in the scattered remnants of the Flotilla and to establish who could make it home and who needed help. With the aid of searchlights, a few sailors were recovered from the waves, some immediately passed up to *Darrow* or *Brackendale* for urgent medical care by the surgeons.

By the time all was ready, the moon had slipped far to the west and faded behind a bank of clouds.

Much later, in the first pale light of dawn, Richard Thorburn stood in the starboard wing of *Brackendale's* bridge and watched his small Flotilla pushing on for the Kent coast. A mile ahead, and listing heavily to port, *Cranbrook* yawed erratically as she tried to maintain some semblance of steering for Dover's eastern entrance. A half-mile off Thorburn's bow, of the seven wooden hulled boats that had taken passage with the 'Hunts', only four were making their way home, casualties amongst their crews making for a long list. One of those returning boats had lost all power and had been forced to take a tow.

Darrow had taken station over on *Brackendale's* port bow and as the light of day revealed, had been well and truly mauled by enemy gunfire. But her Battle Ensign flew proudly from the masthead, a triumphant display of victory, and Thorburn felt the tug of a sympathetic smile. He too had refused to take down *Brackendale's* Ensign, and above his head abaft the bridge, the ragged flag snapped and crackled in the breeze.

The ship twisted with the swell and he watched the small boats riding the waves, undulating through the rippling seas. He'd very deliberately stationed himself astern of the procession to escort the 'little ones' home, after all, if it hadn't been for their courage, *Holstein* might still be at large on the high seas.

'Permission to come on the bridge, sir?'

Thorburn turned to stare at the slight figure in a man's uniform, and smiled.

'You're very welcome, Mister Stokesley. How's the arm?'

'A bit sore, sir, but your Doc Waverley said to give it a month and it'll be as good as new.'

'Marvellous,' Thorburn said, 'now what can I do for you?'

Stokesley stepped forward and although his arm was wrapped in a sling, came smartly to attention.

'I wanted to thank you for stopping to take us aboard.'

Thorburn swallowed, slightly taken aback by the young officer's gratitude. Stokesley's boat had been all but sunk and the least he could do was stop to help. He grinned to cover his embarrassment. 'Well, I didn't think you'd make it back by swimming, thought I'd better lend a hand.'

Stokesley's innocent face softened into a smile. 'Even so, sir, I'll not forget what you did for my crew. We owe you our lives.'

Thorburn coughed and cleared his throat. 'Nonsense,' he said gruffly, 'now I suggest you get below and rest. I've a few things to tend to.'

'Of course, sir. Didn't mean to take up your time,' and with that he wheeled away, and Thorburn watched him go, the smile returning. Stokesley had all the qualities to become a fine officer, good prospects of promotion, if only the dangerous pursuit of skippering a Gunboat let him live long enough.

He turned to the forebridge and gripped the rail, watching intently as *Cranbrook* once again veered awkwardly off bearing.

'Number One?' he called, 'we'll go alongside *Cranbrook*, see what we can do to assist. Have the Special Sea Dutymen stand by.'

'Aye aye, sir,' Armstrong said, and the pipe went out on the tannoy.

'Special Sea Duty men close up. Prepare for ship alongside.'

Thorburn moved to the compass platform and positioned himself at the binnacle.

'I have the bridge, Pilot.'

'Aye aye, sir,' Martin said, and stepped down to the chart table.

'Revs for sixteen knots,' Thorburn ordered to the wheelhouse pipe and looked ahead to where *Cranbrook* weaved uneasily from port to starboard.

'Speed sixteen knots, sir,' came the repeat from the pipe, and he checked the compass.

'Steer two-six-oh degrees,' he said, and looked round the crowded bridge. He found his signaller.

'Smith, signal *Darrow* to take my station,' he called, and seconds later the Aldis lamp chattered as the man called her up.

'*Darrow* acknowledges, sir.'

'Very well. Now make to *Cranbrook*, "Will close your port side." That'll do for now.'

'Aye aye, sir,' Smith said, and again the light flickered under his hands.

Thorburn saw that *Darrow* had slowed to allow *Brackendale* through, and at the same time *Cranbrook's* lamp flickered in response.

Smith talked it through. 'From *Cranbrook*, sir. "Cannot maintain course. Suggest you stay well clear of port side." Message ends, sir.'

'Acknowledge,' Thorburn confirmed, and continued to watch while *Brackendale* closed the gap. Finally they were less than a hundred and fifty feet clear and broadside on to the damaged Hunt's port side. He estimated her to be steaming at no more than six knots and adjusted speed to suit.

Lieutenant-Commander Roger Sullivan, the tough Yorkshireman, appeared on the port wing, a blood stained bandage round his head.

Thorburn cupped his hands. 'Can we do anything to help?' he called.

Sullivan shook his head and shouted in return. 'No, I think we'll make it. The Chief Engineer has worked bloody miracles.'

Thorburn paused, taking in the extensive amount of battle damage, hoping Sullivan was correct.

He called again. 'We'll be standing by if you need us.'

Sullivan waved a hand. 'Thank you!'

Cranbrook tugged to starboard and the gap widened, and Thorburn gave the order for *Brackendale* to stand off on the ship's port quarter. If needed they'd be alongside in minutes. Through his binoculars, Dover Castle appeared from the skeins of misty fog and he estimated it would be another hour before they entered harbour.

Lieutenant Robert Armstrong came to the bridge and leaned on the screen. Thorburn felt his eyes and looked sideways.

'What?' he asked.

Armstrong raised a sardonic eyebrow and tilted his head. 'Remember that signal about half the German navy at sea?'

Thorburn collected his thoughts, remembering the message. 'Yes . . . ?'

'Seems to me it wasn't too far from the truth, at least that's how it feels now. Certainly one or two more than we were led to expect.'

Thorburn grinned at the quiet understatement. 'That, Number One, is what's known as, don't let 'em know too much.' He mimicked a very old, very senior officer; 'not good for morale, eh what?'

Armstrong laughed and looked out over the bows. 'Mmm . . . , something about, "don't frighten the sheep" comes to mind.'

'Exactly that,' Thorburn agreed, and they lapsed into silence, watching the sea and a battle scarred flotilla about to enter harbour.

Jennifer Farbrace yawned behind her hand, it had been a long night. In the quiet of the cellar, the insistent ring of the telephone broke the stillness and she reached for the receiver.

'Captain Pendleton's office.'

'Harbour watch, ma'am. *Brackendale* approaching from the southeast.'

She closed her eyes for a moment, relief surging through her body, then remembered the need for her official response.

'Thank you, and the remainder of the flotilla?'

'Hard to say, ma'am. Those I can see look a bit worse for wear.'

'Alright, I'll inform Captain (D).' She slowly replaced the handset and came to her feet. The wound to her neck gave a sharp reminder that it was not yet healed, but she immediately forgot the discomfort, thinking instead of the many casualties that would have been inflicted on the men in those ships.

She smoothed her skirt into place, checked her appearance in the mirror of her powder compact, and refreshed her lipstick. The puffiness under her eyes couldn't be helped, the strain of waiting for news leaving its mark.

The Captain's door stood ajar so she knocked and entered. He stood at the chart table, eyes fixed on the model ships, most of which now seemed scattered to the four corners of compass.

'*Brackendale's* arriving, sir,' she volunteered.

'Yes,' he said, distracted by something in front of him. 'I fear we've sustained significant losses.'

Jennifer frowned before replying. 'The harbour watch reported no major casualties, sir.'

He looked up, surprise registering on the bearded face.

'Really? You realise we've not heard from *Cranbrook*?'

'Surely *Brackendale* has signalled, sir?'

The Captain shook his head. 'That's the rub, she hasn't signalled either.'

There was a cough at the door and a Telegraphist stood waiting.

'What now?' Pendleton asked wearily.

'Message from your lookout, sir. *Brackendale, Cranbrook* and *Darrow* sighted. *Cranbrook* is listing heavily and down by the head. *Brackendale* appears to be close alongside.'

Jennifer peered at the Captain's bearded face. That message had come from his personal watchkeeper perched high over the cliffs to the east of the castle, a precaution he'd instigated as soon as regaining command as Captain (D). He must have felt her looking and glanced at her, eyes glinting with satisfaction.

'Never doubted it,' he said with a broad grin, an eyebrow raised, daring her to say otherwise.

She smiled secretively, a private gesture between the two of them. 'No, of course not, sir,' she said, and dismissed the Telegraphist with a nod. She watched Pendleton cross the room and retrieve his gold braided cap from the desk, placing it squarely over his forehead. He motioned towards the door.

'Ladies first, let's go and see to their homecoming.'

On the far side of the Channel in the gently undulating countryside of Dunkirk's hinterland, Paul Wingham prepared to bid farewell to Marianne. The village of Armbouts-Cappel had not yet fully woken from slumber, the quiet dawn brightening beneath a layer of grey cloud. Together they walked slowly towards a gate in the white picket fence.

'Will you go back to Dieppe?' he asked.

'Probably, unless Bainbridge decides on somewhere else.'

He smiled and nodded, reaching to open the gate. 'I'm for the coast, back to England. It's all arranged.'

They stood for a moment and looked out over a meadow dotted with red and gold flower heads.

'I wonder,' he asked thoughtfully, 'if we managed to make a difference?'

She met his eyes and slipped a hand into his. 'Of course we did, Paul. You must never doubt what we do.' She came close, voice lowered. 'Everything makes a difference, always. We have to believe that.'

Wingham shrugged. She could be very naïve at times, but it didn't distract from her sense of patriotism. He pulled her in and brushed her lips with his. They parted and stared knowingly into each others eyes. This might be the last time for both of them.

'Look after yourself, Marianne, and be careful around the Boche. They are ruthless when woken.'

'I will,' she said lightly. 'May the angels watch over you, Paul Wingham.'

He nodded and caressed her cheek with his fingers. 'You too,' he said, and stepped out onto the rutted farm track.

Without turning to look back he strode off for his prearranged rendezvous with the local resistance.

Chapter Twenty-Six . . A Simple Truth

Captain James Pendleton made his way out into the grey light of an overcast day, turned left on the pavement and hurried towards the Eastern Arm, the breakwater that stretched out to sea like a disjointed finger from the base of the cliffs. Weaving round a barbed wire entanglement he paused while a sentry checked their identity, and then led them on between two anti-aircraft gun emplacements. It was another fifty yards before he slowed to look round at Jennifer.

He waited while she caught up, made a determined effort to be more considerate and not lengthen his stride, and threaded his way past a heavy gun battery and its oversize searchlight. The khaki uniformed gunners huddled over a large pot of tea and glanced up at the high ranking officer with the elegant woman at his side. Their Corporal snapped up a late salute and turned back to the steaming tea.

Picking his way forward, Pendleton became so intent on not missing his footing on the uneven surface, Jennifer's call took him by surprise.

'Sir! To your left, south-east.'

He looked up and stepped over to the low parapet. There against the brighter horizon he found the low outline of three 'Hunts', a pair of funnels close abreast and a solitary escort out to sea. At this range there was no sign of the M.T.B.s or the Gunboats, and without binoculars it would be a while before they showed up.

Jennifer's footsteps came close and he offered her a broad smile while waving an expansive hand in the direction of the warships.

'There, young lady, you see the victors of that battle. The conquering heroes returned home to a silent welcome.'

'Yes, sir,' was all she said in reply, and the Captain decided to lift her mood.

'Right,' he said forcefully, and pointed to where the breakwater ended at the entrance to the harbour.

'We'll go and wave them in, you'll be able to see for yourself.'

Jennifer's eyes turned to him and he saw her smile, a little faint-hearted, but her first proper smile in hours.

'I'd like that, sir . . . , I'd like it a lot.'

He clapped his hands. 'Good, then let's get on with it.'

Together this time, they walked off towards the final section of the Eastern Arm's defences, a concrete Observation Post purpose built to house the spotters for the harbour's anti-aircraft defences. Hurrying was out of the question, each cautious step determined by the neglected state of the war ravaged surface. Here and there, repairs underfoot were sound enough to quicken their pace, and having skirted another five sandbagged guns they eventually climbed to the flat roof of the building.

And so they stood, side by side, the old bearded Captain and the young Wren officer, waiting for the ships to enter harbour.

Leading Seaman Allun Jones, binoculars raised towards Dover's harbour mouth, called round to the captain.

'Tug coming out, sir.'

Thorburn looked up from the chart table and found the squat, chunky shape of the harbour tug butting clear of the southern breakwater and turning to meet them. For the first time in a long while he turned away from the bridge-screen and sagged into his chair. It was over, they'd made it. The hastily thrown together Flotilla and the men who crewed the ships, victors in battle, survivors. They were back.

At Marine-Oberkommando Nordsee in Wilhelmshaven a message arrived detailing the catastrophic failure of Operation Triton. Shortly thereafter Großadmiral Erich Raeder called the Communications Room and demanded to speak with Admiral Krause. He was left in no doubt that his career hung in the balance. Hitler had apparently thrown a tantrum and swore he would relegate the surface fleet into 'cargo carriers'. Worse followed when he instructed the Kriegsmarine to redirect all resources now allocated to ship building and place those resources in the hands of Admiral Dönitz, Commander in Chief of the U-boat arm.

A crestfallen Krause apologised profusely and promised to find an explanation for the failure. He made a few hurried calls and discovered the defeated remnants of the two flotillas licking their wounds in the harbour at Ostend. He was informed that the most senior surviving officer was Korvettenkapitän Wolfgang Schulze.

Krause gave the order for Schulze to be arrested for 'cowardice in the face of the enemy' and once arrested, the man should be executed by firing squad forthwith.

Korvettenkapitän Wolfgang Schulze died in a small courtyard, stripped of his regalia, blindfolded and tied to a wooden stake. Six bullets found their mark.

Standing with Pendleton on the end of the Eastern Arm, Jennifer watched in silence as the tug came past the end of the breakwater, the towing cable stretched taut to *Cranbrook's* bullseye. The Hunt sat low in the water and what struck her most was the amount of damage to the bridge and forward gun turret.

Slowly, inch by inch, *Cranbrook* squeezed through the entrance, with whatever had happened to her steering forcing the ship to crab sideways. Scorched and blackened she finally limped into harbour and the tug gently pulled her across towards Admiralty Pier.

Jennifer fought to hold back tears, saddened by the sight of so much destruction. *Darrow* came next, pushing through under her own steam, clear evidence of the battle's ferocity disfiguring her upperworks.

Lieutenant-Commander Hudson must have seen Pendleton's 'scrambled egg' and acknowledged him with a salute, promptly returned, and then continued to concentrate on conning the ship to a mooring.

And now it was the turn of the little boats, just four of them in all, the last of which, an M.T.B., had managed to a hitch a tow from a Gunboat. The M.G.B. didn't look much better off herself, tell-tale signs of damage all over the foredeck.

Eventually, it was *Brackendale's* turn to enter harbour and Jennifer straightened, dashing a tear from her cheek. The last thing she wanted was for Richard to see her weakness. This was men's work and not the time for a woman's sensitivity.

Pendleton cleared his throat, twice, before saying, 'She's taken a beating.'

She could only nod, a lump in her throat, not trusting herself to speak. From stem to stern the destroyer's hull had been pock-marked with bullet holes. Daylight glinted through jagged holes in her fo'c'sle, what must be the visible evidence of near misses. She peered up at the bridge, and again the evidence of battle could be seen. The wheelhouse below looked a shambles but she detected someone's face steering the ship. Her eyes swept the fore-bridge looking for Richard's familiar figure, and the fact he didn't appear to be up there only made matters worse. What had happened to him? She spotted Lieutenant Armstrong leaning over the starboard wing, watching the end of the breakwater as the ship approached, but still no sign of Richard. Her legs felt weak, her heart thumping with anguish. Surely he was still in command.

A movement caught her attention, the top of a peaked cap near the port corner of the bridge. And then the figure straightened into full view and her heart leapt. Richard Thorburn stood there, head and shoulders above the splintered screen and talking to someone behind him.

Pendleton interrupted the moment. 'God Almighty! Look at the damage to her starboard quarter.'

Jennifer wrenched her eyes from the bridge to take in *Brackendale's* stern section. The side plates adjacent to the rear gun mount had been buckled and stove in, the guardrail missing for seven or eight feet, and in the centre of the damage a vertical hollow had been scored into the deck. She switched her gaze back to the bridge. Richard was too preoccupied with running the ship to notice the two figures standing below on the Observation Post, but she no longer cared. He was alive, and that was enough.

And she must never let him know she'd suffered; better for him to carry on believing it was just a light hearted relationship than become pressured into thinking he ought somehow make it more permanent.

The small destroyer made it into the safety of Dover harbour and Pendleton turned away.

'We should get back, young lady. Nothing we can do here.'

'Yes, sir,' she said. 'And thank you, sir, I'm glad I was here to see it.'

He stopped and fixed her with a long look. 'You of all people Miss Farbrace, are most welcome. It was the least I could do . . . , and anyway, I wouldn't have missed it for the world.' His face softened, the eyes smiling above the beard, and against all convention Jennifer was moved to touch his arm. She swallowed, unable to find the words.

'It's okay,' he said gruffly. 'I understand.'

She nodded and followed him down the concrete stairway. Once or twice, as they retraced their steps along the breakwater, she glanced across at Richard's ship, now mooring up mid harbour, shore-side of the old rusting freighter. She looked again at the big merchantman, it was still there, and it dawned on her that what had seemed such a long period of time had in fact been but a short interval, too soon for the cargo vessel to have found passage with another convoy.

Jennifer Farbrace shook her head in wonder and followed the Captain onto terra firma.

At lunchtime in *Brackendale's* wardroom, Thorburn sat with his officers as they consumed a cold meal. A vacant seat made for a sombre mood, a reminder of Hardcastle's death. In the background the radio played a variety of light music, finally interrupted by an announcer with the one o'clock news.

George Labatt reached round and turned up the volume.

"This is the BBC, home news," said the voice. "The Admiralty reports that in the early hours of this morning, a small flotilla of Royal Navy warships engaged with a large German force off the coast of Ostend. In a short but fierce skirmish an Armed Raider was destroyed and the remaining German warships suffered considerable damage. Casualties amongst British ships was said to be light. Abroad now, and in the Mediterranean, Malta continues to withstand . . . ." The news reader droned on and Thorburn leaned back with a wry smile. 'If that was a bloody skirmish, God knows what they call a battle.'

Armstrong nodded, tickling a tea leaf from his cup. 'I think, sir,' he said, choosing his words carefully, 'that a battle is described as, a significant engagement.'

Thorburn took a last mouthful of cold sausage and placed his knife and fork neatly together to signify he'd finished. 'Yes,' he said, allowing a severe frown to wrinkle the corner of his eyes. 'I suppose they'd use that for battleships and cruisers. It wouldn't do for little shrimps like us, would it?' And he broke the frown with a broad grin.

Smiles of agreement met his attempt at lifting the mood, and as he lit a cigarette the wardroom relaxed into a chatter of animated conversation. Hardcastle had not been forgotten, but for a time they could live with his absence.

It was seven o'clock that evening when Thorburn answered a knock on his cabin door. 'Come.'

The solid weathered face of Chief Petty Officer Barry Falconer appeared, and he took a tentative pace inside the cabin.. A sling supported his left arm and Thorburn grinned at the unbuttoned jacket. He knew the man's ribs were also encased in three layers of bandages.

'Harbour launch is coming alongside, sir.'

Thorburn leaned back from the desk, gratefully dropped his pen and grinned.

'How's the chest, Cox'n?'

'Fine, sir, as long as I don't laugh, cough or sneeze.'

'In that case,' Thorburn said, stifling a laugh, 'I'll be on my way before I say the wrong thing.'

The Cox'n nodded his thanks, eyes smiling, and retreated from the room. For a moment Thorburn looked at the door after him. He was glad Falconer was back on his feet. In wartime nobody was indispensable, but of all the men under his command, the Cox'n would be hard to replace.

Minutes later he clambered down the Jacob 's ladder and dropped into the waist of the harbour launch. The sun had finally broken through the cloud cover and now the waters of the harbour sparkled under the warming rays. A signal requesting his presence at Pendleton's office had been received shortly after the dead and injured had been transferred to shore, and by lunch time he'd completed a thorough inspection of *Brackendale's* damage. Following the meal in the wardroom he'd hastily compiled a report on the operational details of the mission, been presented with a long list of repairs which concluded with the Chief's verdict on the ship's seaworthiness, and eventually drew breath and stuffed them inside his briefcase.

As the boat turned for Granville Dock he looked back at *Brackendale* and shook his head. The majority of the damage was superficial. Only the point of collision would require dockyard refurbishment and it was likely the ship's company were about to take a lengthy, well earned leave. He smiled grimly to himself and wondered if he might prevail upon the authorities to have the ship fitted with that long overdue radar installation.

Across the harbour, temporarily supported alongside Admiralty Pier, he could see a number of civilians clambering over *Cranbrook's* decks and he guessed they'd been sent from Chatham to give her the once over. As far as *Darrow* was concerned, he suspected she too would also undergo repairs in the Royal Dockyard.

The feathering of the throttle made him look ahead, and the harbour launch slid neatly into the inner basin before being manoeuvred up to her berth.

Briefcase in hand, Thorburn climbed from the boat and headed for the Captain's headquarters.

At the sandbagged entrance, he returned the solitary guard's salute and stepped into the relative darkness of the hallway. It seemed busy, with an inordinate amount of superfluous other ranks, and he hurried through the throng and escaped down to the cellar. Except for the clatter of typewriters all was quiet, and his footsteps echoed in the corridor. He noticed Jennifer's door was closed, hesitated as to whether he should knock and disturb her, thought better of it and instead knocked loudly on the door marked Captain (D). Tired though he was, he straightened his shoulders and attempted to look the part. Debriefs were not really his cup of tea, drawn out affairs with too many questions and not always blessed with decisive answers.

The gruff, deep voice answered. 'Come.'

Touching the door, it swung in and he stopped in surprise. Pendleton stood behind his desk, as he'd expected, but standing at the end was the authoritative figure of Commodore Lawrence T. Collingwood, puffing vigorously at his pipe. He waved away the smoke and gestured at a chair.

'Come and sit, Commander.'

Thorburn felt a movement from behind and Jennifer brushed past to take her place at the desk. He stepped forward to the chair and slowly eased down onto the seat, very aware of being under observation. He lifted the briefcase and flicked a catch.

'Leave that,' Pendleton said shortly, 'I can read all that later.'

Collingwood nodded, puffed some more and tamped down the glowing embers. He perched himself on the corner of the desk and jabbed the stem of the pipe at Thorburn.

'All we want at the moment is your appreciation of how things went.'

Thorburn hesitated, tight lipped, and glanced at Pendleton who gave him a reassuring nod.

'Well, sir . . . , given the circumstances I though the Flotilla carried out your orders, and more specifically my tactics, with a high degree of professionalism. The coordination between *Cranbrook*, *Darrow* and the boats was, in my opinion, exemplary. The torpedo boats pressed home their attacks in the face of overwhelming odds and I've took a report from Sub-Lieutenant Stokesley that it was Lieutenant Holloway who torpedoed *Holstein*.'

'Yes,' Collingwood said, 'and lost his life in the process.'

Thorburn lowered his head, remembering the mayhem, and then wondered if the statement was an implied criticism of his actions.

'Yes, sir,' he said simply.

Pendleton moved across behind Jennifer and peered over her shoulder at the notes. He turned slowly, pondering, and wandered back behind the desk. Thorburn felt his gaze.

'And you, Richard, how do you think *Brackendale* performed?'

'With a great deal more luck than judgement, sir. My plan had been for *Brackendale* to run inshore on contact and take *Holstein* from the port side, splitting the enemy firepower. But we were jumped by that second German flotilla. Luckily one of my lookouts raised a timely alarm and we managed to turn and engage. My gunnery officer can take a lot of credit for turning the tables.'

He saw Pendleton take a swift look at the Commodore, who then asked a question of his own.

'Do you not think it might have been better to hold your force as a single division?'

Thorburn tensed, not liking where this was headed. But he knew in his own mind the decision to split his forces had been correct at the time. He met Collingwood's inquisitive stare and shook his head.

'No, sir, I don't. And given similar circumstances I would make the same choice again.'

The Commodore sat in silence and Thorburn guessed his answer was not what the man wanted to hear, but he remained convinced his strategy had been a good one.

Collingwood came to his feet and very deliberately clamped the stem of his pipe between his teeth. Slowly, he drew back both hands and clapped them solidly together, and then again, and again.

'Well said,' he nodded, by now grinning broadly while continuing to clap. Pendleton too joined in by banging the top of the desk.

Thorburn looked from one to the other, then at Jennifer who couldn't contain the pleasure showing on her face. He blushed, uncomfortable, embarrassed.

Collingwood removed his pipe, tapped it into the marble ashtray, and walked forward, hand outstretched. Thorburn stood to meet him.

'I somehow doubt there was much luck in your judgement, or in those decisions.' He released the handshake and the smile faded into a thoughtful frown.

'You know, Commander,' he said slowly, the blue eyes glinting. 'We in the Service respect long held traditions. We toast the King, salute the White Ensign, and remember gallant ships of the line. But above all else we salute the backbone of the Navy, the small ship we call a destroyer, a man-of-war.' He glanced up at Jennifer, sideways at Pendleton.

'Sometimes we forget a simple truth, that he who commands a King's ship, who devotes himself to the cause of battle . . . , he too is a man of war.' He stepped back and picked up his cap, and Thorburn felt the full force of Collingwood's searching gaze.

'I wish you good luck for the future, Commander. There may well come a time when I call on you again.'

And with that, he nodded courteously to Jennifer, touched his cap to Pendleton, and walked out.

Thorburn sank down onto his chair and looked sheepishly at the floor, not wanting to look up. It was Pendleton who thankfully broke the silence.

'Right then, time you got some shut eye. I've arranged for you and *Darrow* to undergo repairs at Chatham. *Cranbrook* will be pumped out and towed across in the next few days. Any questions?'

Thorburn's mind returned to the battle, to the torpedo boats and Holloway's sacrifice, amongst others.

'I'd like to put forward some names that deserve special recognition. Can it wait awhile?'

Pendleton rubbed his hands together, a visible show of business as usual.

'Of course, m'boy, take all the time you need. Now, if you'll deposit your reports with Miss Farbrace, we'll talk again tomorrow.'

Thorburn delved inside the briefcase, handed over the file, and Jennifer stood to leave for her office.

Pendleton stepped closer and placed a hand on Thorburn's shoulder.

'Well done, Richard, that was a damned fine effort. I know there were many who didn't make it, but we all take our chances. If it's any consolation, their sacrifice will have saved a lot of ships.'

Thorburn stared at him. There were times when Pendleton was hard nosed, ruthless if he had to be. And then there were moments when Thorburn managed to see beneath the tough façade, to the man beneath, the real person with thoughts and emotions. That's why the Captain had earned his loyalty, and Thorburn nodded.

'Yes, sir.' There wasn't much else he could say. He turned and followed Jennifer out to the corridor and into her office. She dropped his report on the desk, closed the door and came to him. He folded her in his arms. The kiss lingered and he allowed himself the soft luxury of her fragrance, the sensuous touch of her lips. She clung to him, arms tight round his neck, then slowly pulled away, eyes searching his.

'I was afraid you weren't coming back.'

Thorburn winked, gave her a small smile. 'I'm not that easy to get rid of.'

Jennifer pouted, screwed up her nose and punched his arm. 'That's not what I meant.'

He grinned and reached for her hands. 'Remember me asking you out for a drink?'

She laughed lightly, fluttering her eyelashes. 'I do, kind sir, but the war somehow got in the way.'

'Well what about now, that's if you feel up to it?'

Jennifer looked down at herself and smoothed her skirt, then touched the bandage on her neck.

'Are you sure? I must look awful, and I only managed a few hours sleep today.' She looked at him pointedly. '*You* kept us awake last night.'

'Oh, sorry,' he said, trying to keep a straight face. 'Somebody'll have to tell the Germans to play in daylight.' He straightened his cap and reached beyond her to open the door.

Jennifer hesitated and inclined her head towards Pendleton's office. 'I'll have to let him know.'

Thorburn peeled back his cuff and tapped the face of his wristwatch.

'I think, Miss Farbrace,' he said with controlled emphasis, 'that your spell in the office is well and truly over. By a couple of hours if I'm not mistaken?'

She shrugged in resignation, and then with a giggle, curtsied and lowered her head.'

'Lead on then, kind sir. Where will you take this poor maiden?'

'Out of here for starters,' he said, and bowed from the waist, sweeping a hand towards the corridor. 'Ladies first.' And together they walked up and out into the evening sun.

He took a few paces and stopped, suddenly at a loss as to where they might go.

'Men!' she said, shaking her head. 'You haven't got a clue, have you?' She pointed towards the Castle and the snake of road leading upwards. 'There's a small Inn up there on the lower slopes. It's run by a widow and she keeps a well stocked bar.' She tapped the side of her nose. 'For the right people, that is.'

'How far?' he asked.

'Ten minute walk,' she said, and strode off along the pavement.

For a long moment he stood and watched her from behind, admiring her elegant poise, that effortless, graceful sway of hips. He knew he should be feeling tired, but had somehow gained a second wind. In spite of everything, he grinned and hurried to catch her. After all, it was his idea.

In Pendleton's office the telephone rang. He reached forward across the desk and put the receiver to his ear. 'Yes?'

He listened intently while the voice on the other end imparted the information, and then, having thanked them for the news, slowly clicked the handset back onto the cradle.

The Captain leaned back in his chair and extracted a cigarette form the packet of Senior Service. Very deliberately he struck a match and brought the flame to the tip, and inhaled deeply. Stroking his beard, deep in thought, he allowed a trickle of blue smoke to fall from his lips.

It had been a very bland message from Captain of Submarines at Parkstone Quay in Harwich. H.M.S. *Trophy* had not been contacted since sinking a U-boat shortly after midnight. She'd not made the rendezvous with her escort for entering harbour, and in the absence of any further communiqué, was 'presumed lost'.

James Pendleton smoked his cigarette and thought it over. No reason to tell Thorburn. There was nothing to be gained in the short term, he'd find out soon enough. He reached down to the desk cupboard, found a bottle of brandy and a tumbler, and poured himself a good double. Silently, he raised the glass in toast and drank to *Trophy's* memory.

Thorburn ushered Jennifer out from the bar and through to a rear door. They sat themselves on a wrought iron bench in the back garden and nursed a couple of gins. The alcohol worked its magic and her head rested contentedly against his shoulder. A golden orb hung low in the sky and silhouetted a few dark clouds with a blaze of pink, and he raised a hand to shield his eyes from the glare. From up here on the slopes he could clearly make out the harbour nestled inside the breakwaters, and it was easy to pick out the distinctive shape of *Brackendale* swinging to her mooring.

He felt Jennifer move, and she too raised a hand to squint at the harbour.

'What are you thinking?' she asked.

He took another mouthful of gin and rolled it round his tongue. In that minute he was remembering the battle, the carnage wreaked upon men and ships, the sounds of gunfire and screams of the wounded. But there was no point in trying to explain it all, and instead, he put an arm round her shoulder and smiled quietly.

'Funny how things turn out.'

'Meaning?' she asked.

'Well, if it hadn't been for *Holstein*, we might not have met again.'

'True,' she said, 'but I'm glad we did. I wonder where you'll be going next?'

Lieutenant-Commander Richard Thorburn chose not to reply. There were times when being ashore and away from the responsibilities of command seemed a welcome relief. But as always when on dry land, he found his thoughts straying elsewhere, towards the ship's loyal crew, the wounded *Brackendale*, and how long before he could put to sea? He put an arm round her shoulders and hugged her close, gently kissing the upturned lips.

'I don't know,' he breathed. Pulling back, he twisted the glass in his fingers and looked wistfully at the destroyer's small shadow nestled in the harbour below, and pursed his lips. Perhaps Collingwood would honour his pledge and call upon a King's ship . . . , and he smiled.

Brackendale, man-of-war.

Novels by Graham John Parry

* * *

(World War II Naval Saga featuring Richard Thorburn)

The Waves of War

Man of War

When D-Day Dawns

* * *

(Present day thriller with Mike Bowman)

A Spy in all but Name

27047510R00170

Printed in Poland
by Amazon Fulfillment
Poland Sp. z o.o., Wrocław